LORI WICK

Moonlight ON THE Millpond

HARVEST HOUSE PUBLISHERS

EUGENE, OREGON

All Scripture quotations are taken from the King James Version of the Bible.

Cover images © Getty Images; George and Monserrate Schwartz/Alamy Images

Cover by Terry Dugan Design, Minneapolis, Minnesota

The Author

LORI WICK is one of the most versatile Christian fiction writers in the market today. Her works include pioneer fiction, a series set in Victorian England, and contemporary novels. Lori's books (more than 4 million copies in print) continue to delight readers and top the Christian best-selling fiction list. Lori and her husband, Bob, live in Wisconsin and are the parents of "the three coolest kids in the world."

MOONLIGHT ON THE MILLPOND
Copyright © 2005 by Lori Wick
Published by Harvest House Publishers
Eugene, Oregon 97402
www.harvesthousepublishers.com

Library of Congress Cataloging-in-Publication Data
Wick, Lori.
  Moonlight on the millpond / Lori Wick.
    p. cm. — (Tucker Mills trilogy ; bk. 1)
  ISBN 0-7369-1158-8 (pbk.)
  1. Brothers and sisters—Fiction. 2. Massachusetts—Fiction. 3. Sawmills—Fiction.
I. Title. II. Series.
  PS3573.I237M66 2005
  813'.54—dc22
                                                  2004029889

Printed in the United States of America

05 06 07 08 09 10 11 12 / BP-CF / 10 9 8 7 6 5 4 3 2 1

For the newest
members of the family:
Max and Rachel.
I love you.

*W*onderful people I wish to thank...

- Mary Margaret, who always rolls with the punches. We have rushed, and we have had time, and you're always up for it. Thank you, my friend, for your faithfulness in the Body, in our friendship, and in our working relationship. I never want to do this without you.

- Dooner (Jeff Muldoon), for the loan of the name. It's one of my favorites of all time.

- Abby, for the covered bridge. I so appreciate you and all your facets. The rare diamond that you are keeps presenting new ones, and each is a delight. Thank you for being both a friend and a daughter every step of the way. Also, thanks for going on that first trip. Those pictures are my favorites.

- Phil, for all the great teaching and wonderful words, even those that wound. Your capacity for love and patience with the Body is precious. Thank you for teaching us what it looks like to pray for all men, for never giving up on us, and for loving a repentant heart as much as God does.

- Tim and Matt, for being grown men who still seek their parents' approval. You guys are so cool. I love you.

- Bob, for not one trip to Massachusetts, but two. You're quite the travel partner, especially when the rain is dumping. Thanks for the amazing amount of work you did on this book. My mother once said that if she could have picked a husband for me from anywhere in the world, you would have been the one. I think we both have great taste.

Prologue

The street quiet, almost oddly so, she waited in the usual place. Their place. The strong emotions that always filled her heart at these times were different tonight. The feelings surging through her were just as strong, but the joy and anticipation were missing. She peeked around the corner to see if he was coming and told herself to breathe when his handsome face came into view.

He noticed nothing amiss until he stepped around the corner to take her into his arms, stopping when he saw the expression on her face.

The small blonde woman looked into the eyes of the man she loved, her heart pounding with grief, knowing that it was all true: She'd been betrayed. She confronted him and then waited, clearly able to see the guilt he could not hide.

"Is it true?" she asked again, hating his silence but terrified of his answer. "Are you married?"

"I can explain," he began hoarsely, but the woman shook her head, and he stopped.

"What could you possibly say?" she whispered. "I love you. You told me you loved me and that we'd be married someday. I was willing to wait forever."

"We can still be together," the man tried again, desperate not to lose her. "My wife need never know."

The hurt gave way to rage. Her blue eyes flashed fire as they drilled into his. Her hand itched to strike him, but she said and did nothing. Instead, she turned away, but before she could go two steps, she stopped. Turning back long enough to say one more thing, she commanded, "Don't contact me or come near me ever again."

She held his eyes until his dropped with shame. Only then did she turn resolutely away. This time she did not stop or look back.

One

Tucker Mills, Massachusetts—1838

Jace Randall's gaze followed the consistent progress of the log as it moved through the saw blade, his eyes probably more watchful than they needed to be. All looked to be in order—he had done everything correctly—but his eyes never wavered from the saw blade or the huge log that was being transfigured methodically into boards.

Jace was new at the job. And his inexperience was causing him fear, fear that he would cost his uncle money rather than be the asset they both planned on. This sudden opportunity had come his way, and it was not one he wanted to squander.

Woody Randall, longtime owner of the Randall Sawmill in Tucker Mills, Massachusetts, had asked Jace, his only nephew, to come and work with him. Jace had read the letter over six times. Never at any point did his uncle ask him to make the trip to Tucker Mills so he could work *for* him. The word *with* was always used, and when Jace accepted the offer, he found out why.

Woody's health was in decline, and as much as that man wanted to live forever, recent events told him there was no chance. He had written to Jace, who lived in Pine River, keeping the letter a bit vague. As soon as Jace accepted, however, Woody's next letter detailed his plans to someday have Jace own the sawmill in Tucker Mills.

The offer wasn't without conditions, but Woody wrote to Jace that he knew him to be hardworking, and he was fairly confident that the younger Randall would have no trouble catching on.

"You're attracting another crowd," Woody called out, lifting his voice slightly to be heard over the noise of the machinery.

Jace glanced behind him. Three of the young ladies from town were walking past the millpond at a snail's pace. Two of them were doing their best to see inside the mill and not be caught in the act. Jace turned away with little more than a glance.

"I'm here to work, not visit with the women."

"Can't you do both?" Woody asked, thumping him in the chest at the same time.

Jace's handsome face split with a grin that he threw in his uncle's direction, but he didn't comment further. If the truth be told, he was very interested in finding a girl, but his sister's last words as he left Pine River had stopped him cold.

The women like you too much, Jace Randall, and you don't always use your head. I know you'll go to Tucker Mills and fall for the first woman who smiles at you. You'll find yourself with a wife and six babies on your hands before you can blink.

Eden Randall, whose every letter asked if he'd found a girl, was a sister ten years his senior who had practically raised him. She liked to be right. Jace savored the few times she was wrong. And so, if it took every fiber of his being to avoid being lassoed and married by one of the local girls, Jace would expend the energy. He'd been in Tucker Mills for more than five months and had yet to give one of them a single glance.

"Get ahold of that board, Jace!" Woody shouted, and Jace realized that he'd allowed his mind to drift. The men worked together for the next ten minutes before shutting down the operation and heading to the house. Almost noon. It was time for dinner.

"You look tired, Doyle," Cathy Shephard said to her husband of many years, watching him eat the midday meal she had brought to him in the store.

"I think I am a little," he said, his tone telling more.

Cathy debated her next comment. He didn't want to discuss his health, of that she was sure, but his skin color was off and his eyes didn't have their usual gleam.

He was rarely irritable or in a poor humor, and Cathy couldn't imagine a man more easy to live with than Doyle Shephard. She had fallen in love with him when she was still a teen; he was five years older. And she still loved him and knew he loved her in return. But right now she wanted to ignore the tone in his voice and press him over the way he felt.

Doyle had opened the store at 8:00 as usual, but there was something missing in his step this day. Cathy didn't work in the store—at least not on a regular basis—but she'd been over that morning to collect some goods and had watched her husband in action. He usually enjoyed the start of each day and greeted customers with enthusiasm, but not today. Today his smile had been just as kind, but his voice lacked strength and his eyes showed strain.

"I can handle things this afternoon," Cathy said midmeal.

"Why would you need to do that?"

"Because you look like you need to rest."

"I'll be all right," Doyle told her, but there was little conviction behind the words.

Cathy let the matter drop. Knowing that her work at home could wait, she made a promise to herself to find excuses to be around the store off and on for the rest of the day. But she wisely kept this plan to herself.

"Where have you been?" Alison Muldoon asked of her 16-year-old daughter when she came in the door a little late.

Hillary Muldoon rolled her eyes. "Greta and Mercy insisted that we crawl past the sawmill so Greta could get a glimpse of Jace Randall."

Alison looked patient and then concerned. "And what do you think of her being so enamored with Jace?"

"I think it's silly." Hillary started setting the table and kept talking. "She doesn't even know him, but she's desperate to have someone special in her life."

Alison nodded but didn't comment.

"And Jace is certainly good looking," Hillary added, causing her mother to look at her. Alison was pleased with what she saw. Hillary wasn't the least bit starry eyed, stating only the facts as she saw them.

"It's awfully quiet around here," Hillary commented. "Where are the boys?"

"They ran a loaf of fresh bread over to old Mr. Sager," Alison told her, referring to her sons. "He's not feeling the best right now."

As if on cue, a commotion sounded outside the door, and the boys trooped noisily into the kitchen.

"He gave us candy," 12-year-old Joshua Muldoon stated, "but we didn't eat it."

"I'm glad of that," his mother told him with an approving look. "Your father will be home any minute for dinner. You can enjoy it later."

"I wanted to lick it," 11-year-old Peter Muldoon admitted, "but Josh said no."

Alison laughed a little over this declaration, loving his honesty. She set a steaming bowl of potatoes on the table and went to the other room to find her five-year-old son, Martin. He was making a stack with his blocks, his hand steady and his eyes intent.

"Your father will be here soon," Alison told him.

"I can show him my blocks," Martin said, hand still steady. But just then the back door opened and closed, sending the tower to the floor.

"Did I do that, Marty?" Douglas Muldoon asked, coming to kiss his wife while speaking to his son.

"It's all right," Martin forgave, but his eyes looked a little sad.

"You can work on it again after dinner," Alison encouraged, stopping him when he would have reached for the blocks again.

Not five minutes later they were gathered around the table to pray. The dishes were passed and the meal began. Douglas waited only until everyone had food on their plates to share his news.

"Thank you, Clara," Jace said to the woman who kept house and cooked the noon dinner for his uncle six days a week. Clara had been on the job for more than 20 years, and although she was sometimes outspoken, she was not unkind. Her husband had worked for Woody until the day of his death.

The table, set and laden with food, invited the men to eat. Clara made her way from the room. Jace barely glanced at her, his gaze going to Woody. They had accomplished much that morning, but on the walk home, Woody's breathing had been labored. He was eating, but his movements were slow and deliberate.

The first time Jace had witnessed this, he'd offered to handle the afternoon workload. Woody had frowned at him and said nothing. Jace had learned not to comment, but his heart grew heavy with the fact that one of these days Woody would not have the energy to go on. Jace wondered just what he would do when that time came and then pushed it from his mind. He still had a lot to learn, and he was in no hurry to see his uncle gone.

"What are you looking so worried about?" Woody had spotted the reflection.

"Just the mill," Jace hedged. "Asa expects his boards this week."

"We'll get it done," Woody said easily, meaning it and not just trying to comfort the younger man.

"How often have orders been late?"

"Never," Woody told him.

Jace felt his heart sink a bit. Logs would come to the sawmill off and on all winter, but cutting didn't usually start until February, making the spring demand for boards overwhelming at times. And the planting had to be done before too much spring passed as well. Woody didn't work the sawmill all year. He was a farmer by trade. Jace couldn't help wondering how the older man had done it all these years.

"Is there dessert?" Woody asked Clara when she came from the kitchen with the coffeepot.

"When is there not dessert, Woody Randall?"

"I remember a day," he teased, "even if you don't."

Clara's hands came to her waist. "The Dresdens' kitchen was on fire!" she reminded him. "I thought the safety of those children might be more important than remembering to put the crumble in to bake."

With that she walked back to the kitchen, ignoring Woody's satisfied chuckle. She returned with a warm pie, taking great delight in putting it on the table close to Woody, its aroma wafting throughout the room.

"You don't deserve it," she told Woody, her eyes sparkling with hidden laughter, "but there it is!"

Woody grinned at her, but Clara only shook her head and moved back to the kitchen. Jace cut large slices for both of them, knowing they were enjoying some of the fruit Clara had put up last summer. Since this was mid-March, it wouldn't be long before she would be planting her garden too.

Thank you for praying, Mother. Alison—thoughtful over Douglas' news—wrote in a letter that afternoon. She continued,

I have something to tell you. Douglas came home for
dinner and announced to the family that he'd received a
letter from the manager of the bank. Someone has given
a large donation through the bank to our small church
family. Doug will meet with the other elders this week to
discuss it. His plan is to be patient and go slowly in
order to develop a path that will work well for the church
family.

    As you may recall from my letters, the church
family is growing here. We love meeting in our home,
and also love the hospitality we're able to offer. We've
been so thankful for the space, but it might be time to
think about having our own building.

    Douglas has such a heart for Tucker Mills. Please
keep praying for us and for hearts to continue to soften.
Please also pray that we will be wise with this gift.
Douglas' main concern is our unity, which affects our
testimony here. He reminded us that we can keep the
work going, no matter where we meet. Our building
matters very little. Praying for the lives of all in Tucker
Mills is of paramount importance.

    I miss you, think of you often, and pray for you. I
know you pray for me.

Your loving daughter,
Alison

Alison reread the letter and realized she hadn't shared a word
about the family. She added a paragraph to let her mother know
how the children were doing and even to say that they might be
able to come to Boston to see her sometime later in the year.

    She closed the letter just as Martin came looking for her. He
had pinched his finger in a cupboard door and wanted the comfort of her lap. Happy to sit in silence with his warm body close
to her, Alison prayed for the little boy in her lap and for their
small church family to never lose its focus: to walk humbly with
their God.

❦

Midafternoon found Jace at Shephard Store looking for a tool that Woody requested. Cathy was working on her own in the store, but Jace caught a glimpse of Doyle in the office—not working but sitting at the desk. Jace called to him, but Doyle only waved and held his place.

"Well, Jace," Cathy greeted him. "What brings you into town?"

"A file. Woody seems to have misplaced the one he likes and wants a new one."

Doyle would have normally handled such a request, but Cathy knew where the tools were stored.

"We have one or two, I think," she said, leading the way to the back. She dug in a drawer and put two long tools on the wooden countertop. The front door opened and closed, telling Cathy that someone else had come in, but she called that she'd be right out and stayed with Jace.

"So how are you?" she asked. Jace had come to be a regular at the store and in their home, visiting them whenever time allowed. Both Doyle and Cathy liked and enjoyed him tremendously.

"I'm okay."

"Just okay?"

"We're awfully busy," he said, sounding tired. "I wonder how it will all get done before we have to be in the fields."

"Woody'll show you." Cathy spoke with supreme confidence. "He's a master."

Jace nodded and looked down at the tools in front of him. He wished Woody would have come on his own. He wasn't exactly sure which one to take. He knew he could return one to Cathy if he took both and let his uncle decide, but he didn't want to have anything else on his mind.

"I'll check on you in a bit," Cathy promised, and seeing he was going to need some time, she moved back to the front of the store.

Jace barely heard her. One of the doors that led into the office was right in front of him, so he decided to slip in and ask Doyle.

"Doyle, do you think Woody would have a preference between these two?"

"Let's see," Doyle said. His voice was weary, but Jace was too distracted to notice. "I like the one with the curve, myself," Doyle told him. "But it all depends on what Woody's going to do with it."

Jace nodded.

"Take both, let him decide, and bring the other one back."

"I think I'll do that. Thanks, Doyle."

The older man waved him on his way, and Jace exited to discuss it with Cathy. Not five minutes later he was back in the wagon, the day's post and files in hand, and headed back to the mill. He felt he'd taken entirely too long, but he was wrong. Woody thought he was back in record time, and with a slight sense of relief, Jace continued the afternoon's work without further delay.

Doyle Shephard closed up shop come evening, wondering when a day had been so long. He was tired, much more than his 48 years should betray, and all he wanted was to lie on the floor and sleep. Even making the effort to leave the store and go to his home some 30 yards away seemed more effort than it was worth.

"Are you hungry, Doyle?" Cathy asked from behind him. He hadn't even heard her and thought she had already gone home.

"Not very," he answered, not wanting to tell her how he really felt.

"Please let me get Doc MacKay, Doyle," she pleaded softly. "He's not too quick to bleed a person. I'll just slip over when the town center grows quiet."

Doyle wanted to argue. He wanted to fight this, but there was no fight left in him. Like an old beast working to carry his last load, Doyle nodded and made his way to the rear door. Once at the house, he completely skipped the parlor, where Cathy had laid out their tea and evening snack, and went straight to the stairway that led to their bedroom. Cathy was behind him the whole way. He lay down on the bed, not bothering with his clothing. So weary was he that he didn't move, not even when he heard Cathy leave or when he heard the door again and realized she was returning with old Doc MacKay.

Jace and Woody worked until sundown, but the walk home still afforded plenty of light. When they arrived, Jace knew that Clara would be gone to her own small home on a corner of the farm, but things would be laid for their evening meal: leftovers from dinner, tea, and something sweet to be enjoyed, perhaps the remainder of the pie.

Tired and a bit labored in his breathing, Woody went directly into the house, but Jace lingered outside. The lowered sun cast a glow over the farm and farmhouse that Jace found irresistible. Not in his wildest dreams had he ever pictured himself living out of the city and in such a beautiful setting. Woody's death could be pushed far from his mind at times like this. Jace was only glad to be here and not back in the stifling heat of the glass factory in Pine River.

That he would someday be living here alone, without his uncle's guidance and company, was not something he chose to dwell on, even as he realized that an opportunity such as this

came along rarely. At times he tried to tell Woody how he felt.
Twice he tried to thank him, but Woody would have none of it.

"You'll work hard or it won't last," Woody had said. "And I'm
not as generous as you might think. I want to die in peace, and I
can't do that if I don't know I have someone who wants to make
this work, someone who is here to carry on."

Well, Jace thought to himself, *I'm certainly that someone.*
Almost from the moment he'd seen Woody's farm, he'd fallen in
love. He hadn't been as keen about the work at the sawmill, but
that was before he'd tried it. Soon he found himself intoxicated
by the smell of freshly sawed wood, and the satisfaction of filling
orders and stacking boards he'd cut himself was like nothing
he'd ever experienced before. His pride grew with each passing
week, and before long he understood why Mr. Vargas, the owner
of the glass factory, had come through on a regular basis. He
cared in a special way. His was the pride and caring of ownership.

"Jace?" Woody called from the house.

"Coming." Jace turned that way, but he didn't hurry. The
evening air was cool, and the sights and aromas were too
tempting. Still looking around as though he'd just moved into
town, Jace walked slowly up the front steps, the town of Pine
River and the boardinghouse he grew up in a distant memory.

"I hope you know," Alison told Douglas as they readied for
bed, "that I did some worrying today."

"Worrying about what?"

"The donation. Will the church family keep it in perspective?
Will the elders agree about what to do?"

She would have gone on, but Douglas' laughter stopped her.

"I don't think it's funny," Alison told him, her dress half off.
"At one point, I was in a terrible state. I wrote Mother a letter,
and that helped, but I was worried off and on all day."

"I couldn't tell when I looked at you over tea this evening."

"By then I was doing better."

Sitting on the edge of their bed, Douglas didn't comment for a moment, thinking he'd done some fretting of his own. It had not been of the same variety as Alison's, but along the lines that some sort of mistake had been made at the bank. They didn't know who had given the money, so he had no real reason to doubt, but Douglas' thoughts had moved to the person who gave. He prayed for this person and tried not to worry that it was too much for him or her, or figure out why the money was given, or why it was done anonymously.

The funding is not important, Father; not really. It would be helpful to be able to give to our families who struggle to get by and maybe some day build a modest meetinghouse, but You know our hearts. You know the best time for this.

"Are you all right?" Alison asked. "Did I say something to discourage you?"

"Not at all." He reached for her hand. "I had my own worries today, and I was still discussing those with the Lord."

Alison sat next to him, her hand still in his. They were quiet for a time, but both were prayerful—not for themselves—but for each other and, as always, for the folks of Tucker Mills who needed the good news that Douglas and Alison believed in with all their hearts.

"It's your heart, Doyle," Doc MacKay told him quietly, not because the situation was dire but because he was a soft-spoken, kind man.

"My heart is fine," Doyle tried to tell him, but MacKay was patient and heard him out. "My back has been troubling me and I'm not sleeping as well. It's probably just that."

"I didn't say you were dying, Doyle," MacKay replied, cutting to the point. He was humble but certain of his estimation as to what was ailing this man. "It might be your back and the fatigue from that, but I think it's your heart, and sooner or later, you'll know yourself."

"What do you mean?" Cathy questioned him anxiously from the other side of the bed, picturing Doyle dropping dead without warning.

"Just that he'll have to rest more or he won't be able to carry on. Your store serves the whole community. Doyle lifts and totes all day, carries heavy loads, runs the stairs, and climbs ladders. His heart is telling him he has to slow down a bit. The beats of his heart are irregular. I don't think his heart is suddenly going to fail him, but it's not the heart of a 25-year-old any longer."

Doc MacKay sat still after this little speech, waiting for further protestations or questions. They took a while to come.

"Cathy knows the store, but she can't do it alone," Doyle pointed out quietly.

"She doesn't have to do it alone, but you've got to slow down. You might have to get someone in to do the hard work your body can't do any longer. And Doyle," the doctor added, "I've seen more than one case of rest that put a man back on his feet. Most doctors would bleed you, but that's not my style. If you'll take it easy for a time and let your heart rest up a bit, you might find you're back to your old self again."

Doyle and Cathy looked at each other, and MacKay knew it was time to take his leave. He put his bag back together, and Cathy walked him to the front door, thanking him several times. She watched him walk down the path and then onto the street before going back upstairs to her spouse. Again they looked at each other.

"Things will have to change," Cathy said, not caring if Doyle fought her, not focusing on anything but keeping him well and alive. "We'll do what we have to do to see to it that your heart gets better."

"And just what do you have in mind, Cathleen Shephard?" Doyle asked, having heard the tone in her voice and knowing she was ready to do battle.

Battle worthy or not, Cathy was not immediately ready for this question. Her mouth opened and closed several times before she found her voice. Her chin rising, she told Doyle in no uncertain terms, "I'll send for Maddie."

Two

Boston

Madalyn Shephard stopped her descent of the stairway, trying to decide if Mrs. Nunley had been calling for her. Hearing nothing else, she finished the steps, turned at the bottom, and headed toward the kitchen. She passed Mr. Nunley on the way, gaining a smile from him because he'd been caught coming from that room.

It was their secret. Mrs. Nunley was firmly of the belief that the master and mistress of the house had no business in the servants' areas, and that included the kitchen. Mr. Nunley, however, was not above sneaking into that room and sampling Sherry's baked goods, all of which were mouthwatering. His waistline never gave evidence of this fact, so his wife was none the wiser.

"Sherry," Maddie said as soon as she entered. "The missus wants cinnamon in her tea this morning. Has she asked for that before? She said you would know."

"I've worked here for six years," Sherry declared, hands flying into the air. "I've never heard of such a thing!"

Maddie shrugged, her look just as confused but not letting the incident upset her. If she'd learned anything by living in someone else's home for almost ten years, it was not to take things too seriously. She had seen the Nunleys leave for an extended trip with a few hour's notice, and she had watched the same people become completely distraught over a slightly over-cooked pork roast. Well, in all fairness, Mrs. Nunley was the only one who ever became upset over what was served. Mr. Nunley was happy to eat anything that was placed in front of him.

He had told Maddie one time that he'd not been born into wealth and well remembered the days when he had nothing at all.

"So can you take care of it?" Maddie finally asked, coming back to the task at hand.

"Yes," Sherry answered, but her tone said there was no pleasure in the task.

"I'll be back in a few minutes to get the tray."

Maddie made her usual morning rounds, checking to see that curtains were open and that the early spring flowers were fresh in the vases. In the process of doing this, she ran into Paige, the Nunleys' teenage daughter, the only one of their children young enough to still be living at home. She was standing in front of the large living room window.

"Are you watching for someone, Paige?" Maddie asked.

"How do we know," Paige replied, turning without warning, "that the iceman doesn't have a dead body in the back of that wagon?"

"Paige," Maddie began, as patient as she'd always been with the youngest Nunley's over-active mind, "you really should be writing these stories down. You could be quite famous."

"Mother would never approve."

"She'd be scandalized at first, and then secretly pleased."

Paige shrugged good-naturedly, a half smile on her pretty mouth. "I can't ever stay with one plot long enough. My mind rushes on to something else."

Maddie smiled at her understandingly and realized she was late getting the tray. She returned to the kitchen and then bore

the beautifully laid tray upstairs, smiling in genuine fondness at
Mrs. Nunley when she reached her bedside.

"Did Sherry manage the cinnamon?"

"Yes, ma'am. You'll have to tell me how you like it. I might
want to try it myself."

"Have a sip of mine," Mrs. Nunley offered, completely out of
character for this staid pillar of society, but Maddie knew something that most people did not: Maddie was Mrs. Nunley's weak-
ness.

Maddie had come to them when she was barely 17 to act as
a companion and nanny to their young children. What no one
had anticipated was how much Maddie herself would be
embraced. Mrs. Nunley loved her as a daughter, and it wasn't
long before she was being shown preferential treatment. Maddie
knew she was a servant in this home, but a treasured one to be
certain.

"That's very good," Maddie said, having taken a sip. "I think
she might have surprised you with those little muffins you like
too," she added, lifting the lid from a small silver chafing dish.

"They smell heavenly. Did you bring the paper?"

"Yes. Where would you like me to start, the front page or
somewhere inside?"

Over the years Maddie's job had changed. As the children
began to grow and move on, Maddie became more and more a
companion and confidant to Mrs. Nunley. They had several rou-
tines they followed, but Mrs. Nunley was not so set in her ways
that she couldn't do without Maddie.

Afternoons were always for Paige. Paige was as close to
Maddie as her mother, and the two seemed content to share her.
Maddie had Sundays and a half day on Tuesday afternoons to
herself. Some weeks seemed to be without end, but for the most
part, Maddie was quite content with her lot.

At the moment she was content indeed. She read to Mrs.
Nunley for an hour, but then Mr. Nunley wanted his wife to
accompany him on business downtown. Maddie saw them out

the door, delighted to find herself free until after lunch. Taking a warm wrap and a letter that the missus wanted posted, she took herself off for a walk.

Tucker Mills

It was after Shephard Store hours, so when Jace arrived in town, he made a beeline for the Shephards' house. He'd not seen the couple for a few days and had finally had the energy to venture out at the end of the workday. He knocked softly on the front door, anxious to know how they were doing. Cathy opened the door for him, delighted to see his face.

"Come to the sitting room," she welcomed. "Doyle, it's Jace."

"Good," Doyle proclaimed, glad to set the newspaper aside. "I'm sick of my own company."

"You look good," Jace told him, having shaken the older man's hand and taken a seat. "I think the rest has been good for you."

"Don't let Cathy hear you say that," he gave in a false whisper. "She's so certain I'm going to rest for a full six months."

"I heard that," Cathy called from the other room, and Jace smiled. It was one of the many things he liked about this couple. They enjoyed each other. They frowned at each other and even argued some, but they clearly delighted in one another's company.

"How are things working with Mic?" Jace asked, referring to their temporary help.

"Don't get him started," Cathy cautioned, coming to the door with a dishtowel and a plate in her hand.

"Let's just say," Doyle put in, "that we're most eager to have Maddie join us."

"What day does she come?"

"We assume she'll come as soon as she gets Cathy's letter. She might be on her way."

Jace nodded, but secretly he wasn't pleased. He wished there was a way for the Shepherds' niece to be there right now. She was needed now. At the same time, Jace asked himself what Maddie Shephard was truly like. Was she a hard worker? He hoped for the Shephards' sake that they weren't blinded by their feelings for her and that she truly would be a help to them when she arrived.

"So tell me about the mill," Doyle ordered eagerly. "Are you about done?"

"We're very close. I never thought I'd say this, but once our work moves to the farm fields, I'm going to miss the mill."

"Well, it comes again in the fall for a bit, and then a full gallop by the end of next winter."

"You should be thankful," Cathy added to Doyle's words. "If our millpond wasn't fed by a river as powerful as the Hastings, you'd be operating only in the spring, no matter what."

"I hadn't thought of that," Jace admitted.

"I remember when my brother and I worked on the Hastings River," Doyle chimed in, beginning to reminisce. "It was back in '09."

"What did you do?"

"We worked the barges that transported wares all up and down the river."

"And that was what year again?" Jace asked.

"I guess we actually started in 1808 and went for four years or so. Why, that was before Maddie was born." Doyle gave a small laugh. "Daniel wasn't even married yet, let alone having children."

"Where is your brother now?"

"He and Vera drowned on that very river. Maddie was just a baby, almost drowned with 'em, but the boat captain grabbed her when she floated past and took her to shore. Dan and Vera were coming to visit us, but they never made it."

"And we raised her," Cathy added, her voice wistful. "We raised Maddie and made her our own. We were heartsick about those deaths, but we had a sickly baby to raise and no time to mourn."

Jace sat quietly and took this in. When he was very young, his own parents had died in a flu epidemic that swept through their area. From that point, he'd been raised by his sister. It was interesting to think that this niece, this woman he'd not yet met, had something in common with him.

"Enough of the past," Doyle said gruffly. "We sound like we're in our dotage, Cathleen! Now, tell us, Jace, what will you plant in the south field this year?"

And that was the end of the reminiscing. Even though Jace had questions about their past life, he knew they would have to wait. He told Doyle and Cathy what Woody had relayed to him, swift to remind them that it was all new for him. He was still in his first year in Tucker Mills.

The change in topic seemed to do the trick. Doyle relaxed in his chair, Cathy began to smile again, and eventually she brought in a tea tray. Jace couldn't remember the last time he'd had such an enjoyable evening.

Boston

"It's not my aunt's arm this time, Mrs. Nunley," Maddie explained, Cathy's letter still between her fingers. "It's Doyle's heart, and he needs to rest for some time."

"Of course you must go," Mrs. Nunley said, hiding her disappointment. She and Mr. Nunley were planning a trip later in the year or early the following year. They had planned to surprise Paige and Maddie by taking them both along. At the moment Mrs. Nunley was so relieved that she'd never mentioned this to Maddie that her face gave a false impression.

"Please, Mrs. Nunley, please tell me you understand. I can't stay when they need me."

"Come here, Maddie," she said gently, taking the younger woman's hand when she drew near. Maddie sat beside her on the settee. "I want you to go, and for as long as you need. I grew quiet only when a stray thought wandered in." Mrs. Nunley paused long enough to brush Maddie's cheek with one soft finger. "You'll go just as soon as the next train leaves. Mr. Nunley will buy your ticket."

"Thank you," Maddie whispered, fearing that her employer would not understand. If Maddie could have given her some element of time, that would have been ideal, but she didn't know when she would be back in Boston. It could be months from now or never, depending on what Doyle and Cathy needed.

It was true that she had moved away at 17 to make a life for herself, but that had not been done with hard feelings or a desire to flee Tucker Mills. Her family needed her, and if she'd been forced to sever all ties with the Nunleys in order to leave, she was willing to do just that.

"Go now and start to pack," Mrs. Nunley told her, giving her hand a squeeze. "I'll send word to Mr. Nunley, and we'll get you on your way."

Maddie thanked her sincerely but didn't linger. She slipped into her own room just minutes later and began to organize her things. She hadn't been working for more than 20 minutes when Paige appeared at her door. Even in a home as large as this one, word seemed to travel fast.

"When do you leave?" Paige asked, tears sounding suspiciously close.

"As soon as I can get a train."

"What am I going to do?"

"Well, you could try writing one of the books you keep thinking up," Maddie teased her gently.

Paige sighed and flopped onto Maddie's bed. The younger girl had always been welcome.

"Why don't I go with you?" Paige asked, eyes on the ceiling and willing herself not to cry.

"For a number of reasons."

"Name one."

"I'll do better than that," Maddie continued as she sorted and packed. "I'll name several: Your parents would never approve. This is not a vacation; it's work. You have never lived in anything but the lap of luxury, and the Shephards do not live that way. And lastly, you would be bored silly when I was working all day and not able to be with you."

Maddie stopped working, and their eyes met. She went on quietly. "I'll miss you—you know that—but I have to go. I want to more than anything. Even if I stayed, my heart would be elsewhere."

"Like with that man," Paige surprised her by saying.

"What made you think of that?"

"Oh, just when you were seeing him, your mind was elsewhere."

"I can believe that," Maddie said, able to speak of it after so many years. "And what a waste of time he turned out to be."

"I'm not ever going to be married!" Paige said, not for the first time. "I'm never going to let a man hurt me like that."

Since Maddie now felt the same way, with maybe slightly less teenage zeal, she could hardly argue with the girl. She opted to say nothing, simply going back to her packing.

"Tell me about Tucker Mills," Paige begged, having stared at the ceiling for a time.

"It's small and wonderful. The people care and work hard."

"And you were born there?"

"No, I was born in Worcester, but my parents died when I was very young, so Doyle and Cathy raised me."

"Don't you call them Aunt and Uncle?" Paige asked in astonishment, knowing that Maddie knew better.

"They never led me to believe that I was their child. I always knew they were my aunt and uncle, but they didn't want those words coming out of my mouth with every sentence, so they've always just been Cathy and Doyle."

"Maddie," Paige said, suddenly voicing another thought, "women don't work in Boston shops. Is it so very different in a small town?"

"Actually, it's not, but folks seem to accept it a little more. I grew up in the store, and Cathy comes and goes throughout the week. It's not normal, but folks will understand, especially with Doyle being ill."

Paige took this in for a quiet moment. When she realized that her mind had drifted, she looked to see that Maddie was almost done. Tears flooded her eyes, tears she could not stop. Maddie saw them and went to her. She put her arms around Paige, truly sorry to be leaving with so little warning but knowing she had no choice. Leaving for Tucker Mills just as soon as she was able was the right thing to do.

Tucker Mills

Woody and Jace started the day very early at the sawmill. The orders were being filled quickly, and both were ready to be done. There was a sense of completeness that came with such tasks, and both men worked hard on the job.

Neither man had heard the train in the early hours, even though it was running way behind and had arrived in the wee hours instead of the afternoon before. They had both awakened early because of it but not attributed the disturbance to the distant sound of the train. Certainly neither one knew that Maddie Shephard had come to town.

It was a cool morning, but Cathy wanted the spring air to rush inside and give the store a good smell, a smell of cleanliness and fresh goods. Her mind was on this when she opened the doors, so she didn't look outside. It was for this reason that she was behind the counter before seeing who had come in.

Weary from the train ride, Maddie stood still and waited to be noticed. It had been a few years since she'd been back. All would probably have looked the same to her, but the only person she could see right now was Cathleen Shephard, who took a moment to become aware of her.

"Maddie," Cathy suddenly whispered, her hand going to her heart and her body moving around the end of the counter all at the same time. "When did you get here? Why didn't you come to the house?"

The women hugged each other for a long time, so long Maddie forgot she'd been asked a question.

"Well?"

"Well what?" Maddie's tired brain tried to think.

"When did you get here? Just now? I didn't hear the train."

"No, it was a few hours ago."

"You poor dear. Were you sitting outside?"

"I wanted to let you sleep," Maddie replied, evading the interrogation. "Now stop with the questions, Cathy, and tell me about Doyle."

Cathy stopped and looked at her, not an ounce of worry on her face.

"As soon as I said I was sending for you, he relaxed. He's been resting ever since."

"And what about you? How are you doing with it all?"

"Well, Mic is some help, and I just do what I can."

Maddie looked into her face. She looked tired but not older. Maddie hoped that was a good sign.

"Who is Mic?"

"A young man we hired until you could come."

Maddie smiled. Weary as she was, there was no dimming the light in those blue eyes.

"Well, I'm here now. I'll take care of you both."

Cathy pulled her back into her arms. They hugged again for a long time, stopping only when Maddie said that as soon as she'd run next door to kiss her uncle and then returned and found an apron, she'd be ready to work.

"Maddie's in town," Woody told Clara over dinner.

"Is she now?" Clara set the coffeepot down, interest in her face. "When did she get in?"

"Just today, according to everyone who stopped by the mill."

"Good. If anyone can get Doyle to take a rest, it's Maddie."

Jace didn't comment on any of this, not because he had something against the Shephards' niece but because his mind was on something else. A young lady had walked past the mill today who had actually caught his eye. He had so conditioned himself not to look even a second time that when his head turned twice today, it gave him pause.

With further inspection, he realized he hadn't seen her face clearly at all, but the color of her dress, a green print that was easy on the eyes, and the graceful way she moved, had stayed on his mind for quite some time.

It might be time, Jace reasoned. *Would Eden actually say she was right if after all this time I sought out some female company?* Almost the moment he mentally raised the question, he knew the answer was yes. It wasn't going to matter when he met someone he thought was special enough for a second look; his sister was just difficult enough to say that she had been right.

The only question that remained for Jace now was, Did he really care what his sister thought, said, or did?

"I missed you," Doyle told his niece at noon over dinner, his voice saying more. Maddie had gone home to eat with him, planning to take food to Cathy later.

"I missed you too," Maddie said in return, acknowledging how wonderful it was to be home again. She wondered how she would finish the day on so little sleep, but her heart knew nothing but delight that she had been able to come so swiftly and find her uncle doing so well.

She had expected worse. She thought Doyle would be sickly looking and pale, but he was neither of these. His eyes were bright and his color good. The only discernable change was his soft-spokenness and eyes that looked as though they wanted to tear every time she smiled at him.

"Was the work too hard?" Doyle suddenly teased.

"I didn't do any work," Maddie teased back. "I spent the whole morning answering questions about my life. I wasn't a help to Cathy at all."

"I find that hard to believe. Tell me, did everyone who wanted answers also buy something?"

"Yes, they did," Maddie said, suddenly realizing.

Doyle laughed over this, and Maddie was struck by the deep contentment she felt. Smiling at her uncle and going back to her meal, she decided that no matter what, she would not stay away this long again.

When Douglas Muldoon moved to Tucker Mills with his family, he went directly into a house that was already built. He'd watched the building of other homes in the village but had never been involved personally.

The donation of funds for their meetinghouse made all questions about such matters come alive. Having not purchased land yet, Douglas was nevertheless asking where one purchased boards or logs to be cut, who in town could build pews, and would the woodcarver expect them to supply their own logs?

Rather than take time on the matter, Douglas began to make a list of all his questions. He didn't know when he would find answers, but it didn't have to be today. Today he had a sermon to work on and no time to consider side issues.

Woody stepped outside the mill, around the corner from the doorway, and leaned against the wall. He rubbed at his aching chest and arms. Jace was working hard over the saw, and for a moment, Woody was glad for the reprieve.

He had laid things out for Jace before he arrived. He wasn't going to be around forever, but not at any time did he want to worry the younger man and distract him to the point where he might be injured on the job. The mill and farming were both dangerous jobs. Jace needed to keep his head at all times. Woody had seen Jace's face full of concern during those times when he'd let his guard down. He knew he was a man of compassion, and he admired him for that, but he also didn't want it to interfere with the task at hand, the important task of learning to take over all that Woody would leave behind.

"Woody!" Jace suddenly called, and that man put his head around the door to see his nephew frowning at the saw. Jace waved him over.

Hoping his face looked as though he hadn't a care in the world, Woody returned to the interior of the sawmill, hoping he would be around long enough to show Jace everything.

The end of the business day could not come fast enough for Maddie. The long hours on the train and the emotions of coming away from Boston so swiftly were all starting to wear on her. In addition, it seemed as though every time someone came in the door, they were there to see her.

She was extremely pleased to see old friends and even meet some new ones, but constantly bringing everyone up to date, all the while trying not to encourage any of the single men, was beginning to take its toll.

A glance at the clock told her she didn't have long to wait. She told herself that a quiet evening was ahead, with a nice tea and snack and then her old bed. An unconscious sigh escaped her, and Cathy heard it.

"I can finish here," the older woman said.

"I'll be fine."

"Go on, Maddie. I can see you're nearly spent."

Their eyes met, and Maddie could see that Cathy was doing well. With a small nod, she did as she was told and made for the rear door, the one that put her just 30 yards from the kitchen door of the house.

Cathy smiled in her wake. One of these days she would tell Maddie what it meant to have her here, and why just her presence gave energy to the older woman. One of these days, but not today.

Three

There was nothing Jace wanted more than a quiet visit with Cathy and Doyle, but on his way into town, he remembered that this was their niece's first day home. He did not want to interrupt such a time, so he opted for the Commons Tavern instead, sat at a quiet table, and ordered a pint.

Franklin served him, and hoping to relax a bit, Jace took a long pull and sat back in his seat. It was a quiet evening—most weeknights were—but it was just lively enough to give Jace a distraction.

This had been one of those evenings when Woody was extremely tired. He had fallen asleep in the rocking chair right after evening tea, coming awake suddenly when there was a noise outside, and then taken himself to bed very early. Growing a little more accustomed to the labor, Jace wasn't fatigued at all. Indeed, he thought the hours alone in the house would be dismal, so he cleaned up and rode one of the horses into town with plans to see the Shephards.

Feeling himself relax, Jace took another drink and realized it was never very far from his mind that this hardworking, generous uncle of his was not long for this world. Jace had been tempted to hold himself back. He had tried to keep some emotional distance when he first arrived in Tucker Mills, but it hadn't worked that way. Woody was too personable, too likeable. Even if it meant a more painful loss, Jace wanted to know this man. He wanted to learn all he could and know he had a friend, no matter how it ended.

"Another one, Jace?" Franklin asked from beyond the counter, and Jace, not normally a heavy drinker, realized he hadn't been all that thirsty but instead in need of company.

"I'm good, thanks."

"I didn't see you, Jace," Carlton, from the livery, called from the table with the checkerboard. "Come on over."

Jace went, but it was for the company alone. He had not forgotten the way that Carlton had beaten him three games straight the last time they'd played together.

Jace lingered in the doorway of Shephard Store on Saturday afternoon, the last day of March, trying to find his bearings. At the moment Cathy was not in sight. However, a woman who could only be Maddie Shephard was behind the counter. And she was nothing like he expected. He'd gone from doubting her ability to help Doyle and Cathy to assuming she was a large, sturdy woman, easily able to step into Doyle's shoes. Neither was the case.

Maddie did not sport muscles that could carry everything the store stocked. Indeed, from what he could see over the top of the counter, Jace would have called her delicate. Right now she was waiting on a woman who was deciding between two bolts of cloth, but every so often, Maddie would lean across the counter top a bit to speak to the little girl at the woman's side, even reaching to touch the tip of the little girl's nose with a small, graceful hand.

Jace took in the blonde curls that escaped the coils of hair at the back of her head and the sparkling blue eyes amid a lovely complexion and almost shook his head. A moment later he spotted Cathy in the rear of the store and went that way.

"You didn't tell me she was pretty."

Cathy heard Jace's voice even though she hadn't seen him come in. In the back room, looking on a low shelf for a certain size clay jug, she turned with a smile.

"She's not pretty," Cathy countered, "she's beautiful."

Jace smiled, unable to argue with her.

"Did you meet her?" Cathy asked.

"Not yet."

"Well, let me find the jug I'm looking for, and I'll come out and do the honors."

Jace was only too happy to meet this young woman, so he waited while Cathy searched. Having poked her head under the back-room counter, she asked why he was in.

"I just need a bit of wire. We won't repair things at the mill until the planting is done, but I've got to jury-rig that crank."

"Here it is!" Cathy exclaimed, making a mental note to add that size to the order list. "Come on, Jace—come and meet Maddie—and then I'll get that wire."

The two walked back out front, only to find that the woman at the counter was now debating among four fabrics. Maddie had moved off to help someone else and was just finishing with that man when her aunt caught her eye.

"Maddie," Cathy said, wasting no time, "meet Jace Randall."

"It's a pleasure, Mr. Randall. My aunt has written about you numerous times."

"Please call me Jace," that man said, thinking she was really quite beautiful.

"I've decided, Maddie," the woman suddenly called.

Maddie smiled her goodbye at the two and went toward the customer. She measured and cut the fabric that was chosen and folded it for the woman to place in her basket. By that time Cathy was finding the wire and other customers had arrived.

Maddie greeted the three young ladies who had entered and asked if she could help.

"We're just looking right now," she was told, and so she went about her business. It took Maddie several minutes to notice what kind of browsing they were doing. All their *looking* seemed to be directed at Jace Randall.

While she was still watching, Jace caught their attention, nodded briefly in their direction, and then glanced at Maddie. Maddie couldn't stop the way her eyes lit with laughter. Wanting to laugh as well, Jace only shook his head in Maddie's direction and turned back to Cathy.

And with no warning, the store grew busier. Two more customers arrived, and Maddie was very occupied. Cathy was run off her feet as well, and when things calmed nearly 30 minutes later, Maddie found herself outside, having just helped a woman load a box of supplies into her wagon. On her way back inside, she found Jace just emerging.

"Did you get everything you needed, Mr. Randall?"

"Yes, and it's Jace."

Maddie nodded, smiled, and suddenly teased, "Did you realize when you came into town that you would also be part of the merchandise?"

Jace only laughed as two young men came out the door behind him. They were doing some looking of their own, only it wasn't at him.

"I see you're also mistaken for dry goods," Jace returned when the men had moved on.

"Only on occasion," Maddie said dismissively, and Jace knew that it was probably more along the lines of daily.

"I'd better get back inside." Maddie was the one to break away.

"Have a good day, Miss Shephard," Jace said with a respectful bow of the head.

Thinking he was as kind as her aunt's letters had indicated, Maddie thanked him and slipped back into the store.

Neither one realized their entire conversation had been observed. Doyle Shephard, sitting by a window in the parlor and working to stay rested and calm, found his pulse quickening. Why had it never occurred to him how perfectly suited Maddie and Jace were? He didn't have an immediate answer, but the question occupied his mind for the remainder of the day.

"You're wondering about the cost of boards, Mr. Muldoon?" Woody clarified.

"That's right. We might be entering into a building project in the foreseeable future, and I was just trying to get an idea. Do you have any prices for us?"

Woody had never talked to this man. When he went to services, it was to the Center Meetinghouse. When he went. However, he patiently explained the cost of cut boards versus the cost of the customer providing his own logs to be cut. If the prices were a surprise, the pastor gave no indication.

Douglas Muldoon listened intently, thanked the sawyer for his time and information, and went back to town. He had brought the small wagon he owned and now drove his horse back in the direction of home.

Douglas reminded himself that he could not worry about this. God had provided the money for their needs, and He would certainly reveal the details in the appropriate time.

Jace fed the livestock early Sunday morning, not paying attention to what he was doing, just going through the motions, his mind far away. Not until the rooster tried to spur him did he realize he'd better attend.

"You could end up in a stew pot," he mumbled to the large, colorful rooster, who clearly knew he was the king of the farm-yard.

Jace was eyed disdainfully for his comment and then com-pletely ignored. He finished the chores without consequence and then went inside for breakfast. He took extra time in cleaning up, and when he arrived in the kitchen, he was dressed to go out.

"You going courtin'?" Woody teased.

"No," Jace said quietly but firmly, working to convince him-self as well as his uncle. "I'm going to services this morning."

Woody stared at him and then asked, "At the meetinghouse?"

This stopped the butter knife in Jace's hand. He set it and the muffin down and stared at his uncle.

"Yes. Where else would I go?"

"There is a Center Meetinghouse right on the green, but then there's a group that meets at the Muldoons', the yellow house in town."

Working to be as nonchalant as he could manage, Jace went back to buttering one of the muffins Clara had left for them. He tried to wait a while, but his mind was too anxious.

"Where do Shephards attend?"

Woody took a sip of his coffee and grinned.

"I wondered what took so long in town yesterday. You met Maddie, didn't you?"

"I might have," Jace hedged, smiling but not willing to be caught outright.

Woody wanted to tease him and draw him along, but he didn't have the heart.

"They attend on the green."

Jace nodded.

"I think I'll go with you," Woody announced, stopping Jace's breakfast again.

"Can I trust you should we happen upon Miss Shephard?"

"Trust me how?" Woody said with a satisfied smile.

"To keep quiet."

Woody only grinned at him, and Jace shook his head, wishing he'd lied to his uncle about where he was headed.

Well now, Doyle thought to himself, noticing that Woody and Jace had slipped into the rear of the meetinghouse. He'd not shared his thoughts with anyone, but he had wondered all day— and some in the night—if Jace had taken any notice of his girl. He hadn't seen Jace in the meetinghouse since he moved there, and he'd not seen Woody since long before his health began to decline. Assuming Jace was there for only one reason, Doyle found himself as satisfied as if he'd managed the whole business himself.

"Join us for dinner," Doyle said hospitably to Woody and Jace once the service ended. "We have plenty."

"Thank you," Woody accepted, amazed at himself. He tended to be a loner and couldn't remember the last time he'd eaten in someone else's home. He glanced at Jace to see what he thought of the idea, but Jace was looking in Maddie's direction, telling Woody he'd done the right thing.

Maddie was not looking their way. She appeared to be making an exit from two young men who were trying to speak to her. There was a smile on her face, but she kept backing away from them. They didn't get the message, however, and kept moving with her. Finally, Doyle spotted them and went to the rescue. In the midst of all of this, Woody also took in the fact that when the young ladies passed by Jace, they did so slowly, hoping to catch his eye. Woody could actually find it in his heart to pity them, but he wasn't at all sad that Jace's gaze went in Maddie's direction.

"I'm sorry if I kept you," Maddie said as she joined the group. "They had questions about Boston."

Maddie said this with such sincerity that for a moment Jace's and Woody's brows both rose. Did she really think they were mostly interested in Boston?

"Woody and Jace are joining us for dinner," Cathy said, telling her it didn't matter.

The Shephards began to walk down the green toward their home, but Woody and Jace retrieved their wagon from the meetinghouse stables and moved it to sit behind the store. They stabled their horse with Doyle's livestock before going to the front door to join the family.

In a very short time the women had made the table comfortable for five, food laid out in plentiful amounts but without the bother of cooking. Cathy always made plenty on Saturday so Sunday could be a true day of rest. She wasn't overly religious herself, but she knew she couldn't get through the week without that day off.

The five were seated a short time later, and cheese, slices of pork, bread, apples, corn cakes, and honey were passed in liberal amounts. Cathy put coffee on to boil. She would also serve the blueberry cobbler she'd made last evening.

"You almost done at the mill, Woody?" Doyle asked.

"It's wrapping up fast, this week I expect. It's time to get into the fields."

"Nickleby started his planting. I think we'll have more frost, but he's sure not."

"What did he put down in his south field?" Woody asked.

Sitting quietly and taking all this in, Jace thought he could almost thank his sister. Having her challenge him about his involvement with females had forced him to monitor the way he responded to them. So many days he found women wandering past the mill, women who were a little easier to ignore because of how forward he found them.

But now he realized he could easily fall into the same category. He wanted to speak with Maddie, hear her voice, and have her eyes meet his, but he did nothing to accomplish this. He sat quietly and ate, speaking only when he was spoken to and not letting his eyes rest on Maddie for more than a moment at a time.

And he was certain this was wise because she didn't seem to notice him at all. He knew that some of his interest was over this very fact. *The one who didn't want you was the one you wanted.* But Jace knew it was more than that. Had this woman wandered by the sawmill to catch his eye, he would have let it be caught, not worrying in the least if Eden could claim the victory.

"How much field planting have you done, Jace?"

"A little," he answered, coming back swiftly. "I used to help on a farm, but that was years past."

"He'll catch on." Woody spoke with confidence, and Jace had all he could do not to look at Maddie.

Had he but known it, he could have looked at Maddie. She was smiling in his direction over the compliment, and his looking wouldn't have made a bit of difference to her. She was not interested in getting married, and no amount of male attention was going to sway her feelings.

"Let me slice that for you, Doyle," Maddie offered, taking the apple from her uncle's hand and using her knife.

"Are the little children in Boston missing you, Maddie?" Woody wished to know.

"Everyone is quite grown up these days," she explained. "I'm really more of a companion to the missus, and I think the family is getting ready to travel, so the timing was very fine."

"Actually, Maddie, I was wondering who was peeling their apples for them," teased Woody. Maddie laughed and continued her work.

Jace watched her hands with the apple, finding himself wondering if her skin was soft. The store was rough work, but she'd only just arrived. Had the work in Boston already taken a toll, or would her hands have known an easier life in that place?

"Coffee's ready," Cathy announced, rising to find mugs while Maddie went for the cobbler and the cream pitcher.

As soon as Maddie stood, Jace relaxed a bit. She was gone from the room for a moment, leaving him free to look around as well as watch for her return, something he did with great pleasure, not missing a thing about the way she moved or looked. Her dress was a soft yellow, not a gingham like Cathy usually wore but a solid color with darker yellow, almost gold, fabric on the collar and cuffs.

Not that he would be caught looking. He was careful to school his features before she had a chance to look his way, realizing that having to be on his toes might make for a long afternoon. It was worth it, however. Right now he couldn't imagine a place he'd rather be.

Maddie was also just where she wanted to be, having had few expectations on the day. All she was looking for was a day off from the store, and she was getting that. When she suddenly found herself alone in the parlor with Jace Randall, she thought little of it. Doyle had remembered something he wanted Woody to see in the store. Cathy had gone with them, Maddie was sure, to keep an eye on her husband's activities. Maddie had slipped up to her room to get some handiwork, and when she emerged, Jace was in the parlor.

"Oh, you're still here, Mr. Randall. I thought you might have gone to the store."

"It's Jace, and I wasn't invited," he said easily, trying not to be disappointed at her lack of interest.

"Would you care for some more coffee?" Maddie answered, even though all she wanted to do was sit down and not think.

"No, I'm fine. Can I get you some?"

"No, thank you."

Maddie took a chair, and Jace sat as well. She set her knitting in her lap and looked across at her guest.

"Don't let me keep you from whatever you're going to do," Jace said as he stood. "I'll just look at some of these books if that's all right."

"Certainly."

Maddie bent her head over her sewing, seeing that her aunt's letters had been correct: Jace Randall was a very kind man, and polite in the bargain. Giving him little attention, she grasped the needles and went to work.

Jace did his level best to read the page from the book he'd selected from the oak shelf, but it wasn't going well at all. While in her room, Maddie had slipped her apron off, unsettling her hair a bit. Her usual wound braids were slightly disheveled, and the little curls that had escaped around her neck were nothing short of distracting.

His own hair was close to the same color, but he'd never thought of his as being attractive. Her hair was so lovely and glossy that he wanted to touch it.

"What book did you choose?" Maddie asked.

"_The Pickwick Papers_ by Charles Dickens."

"I've not read that."

"Nor I."

"I'm sure Doyle won't mind if you take it."

"I might ask him."

"Is there time in your evenings for reading, or do you have equipment to mend?"

"There is some repair work, but there's time to read too."

Maddie nodded, her head dipping now and again to check her edges.

"Do you read much?" Jace asked.

"Not books, but I enjoy the newspaper."

"Boston must have offered plenty of those."

"Yes, daily."

"And what about Tucker Mills? Will our small newspaper be enough for you?"

"I think so. I'm not used to the work in the store just yet, so right now I haven't much energy left for reading at the end of the day."

"I take it this is a little different from your life in Boston?"

Maddie smiled. "I wouldn't know where to begin."

Jace nodded, but he didn't need any further explanation. Mr. Vargas from the glass factory had a wife and two daughters, and they would visit now and again. Their clothing spoke of style and wealth. Maddie Shephard's clothing—especially the dress she'd chosen for today—looked the same way.

"How long will you stay?" Jace asked before he thought that she might not think it his business.

"As long as I'm needed."

Jace nodded, his heart torn. In no way did he want Doyle to be in ill health, but if he was back in the store, Maddie would leave. Jace didn't let this fact panic him, but he did know one thing: No matter when she left Tucker Mills, she wouldn't go without knowing how he felt.

"You've been grinning since we arrived home," Woody teased Jace much later that day.

"Have I?"

"Yes. Something tells me you won't be hanging around on this farm most evenings."

"Well," Jace replied logically, "if I'm going to marry the girl, I can't sit out here all the time."

"Marry her, huh? That bad, is it?"

"Not bad at all," Jace said with a smile. "And I'll do my best to see that you're there for the wedding."

Woody's head went back when he laughed, and Jace felt himself relax, realizing that his uncle's approval on this subject meant quite a bit to him. Not until much later did he wonder what Eden would think, and then he told himself he didn't care.

On Monday morning, Alison Muldoon realized she needed lard. She added that to her list for Shephard Store and saw that the list was getting rather long. She was ready to leave Hillary at home with her brothers and do some shopping, but when Hillary asked to go, Alison took them all along.

The store was quiet when they arrived, and because Alison knew Cathy, she went directly to her. Maddie was across the store, restocking bolts of cloth and cleaning the counter, fixing and straightening items from the morning business. She saw Alison come in, the boys behind her, and then she spotted Hillary.

"Paige!" Maddie said without thinking.

Hillary Muldoon heard her and stopped.

"Excuse me?"

Maddie shook her head and apologized. "I'm sorry, but you so remind me of a girl I know named Paige, that her name just slipped out."

Hillary smiled kindly, aware that Maddie still studied her.

"I'm Maddie Shephard," that lady said, remembering her manners and beginning the formality.

"I'm Hillary Muldoon."

"It's nice to meet you, Hillary. Would you be about 16?"

"Only just."

"And those are your brothers with your mother?"

"Yes."

"Not in school right now?"

"Our teacher grew ill, and now most kids are needed in the fields, so we closed early this year."

"You don't live on a farm?"

"No, my father is a pastor."

"Where is he a pastor?"

"In our home," Hillary explained. "We don't have a meetinghouse yet."

"Where do you live?"

"In the yellow house down the way."

"I know the one."

Hillary smiled at her, liking this woman who seemed young and making her curious about Maddie's age.

"I just realized that I have some mittens that your mother made," Maddie said. "She trades them here at the store, doesn't she?"

"Yes," Hillary said with a bit of pride. "She does beautiful mittens, caps, and scarves."

"And do you knit as well?"

"Not like Mother does, but I'm learning."

"I'm sure you'll be following in her footsteps in no time."

Hillary had no more thanked her when Martin needed some attention. She walked away from Maddie, hoping they would visit again soon.

Four

Doyle was being foolish and knew it, but he didn't want to stop. He had gone across the yard and slipped into the door that led to the office. He then sat on the stairs that led up to storage, giving his ears the opportunity to hear almost everything going on in the store. And he'd been enjoying himself, right up until the moment he heard Maddie offer to carry a bag of feed for a customer.

Doyle's eyes suddenly closed in pain. *She shouldn't be doing that. It's my job. She's too little.*

With the words came real pain, this time from the region of his chest, his heart rate picking up drastically. Moving while he was still able, he rose painfully to his feet, went back out the door, and crossed the yard again.

Once at the house, he wanted to lie down but knew if Cathy checked on him—something she often did—it would upset her to find him in bed. Instead, he made a beeline for the chair by the kitchen fireplace and sat down heavily.

You're an old fool. You're never going to get back down to your store if you pull stunts like that. The speech did not immediately slow his heart, but a few deep breaths and close to 30 minutes later, things seemed back to normal. Only then did strong emotion overtake him. A sob broke in Doyle Shephard's throat, and tears came to his eyes. For a moment there he thought he was going to die; he thought he'd been done for.

"I don't want that," he whispered to the empty room, even as his heart yearned to be out of there and next door. "I don't want to die."

Not willing to fight it anymore, Doyle let his eyes close, falling into blissful sleep. He never even heard Cathy when she checked on him a short time later.

It was not going as Jace had planned. He was supposed to have energy to go to town, but planting the fields was sapping all vigor from his body. Having decided on Sunday to marry Maddie Shephard, it was nothing short of maddening not to have time or physical strength even to see her until Thursday.

Now headed into town, Jace had all he could do not to whip the horse into greater action. He had deliberately waited until near closing, catching Cathy and Maddie in the last 30 minutes of store hours. As he had hoped, things were quiet.

"Well, Jace," Cathy greeted him when he stepped inside.

"How are you, ladies?" Jace spread his smile to encompass both of them.

"Doing well," Cathy replied, hands busy with a task at the counter.

"How is planting?" Maddie asked, having thought about Jace at odd times during the week.

"We've covered plenty of ground, but we're only about a quarter done."

"How are your weeds?" Cathy asked.

"Not bad. Woody says we can attribute it to a dry spring."

A customer came in, and very deliberately Jace moved to Maddie's counter.

"How was your week?" he asked.

"Busy. It's gone very fast."

"It'll be Sunday before you know it."

"A day of rest," Maddie said with a smile, not aware of what that smile did to Jace's heart. "What can I get for you, Mr. Randall?"

"Madalyn," Jace said, his voice low and serious.

Maddie stopped and looked at him, his tone and the use of her full name giving her no choice.

"Please call me Jace."

"You keep telling me that, don't you?"

Jace nodded and smiled a little.

Maddie's gaze softened as she apologized. "I'm sorry. I promise I'll remember."

"And may I call you Maddie?"

"Certainly."

Jace grinned at her, putting every ounce of charm into that smile. Maddie smiled back before saying, "What can I get you, Jace?"

Jace pulled out his list, and the two of them worked until Cathy closed the doors.

"I'd better get going before you lock me in."

"Stay for tea," Cathy invited.

"I'd like that," Jace said, unable to tell them how much, "but Woody is expecting me back. I'll just slip by the house and say hello to Doyle and be on my way. Thanks, Cathy. Thanks, Maddie."

The women bid Jace goodbye, but Maddie stared after him for a long time. Cathy eventually noticed her expression but didn't comment, at least not then, and certainly not to her niece.

"I didn't expect you back so soon," Woody told Jace when he arrived. "Didn't they invite you to tea?"

"They did, but I hadn't told you I was going to be gone into the evening."

Woody's look was telling. "Jace, you're not some smooth-skinned lad who's still answering to his mother. You should have stayed."

Jace shrugged, feeling irritated that he hadn't when Woody made it sound so simple. They took their own tea in near silence until Jace remembered he had a letter. Pulling it from his pocket, he read it, finding that it did nothing to improve his mood.

"Oh, no," he mumbled, putting the paper aside.

"Bad news?"

"Eden's coming." Jace's voice spoke volumes.

"How can she come when she has a boardinghouse to run?"

"One of her tenants already helps her with the cooking, so she just takes over for Eden if she's ever away."

"You don't want her here," Woody stated plainly.

"No."

"Why?" Woody asked bluntly, irritated as well and not sure why.

"Eden thinks my life is her business. She says that because I'm not writing to say how I've been, she's coming to find out for herself."

"That's what I'm talking about, Jace," Woody reiterated, not angry now but wanting his nephew to get the point. "You're your own man, soon to be owner of this farm and the mill. If you don't want Eden to come, tell her. And if she asks things you don't want to answer, ignore her."

Jace nodded, but deep in his heart he knew it wasn't that easy. Eden had all but raised him; she was much more a parent than a sister. And she was subtle. She could gain answers when you were barely aware that you'd been asked a question. And in all fairness to Eden, Jace did love her. Outside of Woody, she was all the family he had.

"Do you mind if she comes?" Jace asked finally.

"Not at all. And if she gets here and runs your life, I'll not say a word. But she won't run mine. And if you're smart, you'll make it very plain in the first five minutes that you no longer need a mother."

Jace's look must have shown skepticism because Woody went on.

"You'll be 25 on your next birthday, Jace, and I've watched you now for months. You're doing fine, and you're going to continue to do so. Eden needs to see that you have grown up."

Jace watched Woody's head go back over his plate and knew that he would hear no more on the matter. It was Jace's first choice to write and tell Eden to stay away, but he thought better of it. Having her come to Tucker Mills might be the best thing. That way she could see that he was fine and not worry—not worry and stay in Pine River. He suspected that her visit was for herself and not her younger brother.

"I have to talk to you," Cathy said that night in the privacy of their bedroom. "Don't turn the light down yet."

Doyle stopped his hand from heading that way and looked with concern at his wife. She'd been whispering.

"What's the matter?"

"Nothing is the matter, but I saw something today."

Doyle waited.

"Jace came in."

"He came to see me," Doyle reminded her.

"Oh, that's right, but this happened before he came over here."

Again Doyle waited.

"I think Jace likes Maddie."

Doyle smiled and reached for the lantern, but Cathy read the look with ease before the room was covered in darkness.

"Doyle Shephard, what do you know?"

"I know what my eyes tell me."

"What have you seen?"

"What you've seen—Jace's interest."

Cathy sighed, a sigh Doyle couldn't place.

"Is this upsetting to you?" he asked.

"I don't know. I watched her with him today, and I think she might have noticed him too, but I don't think she'll let her heart get involved."

"Well, we might have to help with that somewhere down the line."

Cathy's voice told him she was surprised by this answer. "Doyle, she's a grown woman, almost two years older than Jace."

"I'm well aware of everyone's age, Cathleen." Doyle's voice was patient. "We know more about Jace than Maddie does. We know he can be trusted. If we can see that the only thing holding her back is fear, then we need to step in."

Cathy wasn't sure she followed his line of reasoning, but suddenly she was tired. With another sigh, she lay down against the pillow.

"Are you going to worry all night?"

"No, I'm too tired for that."

"Just watch them for now," Doyle advised, "and don't say anything. It will probably all take care of itself."

Again, Cathy wasn't sure this would work, but she didn't argue. Getting a little more comfortable and telling her husband goodnight, she willed herself to fall asleep.

They were spending Sunday together again. With things looking much as they had the week before, Cathy now knew why Doyle had invited Woody and Jace to join them for dinner. And what was more, Cathy suspected that Woody was in the know as well.

"Are you reading your Bible?" Jace asked of Maddie. They were once again on their own in the parlor.

"Not actually reading, but looking for a verse that Mr. Sullins used today."

"Which one?"

"It said something about heaven."

"And you had a question about that?" Jace asked, not wanting to admit that he hadn't heard a word of the sermon for looking at the back of her neck and the intricate coils of braids in her hair.

"I just didn't understand what he meant. It sounded like heaven was only in the apostle Paul's mind, and that makes me wonder if it's a real place or not."

"I wish I could help you, Maddie," Jace apologized, "but I'm not sure I heard that part."

"I didn't hear anything after that," Maddie admitted. "I was too busy trying to figure it out."

"Did you attend church in Boston?"

"If the missus wanted the children to go." Maddie sighed after she said this. "No one there could ever answer my questions."

"What kind of questions?"

"Oh, about death and heaven."

Jace tried not to think about death too often so he knew he couldn't be of any help to her. He had some beliefs, but they were his own, and he was satisfied with that.

"Did you cut your wrist?" Jace suddenly asked.

Maddie looked down at her lap and studied the back of her left wrist. "Yes, I caught it on a wire yesterday. It was clumsy of me."

"I think you're not actually cut out for store work."

Maddie smiled, not in the least offended. "I was over there every day for the first 17 years of my life."

"But Doyle did the heavy work."

"True, but it won't kill me. I'm sure of that."

He didn't love the thought of her hauling crates and merchandise all day, but her hardworking attitude was easy to hear. Farming was hard work for men and women alike. It would include more lifting than was expected in the store. He was glad she wouldn't shy away from the jobs that came with being a farmer's wife.

It occurred to him that he hadn't asked her why she was thinking about heaven and death. He wondered for a moment if Doyle's condition had anything to do with it but then remembered that she'd had questions in Boston as well.

"I think they're done outside," Maddie said absently after hearing the kitchen door. She shut the Bible and listened to footfalls from a distance.

Jace knew a moment of regret. He'd enjoyed being alone with her, not because he was ashamed of his thoughts or what he might do, but because when they were alone, Maddie was somewhat focused on him.

The three other adults joined them a moment later, and Woody said he was ready to go. Jace took his leave as he always did, wondering when he would see Maddie again.

Several hours later Maddie brushed her hair out, thinking about Jace Randall as she readied for bed. Even knowing that she would keep her heart to herself, she had to admit that he was one of the best-looking men she'd ever met.

For a moment, his green eyes swam into her mind, and she thought about the way his hair fell across his forehead, always looking a little messy but also rather fetching.

Maddie sat up straight, the train of her thoughts not amusing her in the least. *What's the matter with you? He's not to be trusted. Not him or any man!*

Ruthlessly pulling with the brush, Maddie finished her hair in a no-nonsense way, turned the light down, and climbed into bed. She wasn't tired enough to fall right to sleep, but that didn't matter. What did matter was that she had a will strong enough to keep Jace Randall completely from her mind.

"Douglas?" Alison called from the stairs before walking all the way down. She checked the parlor and her husband's study and found them both empty. The kitchen was next, but he wasn't there either. The door, however, was not completely closed. Alison put her head out and found her husband standing in the semidark moonlight at the side of their house.

"Douglas?" she whispered as she joined him.

"Come here." He held open his arm, and she slipped under it to be pulled against his side.

"Are you praying for Tucker Mills?" she asked.

"And for us."

"Us the church family or us the Muldoon family?"

She watched him smile before saying, "Yes."

"Do you ever get discouraged?"

"Just with myself," Douglas admitted. "I get impatient for answers and want things to happen. It's too easy to forget that I'm not in charge."

"I pray for you."

"I can tell that you do." He turned his head enough to kiss her brow. "Kids all down?"

"Yes, it's nice and quiet."

"Was that an invitation, Mrs. Muldoon?"

"It might be," she teased as she scooted out from under his arm.

Alison reached the kitchen door ahead of him, but just barely. His own worries and troubles retreating from his mind, Douglas was right on her heels.

Jace was in the fields with Woody when he spotted her. She hadn't said when she was coming, and it was quite a walk from the train station, but she had done it. Eden Randall had come to Tucker Mills.

"I would have picked you up," Jace said as she neared. "You didn't say what day you were arriving."

Eden only smiled, not wanting him to know what week she was coming.

"You've filled out," she commented, touching his arm, "but your face is leaner."

Jace shrugged a little, pleased by her words but not telling her so.

"Hello, Eden," Woody called as he came around the barn.

"Hello, Uncle Woodruff."

"He goes by Woody," Jace said as that man came to shake her hand.

"It's good to see you," Eden told him with a smile.

"Welcome to Tucker Mills," Woody said, surprised at what a fine-looking woman Eden Randall was. From the way Jace had talked, Woody had been expecting a spinsterish old shrew.

"Come inside. Clara's still here. I'm sure she's got the kettle on."

"Clara?" Eden turned to Jace with raised brows, only to find her brother mute. He smiled at her and brought up the rear.

Right then and there, Eden knew fear. Jace had been telling her everything she wanted to know for as long as she could remember. When he'd left Pine River last October, he'd said he would write, but only one letter had come and nearly none of her questions had been answered. She wrote to him every week with inquiries about his life, but nothing came of it. Not even threatening to come to Tucker Mills had forced Jace to write.

And now she'd shown him—as she always did—that she wanted an answer, and he'd not said a word. She didn't think she could lose him this swiftly but suddenly feared that very thing.

"Clara?" Woody called as he stomped his way through the front door. "We've a guest."

Eden's heart calmed a little when an older woman—probably older than Woody and definitely the house help—came down the stairs.

Eden had written to Jace to ask about how they ate and who prepared the meals, but he'd not answered. Well, that was why she was here: to get answers. She was also certain Jace had a girl somewhere in town. And she intended to find all about that as well.

Woody performed the introductions between the women, and completely comfortable with her place at the farm, Clara offered to show Eden to her room. Eden, although very congenial, waited only until she and Clara were alone upstairs to make herself at home.

"I'm going to be here for a few days, and I'd be happy to cook and look after the house for you."

"If that's what Woody wants," Clara said easily.

"I don't think he'll mind."

"Well, he'll be the first to tell you if he does."

Clara led the way back downstairs and to the kitchen. Eden would have liked to freshen up, but she didn't trust Clara to present her suggestion properly, so she came directly behind as the older woman returned to the main level.

"Miss Randall wants to cook for you for a few days, Woody," Clara said, checking a pot on the stove and then turning back to him.

Woody's head came up from the paper he was writing on. Jace also looked up to see his sister near the door, waiting for an answer. Woody looked to Eden for a moment and then to Clara.

"You want a few days off, Clara?"

"Not particularly."

Woody's gaze transferred to his niece. "Thanks for the offer, Eden, but Clara knows the way I like things done."

Both Clara and Woody went back to what they were doing, but Jace had eyes only for his sister. Eden looked to find him smiling hugely at her. She couldn't help but smile back at him, shaking her head a little.

"I'll be upstairs if you need me," Eden announced, not sounding the least put out.

Jace waited just a moment before following her. Once the kitchen was quiet, Woody spoke to Clara again.

"Everything all right, Clara?"

"Everything's fine. You all right?"

"Um hm."

Clara heard the satisfied tone in her employer's reply, and although she didn't comment, she was pleased as well.

"How are things at Randall Boardinghouse?" Jace asked, not knocking as he entered her room.

"Things are fine. May took over for me."

"I figured as much. Did you rent my room?"

"Yes, but it took a while. So what's her name?" Eden dropped all attempts at subtlety and asked outright.

"You don't waste any time do you?"

"No. Are you going to tell me?"

"Believe it or not, Eden, I do not have a string of women in Tucker Mills."

"Not even one?"

"No," Jace answered truthfully.

Eden didn't believe him, but Jace didn't try to persuade her. Even if she stuck around for a good long time, Maddie Shephard was not returning his looks. If Jace kept his eyes to himself, Eden would never be the wiser concerning his feelings.

Almost as soon as he had this thought, Jace felt guilty. Maddie was not some passing fancy. He genuinely cared for this woman and was impressed enough to pursue her. She was the very type of woman he *wanted* Eden to know about, but he knew she would never believe him to be serious.

"I'll find out," Eden suddenly said, causing Jace to wonder what his face had been doing.

"You do that," Jace said, sounding almost bored and causing Eden to doubt but also to hear herself.

"The house is nice, Jace—the whole farm is," Eden said kindly, not wanting there to be anything between them. "I'm happy for you."

"Thanks, Eden. Can you stay a while?"

"A train goes back Monday morning. I was going to stay until then."

"Good. You'll be here through Sunday then; it's the only day things slow down."

Eden nodded, her heart aching with love for this brother who had left the nest. She knew she could be difficult and overbearing, but she believed with all her heart that it was in his best interest.

Clara called them to dinner just a short time later, but in the few minutes they had together, Eden and Jace went back to old times. They were comfortable with each other, occasionally disagreeing but genuinely fond of one another, and until Eden grew bossy, they enjoyed each other's company.

Five

"Any regrets?" Cathy asked of Maddie after David Scales exited the store.

"No, I'm happy for him."

Cathy smiled into Maddie's eyes when she saw how true it was.

David Scales had once cared for Maddie, but that had been after her disappointment, and Maddie had not let any man get close since that time. Kind and charming as David was, Maddie had not wanted his attention. Eventually Cathy's broken arm had healed, and Maddie had returned to Boston. David had met someone new and married. As far as Cathy knew, this was the first contact they'd had in several years.

"You have something on your mind," Maddie commented.

"What makes you say that?"

"I can see it in your eyes."

Cathy smiled a little, her eyes narrowing as she teased her niece.

"I'll have to work around here with my eyes closed from now on."

"Why? What is it you're thinking that you don't want me to know?"

"I just want you to have someone, Maddie. I want you to be loved and cherished."

Maddie was speechless. Her aunt and uncle had never even alluded to wanting such a thing for her, and now to hear Cathy state it plainly was something of a shock.

"I'm doing fine," Maddie felt she should tell her. "Truly I am." Maddie stared at the older woman for a moment. "You don't worry about it, do you, Cathy?"

"Not very often, but at times."

Maddie reached to give her a hug, hearing the door in the process and knowing they were about to be interrupted. "Thank you," she said quietly, releasing her aunt in order to go back to work.

Cathy wasn't sure what had just occurred, but she was glad that Maddie had not been upset by her words. Doyle would ask her if she'd seen or heard anything—he did every night—and usually she had nothing to report. Tonight would be different.

"It's not too far from the farm, is it?" Eden asked as the wagon neared the sawmill.

"No," Jace agreed. "An easy walk if you need to."

Parking the wagon outside, Jace gave his sister a hand and took her inside. He explained the workings of the mill in detail and showed her where logs and boards were stored.

"It's larger than I imagined," Eden said, her head tipped back as she took in the rafters inside the mill. "And when do you run the mill?"

"The bulk of work is late winter into early spring."

Eden was impressed. Tending toward the cynical side, she wasn't impressed by much, but this was excellent. She knew the farm work gave a man plenty to do, but there were some months when a farmer wasn't that busy. Having a sawmill on the side was ideal.

"Well, that's about all I have to show you," Jace said. It was late on her second day, and she'd been all over the farm the day before. "We usually go to services at the Center Meetinghouse on Sunday morning. They start at 10:00."

When Eden nodded, Jace felt himself relax. She hadn't pressed him to take her into town. They would be in town tomorrow, but all the businesses would be closed. Even if Shephards invited them to dinner, Jace thought that would be easier than trying to stand in the store and not look in Maddie's direction.

"How often do you get into town?"

"Probably once every week or two on business, but most weeks I go to the tavern at least once."

"So you really don't have a girl, do you, Jace?"

She had tried to feel him out for two days but gotten nothing. She knew it was time to ask again.

"No, Eden, I don't." Jace's voice was patient. "I would like to get to know someone, but all of this is very hard work, and there hasn't been a lot of time."

"Do you have someone in mind?"

"As a matter of fact, I do," he replied, opting for honesty, "but I'm not discussing it."

There was no missing the hurt she felt over this statement, but Jace hardened his heart. He hadn't even told the girl how he felt, which meant he certainly wasn't going to speak to his sister about it!

"Why won't you tell me?"

"Because right now it's no one's business but my own. If something ever comes of it, then I'll tell you."

Eden knew no end of frustration. She had begun to believe she could go home in peace, thinking he'd been working so hard that he'd not found anyone interesting at all. But obviously he wasn't blind, and Eden didn't know why she'd expected him to be.

"So she doesn't know how you feel?"

Jace turned and walked away, something he'd never done to his sister before. Eden stared after him, her mouth open a little, before following.

Jace stood by the wagon, ready to help her back into the seat. This was all done in complete silence until Jace pointed out another of Woody's property lines to his sister.

So that's the end of it, Eden thought. *The matter is closed, and I get no say. He's found someone, but I'm not to be privy to his thoughts.*

"Did you see it?" Jace asked for the second time.

"Did I see what?"

"I was just showing you where that far field borders."

"I don't think I did."

Jace pulled the wagon to a halt. They were about halfway back to the farm.

"Are you going to be angry at me about this? Are you going to leave angry?"

"I just don't understand," Eden began, but Jace cut her off.

"You don't have to understand. You just have to accept my decision on this."

Eden could only stare at him. "How could you have changed so much in six months?"

"I don't know, but did you really think after the things you said to me that I would share anything with you?"

Eden looked completely lost. "What did I say?"

"That I'd have a wife and half a dozen kids before I knew what hit me."

Eden looked away. She was in the habit of making pronouncements, but she'd never imagined he'd take this one so much to heart.

"Well, it hasn't happened," Jace said. "You never admit that you're wrong, but I don't have a wife, not even close." Jace slapped the reins and sent the team into motion.

"I might have exaggerated the facts, but I *was* right," Eden felt a need to tell him. "You *are* interested in someone, and it's been only six months."

"Eden, I'm a 24-year-old man. What do you expect of me?"

"I don't expect anything, but just so you know, I was right."

"If that makes you feel better, Eden, you go right ahead and believe that."

They arrived at the farmhouse, and Eden could not have been angrier. She allowed Jace to help her down, but as soon as her feet touched the ground, she turned to him in rage.

"And is this what else you've learned here, to disrespect your sister?"

"Is it disrespectful to say what I've been wanting to say for years?"

"I don't believe it."

"Well, you need to," Jace said bluntly. "In the past I've just shut my mouth and let you think you're right, but this time I'm telling you different."

The two glared at each other for a time. When Jace could see she was not going to relent, he turned to take the team inside and settle them for the night. He'd not had them out long, but the other stock had to be fed as well.

Eden could not move for the shock she felt. Jace had always bowed to her wishes, never completely refusing her the way he did today. They'd had words certainly, but he'd eventually done as she instructed. She stood for a long time and felt the shock give way to anger, anger directed not at Jace, but at whoever this woman might be. Eden's thoughts became unreasonable, but she wasn't able to see this.

It's this woman. She's had some sort of changing, wicked influence on Jace. Eden's breathing quickened as her high emotional state began to rage completely out of control. *I might not know today, but someday I'll know who she is. And when I meet her, she'll be sorry she ever met Jace Randall.*

The uneasy truce that had formed between Jace and his sister helped him keep his gaze wholly centered on the pastor Sunday morning. But even at that, Jace was able to observe Maddie as she headed directly to the front of the meetinghouse when the service was over to approach Mr. Sullins. He hoped that man would answer her questions about death and heaven.

His thoughts never far from the incident with his sister, he also found himself hoping it would be at least six more months before his sister came back to Tucker Mills.

"How do we know there is a heaven, Mr. Sullins?" was Maddie's first question. "How do we know we don't just lie in the ground?"

"Heaven is a mystery of God, but we can be reasonably certain it's there," Mr. Sullins explained.

"Why doesn't God tell us for sure?"

"It's not something we need to worry about. Don't forget that He is a benevolent God who gave His Son to love us. You shouldn't worry about heaven being there or not. You should not see God as waiting to pounce on imperfect people.

"Just do your best, Maddie. Do good, make a difference— like you're doing coming to help your aunt and uncle—attend services regularly, and our respectable God will reward you with life in heaven."

"But how can we know?"

"We're as sure as we can be, Maddie," Mr. Sullins responded, his voice sounding so firm that Maddie was afraid to ask anything else.

"Thank you, Mr. Sullins," Maddie said, working to hide her disappointment.

Her effort at covering her discouragement must have worked because the pastor only smiled, patted her shoulder, and moved on his way. Maddie joined her aunt and uncle where they waited outside, pleased that they were alone. She wasn't up to company today, not even Woody and Jace. She felt tired and disappointed, and all she wanted to do was rest.

∞

"I'm sorry we didn't get to meet your sister, Jace," Cathy said to him when he stopped by the store and explained that she'd been there.

"It's probably for the best. She wasn't in the finest mood on Sunday."

"Not feeling well?"

"No, it's not that. I don't think she expected me to grow up, and when I did, she didn't care for it."

Cathy's brows rose. They had allowed Maddie to leave home and go all the way to Boston at the age of 17 because she had a dream, so this was not something to which Cathy could relate.

"Did you quarrel?"

"Yes—about women."

"What women?"

"Not women exactly, more like a woman—one woman. Eden was frustrated when I refused to tell her whom I would like to see more of."

"Do I know this woman?" Cathy's voice had dropped, her heart pounding.

For a moment Jace looked at her and then admitted, "Better than anyone else in town, I would say."

Cathy began to smile but was given no time to speak. Maddie had come into the back room looking for something. Cathy told her where to find the item, and Jace followed her out front.

"Did I see you go up front on Sunday?" Jace had waited around and now asked when Maddie had a moment.

"Yes, I did talk to Mr. Sullins."

"And did it help?"

Maddie only shook her head, her eyes a little sad.

Jace wished he knew what to suggest, but if their pastor couldn't help, who could? It occurred to him that maybe she should leave well enough alone. She wasn't dying. She wouldn't have to worry about heaven or the afterlife for a long time. He would have suggested this to her, but Cathy needed her just then.

Seeing that he wouldn't have any more chance to speak with her or Cathy, he collected his things and went back to the farm. Not until he arrived did he remember that there was one more group in town, even if they didn't have their own meetinghouse. Jace wondered if Maddie had checked with that pastor yet.

"I just realized I haven't seen much of Doyle Shephard in the last few weeks," Douglas mentioned to Alison one morning. "Is he all right?"

"I'm not sure. Doyle and Cathy's niece is here from Boston to help out, so I think he must be taking things a little quieter."

"He's not dead, is he?"

"No, we would have heard."

"I might stop around to see him. He's been such a huge help in the past with so many supplies. Do you know if he can have visitors?"

"I don't, but Cathy will tell you. I'm sure of that."

Douglas went back to his breakfast, but his mind was elsewhere. His small church family didn't even have a meetinghouse, and some folks in town thought them different. Most people didn't stop to find out what he believed, but one day

Doyle Shephard had asked a few questions. Douglas wasn't sure whether he had answered to the man's satisfaction or not. He'd told him that if there was ever another question, he should just come around and see him, but it had never happened.

The next chance Douglas had, he'd stop in and see Doyle. He looked forward to speaking with the older man not only because he genuinely cared for him but also to see if his hunger for God had increased since they'd last talked. Douglas prayed for the owner of the general store, asking God for that very thing.

Jace had finally caught on to the routine. After dinner, Doyle would invite Woody to look at something in the store or barn. Jace knew Doyle enjoyed very few outings these days, and was glad that Woody could be around for a small distraction.

Today, however, Jace wanted to get Maddie out of the house on his own. He had nothing to offer in the barn or store but suggested a walk. To his surprise, she accepted.

It had rained in the night, so things smelled fresh and a little wet. Jace walked along the road, town to his right side and trees to his left, and Maddie just a few feet away.

"Did you make that pie today?" Jace asked.

"No, that one was Cathy's."

"It was certainly good."

"Yes, it was," Maddie had to agree, turning her head a bit to look up at Jace's face. He was seven to eight inches taller than she was, with broad shoulders and a solid build. But her favorite thing about his looks was the way his blond hair fell over his forehead. For a moment Maddie experienced that feeling again, the one that had taken her by surprise on more than one occasion. The one she felt a desperate need to push away. For a moment panic filled her as she asked herself why she had agreed to this walk.

Jace chose that moment to turn and look at Maddie. He caught her staring at him before she had a chance to look away. This alone was enough to strengthen her resolve.

"You need to know, Jace," Maddie burst out without warning, "that I think all men are liars and cheats."

Jace had to stop after this announcement. For the moment he could do nothing else. He looked at Maddie, surprise filling him when he saw her frowning face, but he didn't speak.

Maddie looked right back at him, stunned that he wasn't angry with her. Indeed, his face looked as calm as ever.

"I thought it only fair that I tell you," Maddie said, slightly calmer.

"All men?" Jace checked.

"Yes."

"Doyle Shephard?"

"Well, no," Maddie backed off a bit, her fierce expression gone.

"The Reverend Mr. Sullins?"

"No, not him either, but all young men," she said, lifting her chin in defiance.

"Jace Randall?" that man asked quietly.

"Yes," Maddie managed, but her tone wasn't as certain.

"So your uncle allowed you to go for a walk with a man who's a liar and a cheat?"

"Well, men don't think of these things," Maddie explained logically. "Men don't treat each other that way, only women."

"Do women lie and cheat?"

"Not very often, and certainly not like men do."

"I didn't realize taking a walk with you could be such an education."

"If you're going to make sport of me, Jace Randall, I think the walk is over."

"But I wasn't making sport. I was just commenting. I thought the most we'd talk about would be the weather. I'm glad I was wrong."

Maddie stood in indecision. He hadn't sounded as though he was mocking her, but she had been very insulting and wouldn't have blamed him. Maddie studied his face a bit more. He certainly looked sincere.

"So you still want to walk with me, even though I told you how I feel?"

"Certainly. You're entitled to your opinion. That is, if you're willing to continue walking with a liar and a cheat."

Hearing again how she sounded, Maddie didn't comment but slowly began to move when Jace turned and began to walk. He moved slowly as well, wondering what he could say next. She was wrong. All men were not liars and cheats, and women could certainly be worse, but he wasn't going to persuade her—at least not with words.

"Is it nice to be back in Tucker Mills, or do you miss Boston too much?"

"Um, well, I do miss the family in Boston, but I love Tucker Mills."

"It's a good place to live."

Maddie's head was turned so she could look at Jace. His eyes were on the road, but Maddie could not stop staring at him. Had they really just disagreed and now were conversing normally?

"Watch that stick," Jace warned, and Maddie looked down in time. She sidestepped a thin branch in the road.

All at once that feeling flooded Maddie again. Jace's kindness and solicitude were leading her into a dangerous place. She had to get back to the house. She had to get away.

"I think I need to go home," Maddie announced, much more breathless than the walk merited.

"I'll walk you back," Jace offered.

"You don't have to," Maddie said, sounding panicked.

"Well," Jace said slowly, wishing he knew what was going on, "I'd like to walk you back, and on top of that, my uncle is still at the house."

"Oh, that's right."

Maddie started back, Jace in step beside her, but he could not stay quiet.

"Did I say something, Maddie? Are you upset with me?"

"No, I just need to get back."

She walked swiftly, Jace keeping up. Once at the back door, Maddie stopped and looked at Jace, her expression regretful.

"I do thank you for asking me on a walk. I'm sorry I wasn't very good company."

"I enjoyed it, Maddie," Jace stated honestly. "I hope you'll feel better soon."

The eyes that looked up at him told him she wasn't sure about what she'd done, but the panic was there as well. Jace followed Maddie slowly into the house, and as he expected, his uncle was ready to leave a short time later.

"Did you kiss her?" Woody waited until the farm was in sight and they had plenty of privacy.

Jace didn't answer.

"Well, did you?"

"Why have you never married?" Jace asked.

"Who says I haven't?"

Jace's mouth opened on this. "Have you?"

"No, too cantankerous and greedy."

"You're not the least greedy."

"Not now—now that I've figured out that it's all going to stay here."

Jace wasn't sure what to say.

"So tell me," Woody prompted.

"I hope you know that I never let anyone ask me the questions you get away with," Jace told him straight out.

Woody grinned and said with satisfaction, "You kissed her."

"As a matter of fact, I didn't," Jace said, his voice telling Woody this was serious. "It's going to take more time than I expected."

The remainder of the ride into the farmyard and to the barn was made in near silence. Woody offered to settle the team, something he hadn't done since Jace arrived. Jace thanked him and went inside. He was full of questions with no single answer in sight. For the moment, having time alone in his room was just what he wanted.

"Are you all right?" Doyle asked, opening Maddie's door enough to show his face.

"Yes."

"You sound sad."

"Maybe I am, Doyle, but it's nothing that anyone here has done. I just needed to come home from the walk."

"Jace didn't do anything?"

"No, nothing like that."

"Okay," Doyle said, respecting her privacy. "Do you want Cathy to call you for tea?"

"Yes, thank you."

Doyle shut the door, and Maddie lay down on the bed. It wasn't fair that the treatment of a man who hadn't deserved her love should color her world for all time, but it was turning out that way. Jace's face swam into her mind. She pushed it away. Right now she pushed everything away. Some days it was the only way she could survive.

"Jace, what you have to understand about Maddie is that she's been hurt."

"By whom?"

Jace had come to town midweek and found Cathy alone in the store.

"A man in Boston. She was in love, and he didn't tell her he was married."

Jace nodded calmly, but his mind was racing. This made sense. It explained quite a bit.

"When was this?"

"A long time ago—maybe about a year after she left."

"So that would have made her what, 19?"

"Eighteen."

"And there's been no one in all this time?"

"No."

They both heard Maddie coming down the stairs from the storage rooms and into the office. Cathy went to the office door to see whether she'd found what she went for, and Jace exited the way he'd come. He'd not arrived with much on his list—it was getting harder to come up with things—and right now he just wanted to keep thinking. He couldn't do that around Maddie, and Cathy couldn't tell him any more.

Jace made his way back to the farm, wishing there was some way Maddie would talk to him about what happened to her. He wasn't the type to play games with a woman. For all of Eden's claims that he had no head around women, he'd never used a girl or spent time with someone he hadn't truly cared for.

He had told Woody that this was going to take more time than he expected. Jace was torn between not wanting Doyle to be sick, and fearing that Maddie would return to Boston before he could persuade her that he was not playing games with her heart.

Six

Woody did not come to the breakfast table Thursday morning. He usually beat Jace downstairs, but not so this day. Jace waited only a short time before checking with Clara.

"Did Woody head outside already?"

"I haven't seen him."

Jace weighed his options. He had never invaded the privacy of his uncle's bedroom, but that didn't mean he shouldn't if his health was in question. No matter how well and hearty he seemed most days, Woody Randall was not at his best.

Jace went to the stairway, vaguely aware that Clara followed. She didn't follow Jace into the room after Jace knocked but lingered in the hall.

"Woody?" Jace spoke softly, easing himself quietly inside.

"Yeah," Woody answered with a distinct morning growl.

"Are you all right?"

"My chest hurts."

"I'll go for Doc MacKay."

"No. He'll just tell me what I already know. I just want to rest."

"Okay," Jace said, but he lingered in indecision. "Do you want anything?"

"Some water."

Jace used the pitcher in the room and poured him a glass. Clara had come in by then. She stood at the foot of the bed. A slight wringing of her hands was the only indication she was distressed.

"How's that?"

"Good. I'm just going to sleep for a while, and then I'll join you in the south field."

"It's already raining. I'm just headed to work on the wagon wheel in the barn, so you stay put."

"How heavy do the skies look?"

"I'm not sure. I'll check back with you."

Woody only raised his hand and turned on his side to get comfortable. Jace and Clara cleared the room, but both felt a little lost. Jace stood outside the closed door for a long time, Clara at the top of the stairs.

"I'm going to make his favorite bread," Clara said.

Jace went to her and kept his voice low. "I'm going to run into town just to talk with Doc MacKay. If he confirms what Woody said, I'll come back without him. I'll let you know when I get back."

Clara nodded, and Jace wasted no time in saddling a horse to be on his way. It was a wet ride, but he barely noticed. He wasn't ready to lose his uncle—he'd known that all along—but the current pounding of his heart only accentuated that fact.

Woody expected to fall back to sleep almost immediately. He shifted in bed a few times but still wasn't tired enough to drop off. He usually slept well in the night, and last night had been no exception. Clearly his body had had enough rest.

Swinging his legs over the bed, he slowly sat up. He wasn't sure if he imagined it or not, but he thought his chest might be feeling better. Not sure what to think, he decided that lying around never helped anyone. After drinking the water that was left, he got up and shaved.

"Is anyone here?" Jace stood quietly and called to the empty room. He'd let himself in. The shingle hanging over the door announced the residence of Dr. MacKay, and Jace had just assumed he was welcome.

"Is someone there?" a voice called down the stairs.

"Yes."

"I'll be right with you."

Jace waited only until he'd spotted the man who joined him. His own heart was in danger of stopping, so rattled was he about his uncle.

"I don't think we've ever met," Jace said, the words coming in a rush. "I'm Woody Randall's nephew."

"Is Woody all right?"

"I'm not sure. He said his chest hurt, and he didn't feel like getting up. He said you would only tell him what he already knows, but I wanted to hear that from you."

"I didn't catch your name, son," the kindly old doctor said as he put his hand out.

"Jace Randall, sir," he replied, shaking the offered hand. "Can you come? Is there a need?"

"I can come, but it will only irritate Woody, and he's right." The doctor gave a small smile. "I've told him all there is to know."

Jace nodded, feeling a complete loss for words.

"Is he comfortable?"

"I think so. He wanted to stay in bed, and he wanted some water."

"Then I think you're doing fine. Just follow his lead, Jace. Let him tell you what he wants and doesn't want. And if ever he would want me to come, I will."

"Thank you," Jace said, his voice growing a little thick.

The wise doctor nodded, not the least offended when Jace Randall left without saying goodbye. He was glad to have met the younger Randall. It helped the doctor know that Woody was in good hands.

Jace came to a dead halt when he returned to the farm and found Woody at the worktable in the kitchen. That man was reading the newspaper and drinking coffee. He looked a little tired but overall like himself.

"You're feeling better?" Jace asked, working not to react one way or the other. The man had scared him to death, and it was easy to be irritated about that. At the same time, Jace wanted to send him back to bed.

It came to him that this was Eden's influence coming out in him. Woody was a grown man. He knew whether or not he needed to rest. Jace's desire to send Woody back to bed was for his own peace of mind. He didn't want to worry, and that was more easily accomplished if Woody took things slowly.

"I am better, yes. Did you fix that wheel?" Woody asked, and Jace realized that Clara had not told Woody he'd gone into town.

"No, not yet. I'm going to get a cup of coffee and then get it done."

Clara all but shoved the mug into Jace's hands, having prepared it the moment the words were out of his mouth. Their eyes met for a moment, and Jace read worry in her gaze.

"Thanks, Clara," Jace said, meaning it for much more than the coffee. It was good to have someone else around who cared and worried with him.

"I'll be in the barn," Jace said and made his exit. He was certain that Woody would be on his tail, but he was wrong. When he came from the barn for noon dinner—rain still falling—

Woody was sound asleep in the rocking chair next to the kitchen fireplace.

"Jace, is Woody all right?" Cathy asked the moment she saw him coming into the store. It was the afternoon of the same day, and Jace had been so antsy that Woody had told him to go courting.

Jace had laughed at the idea but also taken him up on it. It was his second wet ride to town that day, but the store was dry and smelled nice. At any rate, a chance to see Maddie was worth any amount of trouble.

"He's all right," Jace assured her. "What made you ask?"

"Doyle saw you going into Doc MacKay's."

Jace nodded. "He didn't go back with me. Woody just needed a little bit of extra rest. He was cantankerous when I left, which I assume is a good sign."

Cathy smiled. "It's that way with Doyle too. Feisty is good; compliant is scary."

"Did you ask?" Maddie was suddenly at her aunt's side, any embarrassment she might have been feeling from their last encounter forgotten in light of Woody's health.

"Yes, he's fine," Cathy told her, and Maddie smiled at Jace.

"We were all worried. I'd better go tell Doyle."

"Why don't I go?" Jace offered, hoping to hang around a bit.

"He would enjoy that," Cathy said, and Jace went back out the front door.

"Cathy," Maddie asked as soon as Jace was gone, "how did you get to be so close to Jace?"

"It just happened, I guess. When he got into town off the train, he came here looking for directions to the farm. Doyle gave him a small basket of goods, just some soap and a few other items. He made a point to come back and thank Doyle again a few days later, and I met him then.

"I could see that he was slightly overwhelmed by all that Woody had been presenting him, but when he came to the store, it wasn't because of the mill; it was just a place to visit and maybe buy something. Doyle took to him right off, and I thought he was so adorable that I was always giving him sweets. I probably treated him like a kid, but he didn't seem to mind."

Cathy's story made Maddie think about Jace for a long time. She hadn't considered how he felt when he'd first come or what a huge position he was attempting to step into. When she'd tried to talk to Doyle about Woody's dying, he didn't want to discuss it, but Maddie thought about such things. She worried and pondered what life would be like in Tucker Mills when Woody was gone. And now that she'd met Jace, he figured into her thinking as well.

A few moments later she realized she still needed to sort the special orders that had been delivered that morning and went back to work, glad for something else to distract her thoughts.

"So he was all right when you went back?" Doyle checked again.

"He certainly was. He was sitting at the kitchen table, drinking coffee and looking at the paper."

"Ya just never know," Doyle said, shaking his head in wonder. "Well, as long as he's doing fine. That's what matters."

"I agree with you. He took it pretty easy today, so maybe it won't be much of a setback."

"How is the planting coming? Are you near done?"

Jace filled him in and noticed that Doyle hung on nearly every word. Jace wondered absently what it would be like to be so closed in, and after watching his uncle and then Doyle, he hoped he would never have to know.

Jace didn't get back down to the store until nearly closing time. Not even looking in Cathy's direction, he went directly to where Maddie was working and pulled out his list.

"A bar of shaving soap," Jace began when she was ready to help him. "A small jug. Clara wants a bag of sugar," and the list went on, about eight items in all. Some things Jace needed, and some he wasn't desperate for at all. Clara liked to come in and do her own shopping, but every so often she would surrender one of her items. This week it was sugar.

Maddie fetched all the items, and Jace handed her the money, saying as he did, "You'd better check that money."

Maddie looked down at the coins in her hand and back at him.

"I might be trying to cheat you."

Maddie's mouth opened when she realized what he was teasing her about. She wanted to be angry, but it wasn't working. A small smile tugged at the corners of her mouth, and she turned away before she could laugh. When she returned with Jace's change, however, he did not let up.

"Is this correct?" He studied the coins. "I don't want you cheating me."

"Jace Randall!" Maddie could not keep her silence. "I can't believe you're teasing me about that."

"About what?" His look was as innocent as he could manage. "I've heard that women can lie and cheat too. Not as much as young men, mind you, but women are capable."

Maddie put a hand over her mouth to keep from laughing. Jace gathered his things, his own eyes brimming with a teasing light. When he was ready to leave, he leaned on the counter, bringing his face close and down to her level.

"Madalyn," he said so softly that she leaned toward him. "Obviously some man has hurt you, but you need to believe that we're not all like that."

Maddie felt trapped by his eyes. She didn't move, not even when he reached up and brushed her chin with one finger. Maddie's head turned to follow Jace's progress out the door, but not until a man came from the back room with a rake in his hand did she come back to earth.

Leaving Cathy to help the man, she went down on her knees behind the counter. Shifting and arranging shelves that were in perfect order, she stopped after a few minutes and allowed the thought of Jace Randall to settle in her mind. Remembering his dark green eyes sent her pulse racing. She felt flushed all over.

In an instant she realized no one had ever affected her in that way, not even the man who'd broken her heart, and she'd been in love with him.

Wanting to dismiss the feeling once and for all, Maddie pushed to her feet and got ready to close the store. She finished her duties, but they were done without joy or relief. Right now she felt nothing except hopelessness in her situation.

Cathy witnessed some of this and was on the verge of asking whether Maddie was all right but held her tongue. It would have been a foolish question to voice. One look at Maddie's face told Cathy that the younger woman was anything but all right.

Planting was over and the crops were settled for the season. A stretch of beautiful weather the first week in May allowed the men to put in long hours and finish the job. Weeding always waited for attention, but as for the growth and health of the crops, that was in God's hands. Each and every farmer hoped for the right amount of rain and sun in order to harvest in the late summer and fall.

The Randalls were no different. Their crops were in, and they were working on equipment and at the mill. They had done almost nothing else but planting for nine days, even missing services on Sunday, but this week had brought some relief, and Jace was already planning to go into town on Friday night. Instead of going to the Commons Tavern, he would stop and see the Shephards and Maddie, someone he hated not seeing for more than a week. He hoped to gain an invitation to visit for a spell.

"I'm tired," Woody said over lunch on Friday. "Why don't you go ahead to the mill and work on the millrace. Beavers tend to get in there every year."

"I'll do it."

Woody gave some instructions to Jace, truly wishing he felt like going himself but wanting to see it done today. They wouldn't be using the mill for a few more months, but he wanted that done so he could check it tomorrow, telling himself that tomorrow he'd feel up to going.

The store was busy, almost like a Saturday. Cathy and Maddie worked until dinner, and then the afternoon picked up again. Some folks just browsed, and some came in to visit. Maddie was putting a flask of vanilla back on the shelf when she overheard Asa mention Jace's name.

"I was out near the sawmill before coming here and saw Jace Randall fall in the millpond. Tripped up and went in head first, he did."

Maddie heard nothing else. Her heart felt as though it were going to stop in her chest. It didn't really register with her that there were people in the store and that Cathy needed her help. Jace had fallen into the pond and she had to go.

She slipped out the side door and managed to keep her walk steady until the edge of town. She even waited until a line of trees hid her before breaking into a run, but run she did. She made the mill in record time, her chest heaving, her mind racing.

Jace didn't see her arrive but suddenly looked up to find her in the wide doorway, somewhat disheveled and out of breath.

"What are you doing here?" Jace asked, still dripping on the sawmill floor and thinking Doyle might be sick.

"Asa came in. He said you fell in the millpond."

"I did fall in."

"I thought you'd drowned!"

Jace nodded, compassion filling him. "You don't swim, do you, Maddie?"

Maddie could only shake her head no, too upset and out of breath to say more.

"I swim," he reassured her kindly. "I swim very well."

"You might have drowned," she repeated.

"Not unless I'd hit my head on something, and that wasn't the case. I was leaning over working on the millrace and lost my balance. That's all."

Maddie nodded, unable to look at him. She glanced around the doorframe, aware that he was headed her way.

"Were you worried?" he asked softly when he stopped in front of her.

"Of course not," Maddie said, eyes still averted.

"I think you were."

Maddie finally looked at him.

"And I think you have entirely too big an opinion of yourself, Jace Randall."

Jace smiled slowly.

"So I'm to believe that you ran all the way down here for what reason?"

After casting around for something to say, Maddie tried, "I just thought someone should let Woody know if you had indeed drowned."

Jace smiled again, his eyes knowing.

"I have to get back to the store," Maddie said, knowing retreat was her only hope.

"I'll take you," Jace offered, suddenly serious, but Maddie was backing away.

"I've got to go."

Jace didn't press her, but then he didn't need to. He'd found out in a most unexpected way all he needed to know.

"I'm going into town tonight," Jace told Woody over tea that evening, still thinking about the way Maddie had come to the mill.

"To the tavern?" Woody asked, his voice knowing.

"Maybe," Jace said cryptically.

"Unless you find some other place to go?" Woody guessed.

Jace didn't need to answer. The smile he tried to hide gave him away. The smile faded swiftly, however, when Woody reached up and rubbed at his chest, his face a little pained.

"On second thought, I might just stay here."

Woody looked at him with surprise and found Jace's gaze trained on him.

"Not for me, you're not," Woody put in plainly.

"I think I can make that decision myself," Jace countered.

Woody sighed. "Jace, I don't expect you to center your life on me."

"That's not what I'm doing, but you're not at your best right now, and I'm not expected in town, so my plans are easily changed."

"Go to town, Jace," Woody commanded firmly, thinking that was the end of it.

"What I do with this farm is your business, Woody Randall. What I do with my time is my own."

Woody looked at him, realizing this was exactly what he'd wanted for his heir, but he never reckoned on it being directed at him.

Woody sighed and Jace heard it. He didn't care if the older man didn't approve. He didn't want to live with the horrible feeling he would have if Woody died while he was away. He realized it could happen at any time, but when it seemed this obvious, he knew he would be foolish to leave.

It made for a long evening. Woody fell asleep fairly early, but Jace was strong in his resolve. Nearly as bored as he could imagine, he even got out the book he'd borrowed from Doyle and began to read.

"I need a favor, Clara," Jace said on Saturday morning when Woody had already gone outside.

"As if I don't do enough around here," Clara replied sarcastically, catching Jace off guard. For a moment he stopped and then realized she was teasing.

"I need a picnic lunch," he plunged in and told her, "for tomorrow."

Clara smiled. "Do I get to know whom you're taking?"

Jace smiled back. "As if you don't already."

Still grinning, Clara turned back to the pan she was washing. "I'll leave it for you in the buttery."

"Thanks, Clara." Jace kissed her cheek, surprising her mouth wide open.

But Jace didn't see how he'd startled her. He was already turning toward the door, hoping that Woody was at his best all day. He had to go into town tonight and ask a certain lady to join him on an outing after services tomorrow. And for that reason alone, he desperately needed his uncle to be in top form, at least for the next two days.

Tea was over on Saturday night by the time Jace arrived at the Shephard house. Cathy was handing dishes to Doyle to dry, and Maddie was putting the last touches on some muffins they would enjoy the next day.

Doyle answered the knock, pleased to see Jace, and invited him in.

"You just missed tea," Cathy told him.

"I just had my tea, thank you, Cathy. I'm actually here to ask Maddie a question."

This brought all the Shephards to attention. They looked at Jace as a threesome—two with pleasure and one with dread.

"Maddie," Jace began, his palms sweating as they held his hat, "would you accompany me on a picnic tomorrow after services?"

"Well," Maddie hedged, not wanting to look at her uncle and aunt. "I'm not sure that I'm free."

"Of course you are," Cathy put in, and Maddie turned surprised eyes to her.

"I thought we would leave right after services," Jace explained. "I'll have the wagon."

"I'm not sure that I can, Jace," Maddie began.

"Why not?" Doyle chimed in this time, really causing Maddie's eyes to widen.

"Well, then," Jace said, working not to smile. "Tomorrow, Maddie?"

"All right," she said, unable to believe those words had come out of her mouth.

Jace was gone just moments later, and Maddie stood still, but only until she found her voice. She rounded on her aunt and uncle, feeling utterly betrayed and determined that they would know it.

Seven

"What happened here just now?" Maddie asked, her voice tight with frustration.

"You agreed to go on a picnic with Jace," Cathy spoke up.

"I agreed, or you and Doyle agreed?"

"Either way, it's a good idea," Doyle put in.

Maddie's mouth opened. "How can you say that? You know how I feel. I've never felt so betrayed in all my life."

This silenced Doyle and Cathy. Maddie's feeling betrayed was never part of the plan. Cathy was sick at the thought of it.

"I'll go after him," Cathy said, starting to remove her apron. "I'll tell him we made a mistake."

Maddie looked into the crushed faces before her and shook her head.

"Please, Cathy," she began, stopping her aunt's movements. "Just tell me why you both want me to do this. Please just explain it to me."

"We think Jace is special, and we can see that he cares for you. We thought you might be feeling the same way."

Maddie heard these gently spoken words and realized something. They had never interfered. They had never tried to pair her off or do any matchmaking. That they were doing so now was something she had to take notice of. And on top of all of that, she *was* noticing Jace. It would be a lie to say anything else.

"I'll go with Jace tomorrow," Maddie said, doing her best to cover all annoyance. She couldn't take their crushed faces any longer, and as always, Doyle's health lingered in her mind. "But you need to understand that I'm not making any promises. I think Jace might be special too, but that doesn't mean I trust him. I would never deliberately hurt him, but if my rejection of him does that, I'll not feel guilt."

"We don't expect any more than that, Maddie," Doyle told her. "We want you to be honest about your feelings, and if they don't include Jace, then he'll have to learn to live with it."

"And we don't think he's the type to play games with your heart, Maddie," Cathy added. "We would not have welcomed him in the first place if he were that sort of person."

Maddie nodded, hoping they were right. It had been years ago, she knew that, but some things you don't overcome. She honestly didn't think her heart could take that kind of treatment again.

Jace didn't know when he'd been so nervous. He was ready for services a full hour early, the picnic basket prepared and waiting, and all he could do was pace.

Woody would be going on his own, giving Jace the wagon. He wasn't sure his uncle felt that well, but Jace thought he might be putting on a good front so that Jace would keep the date.

In a last-minute, desperate move just before he went out the door, he slipped a small flask of Woody's liquor into the basket. Not even when he'd come to Tucker Mills on the train had he been this nervous. As excited as he was to have Maddie Shephard all to himself, he wondered if he'd have the wits about him to say anything intelligent.

"You're going to be late," Woody said, already to the door.

Jace shook himself. He'd paced himself into a standstill and was now behind schedule. He went out the door knowing he mustn't dare but wondering if he might need a drink from that flask just to get into town.

Maddie was utterly silent on the wagon seat next to Jace. Jace kept the team at an easy pace, not having revealed where they were going, but Maddie noticed they were headed in the direction of the mill.

"Did you have anything to ask Mr. Sullins this morning?" Jace asked.

"No," Maddie said, not wanting to admit that she'd heard little of the sermon.

"I hope you didn't delay your questions on account of me. I would have waited."

"No, I didn't have questions this morning."

Jace wondered if it was going to be this strained the whole time. He knew he ducked out on her answer last night when she said yes even though he could tell she was doubting.

His eyes shifted every now and then to look at her, but she kept her eyes straight ahead, and there was no eye contact.

Jace had driven the team past the mill and the farm to a nice grassy area of unknown ownership. Woody was friendly with all his neighbors, so Jace felt confident that he was welcome. When he finally stopped the team, he helped Maddie down from the seat. Clara had set out a quilt, and Jace grabbed that along with the basket.

The field was open and huge. The grass wasn't overly long, and Jace took them only a little ways into the field before he set up. Maddie sat on the blanket as soon as it was spread out and let Jace do the rest. He began to unload food, and it seemed to her that there was no end.

Maddie was impressed with the picnic—she couldn't help but be. Clara had made fried chicken, honey rolls, and cheese biscuits. She had cut up small pieces of salted pork and mixed them with apples and raisins. There were cookies, tarts, and a small jug of tea.

"Thank you," Maddie said when Jace loaded a plate and handed it to her. "It all looks very good."

"I think Clara outdid herself," Jace commented, starting on his own plate.

And with that, conversation nearly died. Maddie would only glance in Jace's direction, and she initiated no conversation at all. He hated it when women threw themselves at him, but it would have helped if Maddie had at least spoken to him.

Jace knew it was his own fault. He could tell that she didn't want to go the night before and was probably with him now only to please her aunt and uncle.

"Is your food all right?" Jace finally tried.

"Yes, thank you."

These stilted words were no more uttered than Jace watched her fold her arms and shiver a little.

"Are you cold?" Jace asked, noticing the way she huddled into herself a bit.

"A little," Maddie admitted.

"My jacket is in the wagon. I'll get it for you."

Maddie watched him leave, not sure how she felt about all of this. She reached for a bit of pork on her plate and proceeded to swallow it wrong. Working to dislodge the bit of meat, she reached for the small brown flask that Jace had put next to the tea and took a sip. It didn't help clear the pork away, but she felt almost instantly warmer. Coughing a little, she took another sip, enjoying how swiftly the coolness of the day melted away.

The third time she tipped the flask, she took a healthy swig, feeling heat course through her even as she found it a little hard on the throat. She was coughing when Jace returned.

"Swallow wrong?" he asked, setting the coat on her shoulders.

Maddie replied in a hoarse voice as Jace went back to his plate. He'd only taken a few bites when he looked to find Maddie smiling at him. Jace smiled in return.

"Warmer?" he asked.

"Much," Maddie answered, her smile softening.

Jace's heart did a flip in his chest. Had he known the jacket would do that for her, he'd have given it to her when they started out.

"Would you like more food?" Jace offered, gaining another smile for his efforts.

"I like your hair," Maddie said, and Jace reached in time to keep her plate from sliding off her lap.

Maddie never even noticed. She was still smiling at Jace, whose heart had begun to freeze inside of him. His mind raced with several questions. Could he have been that wrong? Could she have fooled everyone? Was the sweet, shy Maddie Shephard not as shy as she pretended to be? Jace put both plates aside, suddenly not hungry at all. As he did this, he noticed Maddie reaching for the flask.

"Maddie." His voice stopped her. "Have you been drinking that?"

"I think it's strong tea," she told him. "It makes my insides all warm." This said, Maddie smiled at him and asked, "Is your hair soft?"

"Oh, no," Jace whispered, not having to question any longer. He took the flask from Maddie's grasp and held her hands with his own.

"Listen to me, Maddie," Jace commanded. "Do you feel all right?"

"I like you, Jace," she said in return. "You're so sweet and handsome."

If it hadn't been so scary, Jace might have laughed.

"Do you know what we need to do?" Jace asked, coming to his feet. "We need to take a little walk. Can you get up, Maddie? Come on. Get to your feet."

Maddie did as he asked, but she didn't feel very steady. She fell against Jace once she was on her feet, hands going to his chest as she looked up into his eyes. Maddie smiled and reached up to brush her fingers through the hair that always hung on his brow.

"Oh, mercy," Jace muttered. "Come on, Maddie. Let's walk a bit. Can you do that?"

It was slow going, but Jace managed to keep her on her feet. He thought he'd give much for a pot of coffee right now, but the best he could do was to keep her active in order to drive back into town. If she was grinning and falling all over him when they returned to the house, her reputation would be shot.

"Look at the trees, Maddie," Jace said to her, trying to distract the way she wanted to smile at him. "Why don't we go over to that small group of trees and look at the leaves."

Maddie only giggled and tried to keep step with him. Jace managed to get her to the trees and had her lean against one. He took a step back, making sure she was steady, and then moved away.

"Why are you over there?" Maddie asked.

"It's better this way," Jace said, but she only pushed away from the tree and tried to come toward him. Her feet tangled, and she nearly fell before Jace caught her. Again, her head tipped back and she smiled at him. Feeling her body against him, Jace looked down into her beautiful face and gave up. He lowered his head and kissed her the way he'd wanted to do for weeks.

Maddie was completely relaxed in his arms. Her own arms came up to encircle his neck, and she fell completely against him. Jace's senses swam until he remembered she was not herself. He tried to break the kiss, but Maddie was holding on tight. He eventually had to remove her arms and put her away from him.

She was still smiling when he tried to march her back out to the field, wondering what he had hoped to accomplish by heading into the privacy of the trees. For the next hour they walked around the field until Jace could see that she was standing well on her own. He eventually led her back to the blanket and talked her into having some more food.

"I'm tired," Maddie said at one point. "I probably haven't been very good company today."

Nothing could be further from the truth, Jace could have said, but he kept silent and gave her some tea to drink.

When Maddie began to yawn, Jace knew he needed to get her back. She was still wearing his coat, which he took back, and the coolness returning seemed to wake her up a little more.

"I think we'll head back now, Maddie," Jace said, not sure if he was disappointed about the afternoon. To his surprise Maddie seemed to smile at him with complete lucidity.

"Thank you for the picnic, Jace. I enjoyed it."

The trip back was not as silent as the trip out, but Jace wished he knew whether this was the real Maddie or not. Had she finally relaxed with him, or was there still enough alcohol in her system to impair judgment?

Jace honestly couldn't tell. He returned her to the house, walked her up the front path, and even spoke to Cathy and Doyle for a few minutes. Maddie wore a faint smile all the way home. Jace wanted to be excited by the smile, but something held him back. He left Shephards before deciding if he should tell Cathy and Doyle about the incident.

"Drunk?" Woody asked for the third time. "She was drunk?"

"Yes, you heard me right. I couldn't believe it."

"And what kind of drunk was she?"

"The smiling kind."

"Amorous," Woody interpreted correctly.

"Don't get any ideas."

"So you didn't take advantage at all?"

"I did a little."

"And you feel guilty."

"Completely."

If Woody had wondered if Jace's feelings were real, he wondered no more. A man felt no guilt when he was able to kiss or hold a woman he didn't care about. Jace looked miserable.

"You'll have to go this week and see her. See how she is and how she responds to you."

Jace nodded, trying to think it through, and then something struck him.

"How do you know so much about women when you haven't been married?"

"They're not that hard to figure out."

Jace's mouth swung open. "You must be the only man in creation to feel that way."

Woody only laughed, completely sure of himself. Jace shook his head, wondering yet again how he got into these conversations with his uncle. Woody was always completely forthright with his questions, which tended to disarm Jace and gain honest answers. If Jace was candid, however, he always felt better for having spoken of it. As to whether or not he agreed with Woody's opinion, that was another matter entirely.

"I haven't seen you out and about, Doyle," Douglas explained when both Doyle and Cathy made him welcome. "I wondered how you were doing."

"I'm taking it slow these days," Doyle was able to say, still surprised at himself that he wasn't more frustrated with the fact. "Old Doc MacKay says it's my heart, and taking it easy might do the trick."

"Have you been in quite a bit of pain?"

"Off and on."

Douglas nodded. "Alison tells me she's seen your niece in the store."

"Maddie is the only reason he's able to stay so calm," Cathy put in.

Douglas smiled, but he was thinking how hard it must be to be cooped up all day.

"Are you getting more reading done?" Douglas asked.

"No." Even Doyle seemed surprised by his own answer. "I spend much of my time by the parlor window." He grinned a little. "I can tell you that Turtle Bates comes past here every day about 10:00, even on days he doesn't need to shop. And the Canton boys come by closer to noon. They never look angelic enough for my taste, but I never witness the things I hear about."

Douglas laughed.

"How have you been, Mr. Muldoon?" Cathy asked.

"I'm doing well. I've been thinking about you folks a lot. Is there anything you'd like for me to pray about?"

Without missing a beat, Doyle said, "And I think Alice Houston and that Bluel fellow are sweet on each other."

Douglas nodded and smiled in his direction, knowing he had his answer. There was no hunger in Doyle Shephard for the spiritual things Douglas would love to introduce to him. Douglas didn't rush away, and although Doyle had no requests, Douglas still prayed.

Cathy didn't try to ask any more questions of him, and Douglas listened for an hour as Doyle shared, but by the time the pastor took his leave, he sensed that God had answered his prayer. He had asked God to put hunger in Doyle's life and Cathy's too. And now he asked God to help him keep the friendship alive.

∞

"Well, hello, Hillary," Maddie greeted when that girl came in the front door.

"Hello, Miss Shephard. How are you?"

"I'm very well. How about yourself?"

"I'm fine. My father is visiting with Mr. Shephard, so I came with him to fill a list for my mother."

Maddie smiled, now understanding her serious face. She was on a mission.

"Put your basket here, Hillary," Maddie invited, "and tell me what you need."

"Lemon oil and lard," Hillary began, and Maddie started to put things on the counter. They worked together for about 20 minutes before Hillary said they'd covered the list.

"It was kind of your father to visit Doyle," Maddie mentioned, helping Hillary arrange the things in her basket.

"He likes your uncle. We all do."

Maddie smiled, pleased but not very surprised. Everyone in town liked Doyle Shephard.

"Is he feeling better?" Hillary asked.

"Well, he's taking it slow, and that might help in time."

Hillary nodded, not willing to intrude but also not willing to admit that she didn't know what was wrong with Doyle Shephard.

"Why didn't you visit him too?" Maddie asked.

"Well, sometimes folks like to talk about spiritual things with my father, and that can be private."

"What type of things do they discuss with him?" Maddie asked, suddenly very interested—not for Doyle but for herself.

Hillary answered artlessly, which was her way. "Oh, they ask about life, death, heaven, and hell—those types of things."

Maddie knew no end of frustration when they were joined by another customer. She wanted to ask Hillary more on those very subjects but couldn't.

"Feel free to browse, Hillary," Maddie directed, hoping the younger girl would stay for a while.

"Thank you."

Hillary left her basket on the end of the counter and did look around. She had never been in on her own before and found it to be a wonderful treat. There wasn't enough time, however. Her father showed up long before she'd seen it all, saying he was ready to go. Maddie was still working with a customer.

"How was your visit?" Hillary asked her father.

"It was enlightening," he said thoughtfully. "Did you have a good time in the store?"

"Yes," Hillary told him, thinking about the browsing she had done, the dishes and fabric she'd seen. It never even occurred to her to mention her conversation with Maddie. She hadn't noticed anything unusual or important.

Little did the Muldoons know that Maddie finished with her customer just after they left the store and walked all the way out on the road, only to find them too far down the green.

Maddie was thoughtful as she went back inside. She had thought she'd spoken with all the pastors she knew. She'd completely forgotten Douglas Muldoon.

Jace timed his visit again near the end of the day. Maddie was alone—she'd been on her own most of the day—and working on the jewelry display that sat on the counter. She liked having quiet intervals to do small jobs but was also pleased to see Jace.

"Well, Mr. Randall." She turned when she heard the door. "What brings you to town this evening?"

Jace thought her voice and face were open and friendly, but the question threw him a bit.

"I just happened by," he improvised, hoping to keep that smile on her face. "Just passing through, you might say."

Maddie smiled at him, and Jace relaxed. Maybe his uncle knew more about women than he realized.

"Have you had a busy day?"

"Not very," Maddie told him, glad for the fact. Cathy had butchered a hog and wasn't available. It was nice that things had been quiet. "How about your day?"

"Well, the rain always changes the schedule. Field work was out, and there's only so much to be done at the barn and the mill right now."

Maddie nodded, not seeming to be put out when Jace came close. He looked at the jewelry she was arranging and pointed to a bracelet.

"This one reminds me of one my mother had."

"I think that's the prettiest one," Maddie said, smiling in pleasure and then turning to look at Jace. "Is your mother still alive?"

"No, she and my father died when I was young."

"Who raised you?"

"My sister. She was in town a few weeks back, but I didn't get a chance to introduce you."

"Is she quite a bit older than you are?"

"Ten years."

It wasn't a romantic conversation in the least, but suddenly their eyes caught and held. Maddie had thought about him so much since Sunday. She had not enjoyed a man's company for many years, and Jace had been such a gentleman.

Jace misunderstood the yearning he saw in her eyes. He looked at her for long moments before lowering his head. Maddie hesitated only a few seconds before moving her head away from him.

"What are you doing?"

"I was going to kiss you," Jace admitted.

"Why would you do that?"

Jace looked surprised but still said, "You didn't object on our picnic; I didn't think you would object now."

A thundercloud covered her face. It was swift and fierce.

"Jace Randall! We did no such thing!"

"What?" Jace's mouth swung open in surprise.

"Is that what you tell people?" she attacked. "That I kissed you?"

"I do not talk to other people about us." Jace's voice had grown cold as his own anger mounted. "But we did kiss, and now you're pretending we didn't. What game are you playing, Maddie?"

"*Me?*" she all but screeched at him. "I ought to slap your face."

"You'd better not slap me until you're willing to explain to me what that was on Sunday if it wasn't a kiss."

"Get out" was all Maddie would say.

"Gladly," Jace slapped the hat back on his head, turned on his heel, and stalked out.

Maddie had all she could do not to throw something at his back. She didn't know the last time she'd been so angry. When Cathy checked on her an hour later, she was still slamming drawers and cupboard doors.

Jace couldn't remember the last time he'd had such a headache. He felt betrayed and almost used. Why would Maddie play such childish games with him? It had been true that she wasn't at her best, but to deny the whole thing seemed very juvenile to his mind.

He shook his head, but that only made it hurt more. Woody thought he understood women. *Just go see her and see how she responds to you.* Jace remembered the words with disgust. She had responded just fine until the games began.

It was all Jace could do not to turn around and remind her that *men* were supposed to be the ones who lied and cheated. He wondered how she would view her own behavior. If that wasn't lying and cheating, he didn't know what was.

Jace suddenly stopped his horse. He'd been letting the animal find its own way home, barely even holding the reins.

"What if she doesn't know?" he whispered, not paying any attention to who might be around listening to him talk to himself. "What if she can't recall what we did?"

If Jace thought his head hurt before, he didn't know what to think now. And suddenly he was thirsty. Changing the direction of his mount, he headed back to town and the Commons Tavern.

He needed to sit with a tall mug and think this through. He wouldn't get drunk, even though it was tempting. He might just need to head back to the Shephards and confront Maddie again. And for that he certainly needed a clear head.

Eight

Two things were obvious to Doyle and Cathy: Maddie was upset about something, and she wasn't ready to talk about it. Her demeanor was quiet and sober during tea, and her answers to their questions were nothing more than monosyllabic replies.

It had never been their policy to pressure her into talking, but tonight they were both tempted. The mystery began to unravel as they worked on the dishes. A knock on the door startled Maddie into suddenly throwing her dishtowel onto the table.

"If that's Jace, I don't want to see him."

"Why not?" Doyle asked.

"Because he's like all other men," Maddie said, her face growing dark again.

Confused, Doyle and Cathy looked at each other before the knock sounded again. Cathy went to the door, and just as she dreaded, Jace was standing there.

"Good evening, Cathy," Jace's voice saying it was anything but. "I need to speak with Madalyn."

"She doesn't want to see you, Jace," Cathy said, her voice quiet with regret.

"Is that right? Well, you may tell her that I'm not leaving until I've gotten some things off my chest."

He looked so fierce—more handsome than ever—that Cathy almost smiled.

"Come in," she invited him and watched him take a chair in the parlor. Before she could get out of the room, Maddie had joined them.

"I told you I didn't want to see him," Maddie took one look at Jace and accused her aunt.

"This has nothing to do with Cathy," Jace cut in. "And I'm not leaving until you've heard me out."

Maddie would have spoken but she heard the door just then and turned to see that Cathy had deserted her ship. She had gone back to the kitchen, where Doyle waited, and shut the parlor door behind her.

"What do you remember about the picnic?" Jace asked her when she turned back to glare at him.

"What?" Maddie said, immediately disarmed.

"What do you remember about our picnic? What did we do? What did we talk about?"

"I don't know." She sounded as frustrated as she was. "We were in the wagon and then we stopped at the field. You had food for us."

"Do you remember the little brown flask?"

Maddie heard Jace's quiet, serious voice, looked into his face, and calmed some, even going so far as to take a seat. She didn't want to argue with this man, and if his face was any indication, he was as miserable as she.

"A little brown flask?"

"Yes, you drank out of it."

"I remember now. I nearly choked, but then I was warmer."

"Maddie, how much alcohol do you normally drink?"

"I don't drink any alcohol, not even hard cider. I don't like the way it tastes."

Jace stared at her, desperately regretting what had happened. Maddie looked back at him for a full minute, her eyes growing wide when she realized what he was saying. Her hand came to her face, her mind desperately trying to remember.

"I can't remember a thing," she whispered. "I recall eating and then getting cold, and then we were home, and I thought how nice you had been."

Jace's expression changed to one of regret. Seeing it, Maddie rose slowly, her own face losing all color.

"Jace, did we…?" she couldn't finish the question, so horrifying were her thoughts.

"No." Jace's voice was completely tender as he rose and went to her. He took her hand. "We kissed. I swear to you that is all we did. I didn't plan for that to happen, but you fell against me, and it did. I'm sorry."

The candle wasn't lending much light, but as Maddie looked up at him, she had all the light she needed to see that his heart was real. The regret in his eyes was genuine, and he'd not been playing games with her in the store.

"I'm sorry I was angry with you," Maddie whispered.

"It's all right. I knew you weren't yourself, but I didn't realize you didn't remember."

They stood and looked at each other for a long time. Finally Jace spoke, his voice low.

"I want you to know how much I want to kiss you again, but I won't do that until I know it's what you want as well."

"What about now?" Maddie asked, nearly breaking Jace's resolve.

"Now would work." They were both still whispering. "But when the time comes I want two things."

"What are they?"

"I don't want to be interrupted, and I want you to remember every moment."

Maddie's whole frame flushed with warmth. How had she thought this man anything but wonderful? She leaned toward him, and Jace almost leaned as well, but a noise in the kitchen stopped them.

"Some other time," Jace said quietly, reaching with one finger to stroke down her soft cheek.

Maddie smiled up at him, and Jace touched the end of her nose before smiling as well.

"You, Miss Shephard," he whispered, "are very beautiful."

Maddie's eyes sparkled up at him, and Jace reclaimed her hand.

"Let's go see Doyle and Cathy. They need to know we're not in here killing each other."

Maddie led the way. They joined the couple in the kitchen, who could immediately tell that fences had been mended. The four of them took the parlor a short time later and talked for many hours. It was getting late before Jace took his leave, but tired as they all were, they agreed that they would do it again, taking up where they had finished.

"What changed?" Cathy asked as soon as Maddie came to the breakfast table the next morning.

Maddie was very sleepy, so for a few seconds she only stared at her aunt.

"Is there coffee?" she finally asked.

Cathy poured her a mug, and Maddie sat at the table in the kitchen.

"Are you talking about Jace and me?" Maddie asked after a little more time.

"Yes. After tea last night you didn't even want to see him, and then you watched each other all evening. Did something happen on the picnic?"

"Yes, something did happen," Maddie admitted, and then realized she didn't want to elaborate. "I misjudged Jace," she ended up saying. "I didn't think he could be trusted, but I was all wrong."

"Madalyn." Cathy used her full name and sat down to put their eyes level. "We think Jace is as fine a young man as you can find, but we won't push you anymore. We never meant to push you. We don't want you to ever be hurt again."

Maddie smiled at her. "It's all right, Cathy. Jace and I are fine. I don't feel pushed by you anymore, but I'm glad you told me to go on the picnic. I might not have ever allowed Jace to get close, and that would have been a great loss."

"Are you sure?" her aunt asked, studying her eyes with great care.

"Very sure."

Giving Maddie's hand a squeeze, Cathy nodded as relief filled her. She had lain awake a long time in the night, trying to work it all out in her mind. She wanted Maddie to have someone, of that she was certain, but until Jace had come and the two had talked, she couldn't be sure he was the one.

Now watching Maddie, sleepy as she was, and smiling at nothing in particular as she drank her coffee, Cathy allowed herself to dream.

The letter started, *My Dearest Madalyn, I can't believe how long you've been gone.* Maddie smiled at Paige's dramatics and then sat back to enjoy herself.

> *Did you know there are 96 stairs in this house? I counted each and every one! Is that not the most pathetic thing you've ever heard? I've never been so bored in all my 16 years. Celeste came today and brought the baby.*

Paige changed subjects just that fast, telling of her sister and niece.

> *I think the baby looks like me and a monkey at the same time. Don't tell Celeste or Mother I said that. I've always heard that babies are beautiful, but the only*

beauty I see is in her eyes—they resemble mine. The rest looks like a small ape. We did not go on a trip. Did you know Mother was planning one? We were all set to go, but things came up at the office for Father. One of the partners died and left a terrible mess of paperwork and possibly some underhanded dealings. I always thought his eyes were shifty. I've decided to write that book. You know, the one you've been telling me to write. It will take place by the sea and involve a most vile murder. What do you think?

Maddie didn't know what to think, but she did laugh. She laughed so hard that tears came to her eyes. She waited only until she could breathe again to start a letter in return. She owed one to the missus as well but would cover Paige first. How she missed that precocious teen.

Maddie couldn't remember what she did wrong. She had run upstairs to get a tin of oil, planning to head right back down to the store. She wasn't in a particular hurry, and she didn't feel very distracted, but that didn't change what happened.

One moment she was three treads down, and the next moment she was in a heap at the bottom. The pain in her head and shoulder did not register right away, but when it did, she groaned and gasped a little. Moving her neck slowly in a circle, she didn't think anything was broken, but she was so sore she wondered how she would get up.

"Cathy?" a female voice called from out front.

"I'll be with you in a moment," Maddie called back, hoping it was true.

Maddie pushed to her knees and then to her feet. She dusted herself off, smoothed her apron and hair, and forced her legs to take her out front, hoping she looked more normal than she felt.

The woman in the store was a stranger to her, and she wasn't looking for much. Maddie filled her order in less than ten minutes, relieved to see her go. As soon as she was alone, she slipped out by the stove in the middle of the room and took a seat. Not until that moment did she notice the trembling.

Half of Maddie's heart hoped that Cathy would not arrive unexpectedly. She would know something had happened. But the other half wanted her to come, and that half wanted someone to hug her and tell her the strange, unsettled feeling that resulted from a nasty fall would soon be gone.

Her heart was still in a muddle when David Scales walked in.

"Well, Maddie," he said kindly, "on your own just now?"

"Yes." She rose, trying to keep the grimace from her face. "Cathy is working at home today."

"Any word on when Doyle will be back on his feet?"

"No, but he's doing well." Maddie forced her mind to think about Doyle. "I feel like he'll be back to himself in no time."

"I'm glad to hear it," David told her, and then just stared at her. Maddie caught it and looked back.

"Is something wrong?" Maddie asked.

"I was going to ask you the same thing."

Hoping to distract his thoughts, Maddie smiled at him and asked what he needed. David fell for it. He gave his list to her, a rather long one, and didn't seem to notice her again. Maddie was glad. She didn't want to tell anyone what had happened for fear that it would get back to her aunt and uncle. As soon as David left, Maddie went to one of the mirrors hanging on the wall and put herself into complete order.

She turned away from the glass, determined to look and act normal for the rest of the day.

"I think I'm ready to go back to the store," Doyle announced as he entered the kitchen where Cathy was dipping candles.

Cathy turned slowly toward her husband, not sure how to reply. She stared at the man she loved, the man she shared a life with and who worried her no small amount.

"Say something," Doyle commanded.

Cathy's mind scrambled. "Why do you think you're ready?"

"I feel good."

"How good?"

"Very good."

Cathy smiled at his earnest tone, some of her fear receding, but still she said, "It's only been two months, Doyle. It's not enough time."

He looked as frustrated as he felt, and Cathy expected this response from the man she knew so well. He had wanted her to speak but didn't really want to hear the words. And she didn't know what to say next. Would more words get her into trouble, or was he ready to listen?

The questions were taken from Cathy's hands when Doyle turned and left the room. He didn't slam doors or appear to be pouting, but Cathy knew that, at least for the moment, the subject was closed.

Maddie could hardly believe the day had come to an end. She didn't know what time it had been when she fell, but her body ached much more now, making the the rest of the day feel like a week instead of several hours.

She closed the front door with a great deal of satisfaction but didn't reach the side door in time. Jace was suddenly there, his hat coming off as he smiled at her. She had not seen him on Sunday—Woody had been down—so her heart was torn. She wanted to see him, but she also wanted to crawl into bed and stay there for the rest of the week.

"How are you?"

"Fine," she lied with a smile, thinking that her back had never hurt so much.

"Long day?" he asked, noticing the strained look on her face.

"It was," she admitted, warming a little to his caring tone. "How is Woody feeling?"

"Better. He manages to rally every time."

"I'm glad," Maddie said sincerely, but Jace caught a tone that put him on his guard. He wasn't certain, but it seemed as though she wasn't overly pleased to see him. He'd been so certain she understood about Woody, but maybe he'd misread the situation.

"Is everything all right?" Jace tried again, not wanting to jump to any conclusions.

Maddie looked away, and Jace's heart sank. He had thought that having her was too good to be true and knew that his fears were becoming reality.

"I'm just weary," she said, but her voice said more.

"I think it's more than being tired," Jace said, working to keep his voice normal when he felt anxiety rising inside.

Maddie didn't look at him when she answered. "Have you ever fallen and found it to be unsettling? Did it shake you up?"

"You fell?"

Maddie nodded, still able to see the stairs, banister, and ceiling all rushing up in her mind.

"Where did you fall?"

"Down the stairs."

Jace's heart jolted as he moved so he could see her face. "Where on the stairs?

"Near the top," Maddie said, finally looking at him.

Moving slowly and carefully, Jace put his arms around her.

"Come here," he whispered. "Let me hold you."

Maddie let herself relax against him, once she realized he wasn't going to squeeze her.

"Feel better?" he asked after several moments of silence.

"Much," she said, her eyes closed, her head pillowed against him, thinking she never wanted to move.

"I'm surprised Cathy let you finish the day on your own," Jace commented, his hands warm and gentle on her back.

"She doesn't know," Maddie admitted, feeling Jace stiffen. He shifted enough to see her face.

"You were here alone?"

Maddie nodded. "A customer came in, but I didn't tell anyone."

"You have to tell Cathy."

"That's the last thing I can do. Doyle needs her, and she doesn't need to worry about me right now."

Jace opened his mouth and shut it. He wanted to argue but realized he couldn't. Maddie stood looking up at him until Jace forgot all about her fall. He looked into her eyes and drew her close again. His head was lowering when she gasped.

"I'm sorry," he said, coming back to earth in a hurry. "I didn't mean to crush you."

"I must have a bruise on my side," Maddie said, her voice still breathless.

Jace looked down at her with regret. The kiss was forgotten; he was only sorry she'd hurt herself.

"I'll walk you home," he offered.

"Will you stay for tea?"

"What do you think?" he teased, smiling a little.

"I think you're so fresh that Cathy will chase you off with the broom."

The image caused Jace to laugh, and even though Maddie chuckled, she remembered her aches and pains just then. Not wanting to delay a moment longer, she led the way out of the store and across to the house, hoping that Cathy would not need much help with tea and that no one would notice when she went to bed early.

∞

"I think you're angry with me," Cathy said to Doyle after the lantern was turned low and then off.

"I'm not," he said, but Cathy knew he was put out. He'd been quiet, even during Jace's visit, and had wanted to turn in early.

"You can be angry with me," Cathy told him. "I just need to know about it."

Doyle didn't answer for a long time. Cathy knew she wouldn't sleep if he left it like that, but she also knew she couldn't force the words out of him.

In the next instant she was angry herself. Why would he close her out? She had done everything in her power to make him comfortable and put him back on his feet. She deserved better than to be treated as though it was her fault.

"Cathy," Doyle said in the dark, his voice having changed. "I can feel you getting angry over there."

"And what if I am?" she said to him, flouncing a bit on the pillow. "I've worked hard to take care of you, and you want to throw it all away!"

Doyle didn't speak, but he was smiling in the dark, having just come to the same conclusion. He lay still for a moment but knew he would have to make amends.

Cathy felt his hand on her back—her lower back—his fingers kneading gently where she always ached the most. She almost moved from his touch, but her anger cooled when she saw it for the apology that it was.

In the next few minutes, Doyle rolled onto his side to reach her with both hands. Cathy relaxed under his ministrations until he came close enough to put his lips against her neck.

"Your heart," she said softly, not wanting to even mention it.

"My heart can go ahead and stop in my chest if I can't even touch my wife."

Cathy turned to him, her arms going around him, to welcome his embrace.

∞

Standing before the tall mirror in her room, Maddie stared at the bruises on her body, knowing that Cathy would be very upset if she knew. It looked as though someone had beaten her. Her side was nearly black, and her back wasn't much better. Her upper arm and shoulder sported dark marks, as did the side of her neck.

Maddie planned on wearing high-necked clothing for the next few days and mentally prepared for the work it would take to keep this from Doyle and Cathy. She had thought for a few moments that Jace was going to let something slip, but he'd kept his mouth shut.

With a sigh of relief, Maddie slipped into bed, only to find that every position she attempted caused pain. She had expected to feel so good when she lay down that her disappointment was keen. It was some time before she was able to fall asleep.

Alison stood by the tall spinning wheel, her eyes on the fluffy strips of wool as it spun its way into the thick yarn that she would use for mittens, hats, scarves, and socks. It was a long time before people would need such things, but she liked to get a head start because she traded goods with Doyle Shephard during the winter. He liked the patterns she put in her goods, and he knew her quality was excellent. During the summer Douglas would do odd jobs to gain a little more income, but that became harder in the winter, and having things to trade at the general store had become a lifeline.

Aside from all of that, she loved doing it. She loved working with her hands and seeing the end product of her hard work. It didn't matter if it was a perfect pair of children's mittens with a scarf and cap to match or a pot full of stew—Alison Muldoon loved to work with the hands God had given her.

Just then the room tilted a little, and Alison let the wool drop. She put her hand on the frame of the loom that stood just behind her, trying to get her balance. She closed her eyes for a moment, but that only made things worse. Her stomach rolled, and she mentally tried to talk herself out of being sick.

It was the second time today this had happened. She knew what it meant, and she couldn't have been more pleased. Well, she could have been a *little* more pleased. She knew the nausea would last for a few more weeks, and then she would be much more comfortable.

Some minutes passed before she went back to work. She felt a little odd but decided to ignore it. The bigger question in her mind right then was when to tell Douglas and the children. The biggest question in her mind was whether this baby would make it full term.

"Are you up to going this morning?" Jace asked Woody on Sunday morning. The day before had not been a good one. The older man had spent some time in bed in the middle of the day.

"That depends," Woody said, his eyes sparkling a little.

"On what?"

"On whether you'll go if I don't."

Jace's hands came to his hips. "We've been over this before," he began.

"I'm going," Woody cut him off.

"But are you up to it?"

"Certainly. I just had to see if I could bait you."

"I'll tell you something right now, Woody Randall," Jace stated sternly. "You're not going to die. You're never going to die, because you're too ornery."

Jace didn't know that Woody could manage such an innocent expression. The younger man's head went back as he laughed. Nevertheless, he took his uncle's antics as a good sign. Good to his word, Woody was ready ahead of Jace, and the two men left on time for the meetinghouse.

Nine

Jace's distraction with Maddie made him completely blind to the efforts of Doyle Shephard and Woody Randall. Once again, Jace and Woody had been invited to Sunday dinner with the Shephards. It was a great meal with lively conversation and laughter.

When Jace found himself alone in the store with Maddie after dinner, he actually believed he had maneuvered it on his own. He completely missed the way Doyle suggested that Maddie show Jace the new saws at the store, and then the way Woody said he needed to stay still and put his feet up for a time.

Jace's heart raced as he followed the shapely woman upstairs to the storage rooms above. His mind was not on any merchandise the store carried but on keeping the promise he'd made to Maddie a few weeks back.

"I think this is what Doyle wanted you to see," Maddie said, not suspicious of anything. "He's had these for some time now but not put them out. He must want you to see them first."

Jace forced himself to look at the saws, but his concentration didn't last long. Maddie stood nearby as innocent as she could be, but Jace was too aware of her presence. He glanced up, and when she smiled at him, he gave up all pretense.

"How awake are you today?" he asked.

"How awake am I?" Maddie questioned in confusion.

"Um hm. Are you a little tired or sleepy?"

"No, not at all." She still frowned at him in question.

"How about your bruises? Feeling better?"

"Yes, I barely notice them."

Jace didn't say anything after that, only staring at her until Maddie took a step back.

"You're going the wrong way, Miss Shephard," he said softly. "You need to move over here."

"I don't know if that's a good idea," Maddie said, her heart beating fast for more than one reason. She was a little scared but also excited.

"I don't mind chasing you," Jace told her, moving a step closer to her. "I don't mind at all, but somehow I don't think you need to be chased."

"Is that right?" Maddie's chin suddenly rose in the air. "A girl has one little indiscretion that is no fault of her own, and now you think she wants to be caught."

Jace smiled. She was so lovely and delightful. And when she smiled or teased him, her eyes commanded his complete attention.

"What are you grinning at?" Maddie demanded. "All I have to do is move to the stairs and out the door and this conversation is over."

"You'll never make it," Jace told her, and Maddie could see he was right. Nevertheless, she had to try. She scooted toward the stairs, only to be caught in five steps, Jace's arms coming around her.

If she expected him to be rough, she was surprised. He caught her with complete gentleness, his hand to her wrist, before pulling her against him. Maddie deliberately let her head fall back as she looked up at him. Jace needed no other invitation.

He kissed and held her for a long time. And between kisses, he whispered soft words to her, telling her how beautiful she was, how soft and desirable. Maddie didn't resist. She had no thoughts of resisting. She kissed Jace right back, her arms tight around his neck, wishing it could last forever.

When at last they broke apart, they were both breathless, standing a few feet apart, knowing that to continue would be serious.

"I think it's time," Jace told her.

"For me to go down the stairs?"

"Yes."

Maddie nodded and moved on her way, her legs shaking a little. Jace remembered at the last minute to look one more time at the saws, fearing Doyle would ask what he thought.

He need not have worried. Back at the house, the others were in conversation so deep that they appeared not to notice the younger couple returning. Jace found himself relieved by this, since he didn't notice Maddie's hair until they were back in the parlor. One look at her and anyone would know that they had done more than talk.

Much as he wanted to be with her, Jace was all too pleased to exit when Woody said he was ready to head for home.

Much to Maddie's surprise, she fell asleep almost instantly that night. It had been a wonderful day, a day she wanted to lie still and think about, but her body had other ideas. Unfortunately sleep lasted only halfway through the night. A noise woke her, and with it came worry. And not just worry, but panic.

I don't really know him! Maddie told herself, her heart rate speeding up. *He's going to make me fall in love with him and then leave. I'll just get hurt again. I'm sure of it. He'll turn out to be just like Cliff from Boston. He tells me he loves me, but he doesn't; not truly.*

Maddie lay in the dark, miserable and sure that the misery was only going to grow. She listened carefully, hoping that Doyle or Cathy might be up, but the house was silent. She felt desperate to talk but didn't want to wake anyone.

It made for a very long night. Alone and lonely, Maddie lay in her bed and remembered every lie Cliff had whispered to her. By morning, she had all but convinced herself that Jace was the same type of man.

Douglas Muldoon was at the store bright and early on Tuesday morning. He didn't have a lot of money in his pocket, but he was still determined to find a small gift for Alison. She hadn't been feeling well lately, and he wanted a little something to show her that he noticed how hard she worked, even when she was tired.

Cathy was planning to man the store that morning but had developed a sudden headache. Maddie had been happy to go instead, and when Mr. Muldoon walked in, she greeted him without making any connection to Hillary.

"Good morning. May I help you?"

"Good morning," he said kindly, realizing he'd been expecting Cathy. "You must be Miss Shephard."

"I am Miss Shephard, but you can call me Maddie."

"My daughter, Hillary, tells me you're a very great help."

"Are you Mr. Muldoon?" Maddie asked, taken by surprise but thinking swiftly.

"I am."

"It's a pleasure to meet you, Mr. Muldoon. I like your Hillary very much."

"I like her too," he said with a smile, and Maddie laughed.

"What can I help you with today?"

"Well, I'm looking for a small gift for my wife. Just a little something to make her smile."

"Is she sad?" Maddie asked without thinking that she might be prying.

"Not at all," Douglas answered with another smile. "I just want her to know how much I appreciate her."

Thinking he was nothing like she expected, Maddie stared at him for a moment, and then wondered if she'd misunderstood; maybe Hillary had not said her father was a pastor.

"That's very kind of you," Maddie said softly, genuinely impressed. "Does she like ribbon or maybe a bit of lace?"

"I was rather hoping to find something she wouldn't choose for herself."

Maddie thought for a moment and then took a small bottle from the shelf.

"This is a perfume bottle. Would she enjoy something like that?"

"I don't know. She isn't overly fond of scents for the skin."

"All right," Maddie continued, still thinking. "How about a crystal ink pot? We have clear or two colors of blue. Does she enjoy writing letters?"

"She enjoys writing letters very much," Douglas answered with pleasure. "I wouldn't have thought of that."

"Then maybe she wouldn't think to buy it either," Maddie suggested.

Douglas agreed to the light blue ink pot and counted out the money. While the transaction was taking place, he said, "I think Hillary was right."

"About what?"

"About what a great help you are."

Maddie smiled, but her mind was still on who this man was. She knew she had to be careful, but he didn't seem the type to offend too easily.

"Did Hillary tell me that you're a pastor?"

"Guilty as charged," he said, causing Maddie to laugh a bit but also giving her the boldness to say, "May I ask you a question?"

"Certainly."

"Does anyone ever ask you about heaven?"

Douglas nodded and said, "Often."

"So you believe heaven exists?" Maddie leaned a bit across the counter, not even aware she was doing so.

"I'm so glad you asked me," Douglas surprised her by saying. "I do believe heaven exists, but only because of the way I view the Bible. Does that make sense, Maddie?"

"Not exactly."

"Well, I don't base my belief on some blind hope or empty promise. In Scripture, God and Jesus speak repeatedly about heaven, so I can be confident it's there."

Maddie had never thought about it from that angle. She stared at Douglas Muldoon for several seconds, working on this new thought.

"May I ask you a question, Maddie?"

"Yes, of course."

"Do you believe heaven is there?"

"I don't know," she answered honestly, although it embarrassed her to admit it.

Douglas nodded. "May I make a suggestion?"

"Please."

"Don't start by trying to pin down the existence of heaven, start by figuring out how you view God's Word."

"Why would I start there?"

"Here's my reasoning: I find that the way I feel about the author of a book gives me a bias as I read. If from experience I know they have good things to say, I read with an open mind. I believe the Bible to be the Word of God, which makes me sit up and listen to every word inside, whether it be about heaven or some other subject."

"I've been going about this all wrong," Maddie said, and Douglas could tell she was speaking mainly to herself. He might have left her on her own to think, but she was still holding the ink pot she'd wrapped in paper for him.

"Maddie?" Douglas finally spoke up.

"Oh, I'm sorry. Here's your package."

"Did I say something to upset you, because that wasn't my intent."

"No, nothing like that. I just hadn't viewed it from that angle before, and it takes some getting used to."

"Maddie," Douglas said, his voice turning warm with compassion and caring. "If you have any more questions, I'd be happy to hear them. Anytime, actually."

"You don't mind questions? You don't think I'm faithless?"

"We haven't talked about what you put your faith in, Maddie, so I wouldn't try to figure that out. But I don't think it's wrong to ask questions, not in the least. In fact, Jesus Christ was the most magnificent question-asker of all time."

Maddie thanked Douglas and then watched as he went on his way. She, however, did not immediately go back to work. It occurred to her that she might have learned more in a 20-minute conversation with Mr. Muldoon than she had in six months of meetinghouse visits.

Not knowing what to do with the thought, Maddie picked up the broom and did a little cleaning. Someone had finally answered some of her questions, but she didn't feel any more settled than before. Until another customer entered the store, Maddie asked herself why she seemed so hard to please.

Jace had been pleased when Maddie said she wanted to go for a walk on Sunday afternoon, but they were only a few steps out the door before he realized all was not well. For some minutes he was weary of finding a different woman every time they met, but he pushed this thought aside, working to give her the benefit of the doubt. He wanted to hear what she had to say with the intent of keeping their relationship alive. He'd only just come to this conclusion when she stopped and faced him.

"What do I really know about you?"

"What do you want to know about me?" Jace was able to ask calmly, having settled down a bit in his mind.

"Are you married?"

"No."

"Have you been married?"

"No."

"Have you been with a lot of girls?"

"What do you mean when you say *been with?*"

This question frustrated her, and Jace had to put his hand up to stop her from speaking.

"I'm not trying to duck out of the question, Maddie, but I don't know exactly what you want to know."

"Have you made promises to girls?" Her hand came up and she counted on her fingers. "Have you kissed them and left? Have you acted like you were in love and then changed your mind?"

Jace thought for a moment and then began. "I have never made a promise to a girl that I haven't kept. I have kissed girls I no longer wish to see, but love is a new emotion for me when it comes to women."

Maddie didn't know what that meant. Was he saying he loved her? She was afraid to ask. Choosing not to comment at all, she turned and started on their walk again, but she wasn't agitated this time, only thoughtful.

"Do I get to ask some questions?" Jace wished to know.

"I guess so."

"All right—then you answer the same ones for me."

Maddie thought it only fair, even though she didn't want to talk about herself.

"I've not made promises I haven't kept," she began, but Jace cut her off.

"Are you married?"

"Oh, I forgot about that. No, I'm not married and have never been married. I did know a man once, and I loved him, but he lied to me and I haven't been with anyone else."

"What did he lie about?"

"He said he loved me and we would be married, but he was already married."

"Did you kiss him?"

"Yes."

"Did you do more than kiss?"

"Jace Randall!" Maddie stopped to confront him. "I didn't ask you that."

"But you could have."

Maddie glared at him but still said, "No."

Jace nodded.

"Your turn," she continued.

"No."

"But you wanted to," she accused him, still trying to gain the upper hand.

"Every man wants to, Madalyn," he said without apology. "Make no mistake about that."

Maddie looked away. She knew all this to be true but was suddenly sorry she had brought it up. Jace read her face and, seeing that she was unhappy, determined to make amends.

"I'm not playing games with you, Maddie. I'm not kissing you and saying sweet things to you with the intent to use you and throw you away. I've never done that to any woman, and I certainly wouldn't do it to you."

Maddie looked up at him.

"In fact, if anyone is in danger of being hurt in this, it's me. You don't live in Tucker Mills—I do. I dread the day you come and tell me you're going back Boston. I don't know if I'll be able to stand that."

Maddie had never even considered this. She thought that Doyle would need at least six months' rest, and she'd only been home for two. But then she realized she'd never shared this with

Jace. She knew she was going to be around for a time, if not for-ever. He didn't.

And what if he asked her to stay? What if things grew very serious? As serious as those kisses they'd shared in the store-room?

"I'm not going anywhere right now, Jace." Maddie knew it was only fair to tell him.

"And later?"

"I have no set plans, and I don't wish to surprise anyone."

"So you're saying you'll be here?"

Maddie took a moment to think about this. "As long as I'm needed or wanted, I'll be in Tucker Mills."

Jace smiled. That was exactly what he wanted to hear. He felt himself relax. There was never going to be a time when he didn't want her.

"What is that smile for?"

"Nothing." Jace looked away, spotting an area of trees that would give them some privacy. "Why don't we walk over here?" he suggested, but Maddie shook her head.

"I think we'll head back."

"We don't have to. Woody stayed home today."

"It's not Woody I'm thinking of. It's my own reputation."

"You weren't thinking about your reputation a week ago."

Before he could catch her smiling over the memory, Maddie turned and started back toward the house. Jace fell into step beside her but didn't speak. He didn't need to. With a single glance, Maddie could see by his face that he was pleased. She also knew that that look would mean she would have to keep her distance for the rest of the day.

Douglas waited until bedtime on Sunday to give Alison the gift. She was tired—they both were—but he was so pleased about what he'd found in the middle of the week that he didn't want to wait any longer.

"I have something for you," he said, climbing into bed after her.

Alison turned to look at him, her book still in her hand.

"For me?"

"Um hm. A little gift I picked up."

Alison set her book down on the table by the bed and rolled to look at her husband.

"Why did you do that?" she asked, her voice pleased.

"Well, you've been tired lately and not feeling well, and I want to thank you."

"For what?"

"For never complaining, and for all the hard work you do."

Alison smiled at him. She had waited to share her news for two reasons. She had wanted the time to be special and also had the silly notion that talking about it would more likely result in another miscarriage.

"Dooner," Alison began, using his old nickname. "I need to tell you something."

"Okay."

"I think I'm expecting."

Douglas looked into her eyes and called himself a blind fool.

"Of course you are," he said with wonder. "How could I have missed it?"

"It's all right."

Douglas put his arms around her and pulled her close, kissing her temple when she was settled against him.

"How do you feel?"

"Like always."

"Are you afraid?"

"A little. The children are older now, and should I lose the baby, there's always so much blood. I don't want to scare them."

For a moment Douglas knew his own fear. She had miscarried once after Hillary and twice since Martin was born. There *had* been a lot of blood and no guarantees that she would live through the ordeal.

"What did you get me?" Alison asked.

"It's silly now. You're giving me a baby, and I bought you a crystal ink pot."

"A crystal one?" Alison asked, coming up on one elbow to smile at him.

Douglas' doubts melted in the light of her pleasure.

"I've seen those but never thought I would have one for myself."

Douglas reached down on his side of the bed and handed the wrapped package to her.

"Well, now you do," he told her with great satisfaction.

Without even unwrapping the gift, Alison put her arms around his neck, kissed him, and told him how much he was loved. Douglas held her right back, asking God for grace and peace as He did His will in their lives and the life of this unborn child.

Jace couldn't stay away. He didn't have time to see Maddie on Tuesday evening and he was tired, but spring was in the air, and he went anyway. What he didn't expect to see was Maddie with another man. His steps slowed as he approached the store, and as he watched, the man reached up and touched Maddie's ear. Jace watched her laugh and then put a hand on his arm.

A foreign emotion filled him. He'd never known jealousy before and didn't immediately recognize the source. He knew Maddie was not the type of woman to play false with him, but what he'd just seen gave him pause.

How well did he really know her? Doyle and Cathy were honorable people, and Maddie seemed to be the same, but she'd spent many years away from home. Was she still the woman that

Shephards had raised her to be? Or had an experience with one man made it impossible for her to commit to him or any other man, no matter how much she might wish to.

Jace shook his head. He knew that Cathy would not do that to him. She had told him that Maddie hadn't been interested in anyone since the man she loved in Boston.

Choosing not to read more into the situation when he had little or no facts, Jace finished walking to the store. As he hoped and expected, Maddie was just closing up and invited him to tea. And it turned out to be a good evening. Maddie was completely normal, and as long as Jace didn't think about what he'd seen outside the store, he was normal as well.

Ten

Jace sat against the headboard of his bed, thinking about the evening. He had a full day of work starting early in the morning, and he was tired from the day right now, but sleep would not come.

He wanted to know where he stood with Maddie Shephard. He knew that some women threw kisses away while others only kissed men they wanted to marry. With Maddie he simply couldn't tell. She seemed drawn to him, and she certainly enjoyed the kisses they shared, but at times she looked at him with complete distrust, almost anger. He knew that he had another man to thank for that, but who had she been so familiar with today? Jace let his head fall back against the wall, wishing answers would come from the sky.

He stayed this way for a time before reaching toward the small dresser that sat near his bed. He opened the top drawer and felt around until he found it. Jace pulled his mother's bracelet from inside and cradled it in his hand, letting the candlelight bounce and sparkle as it caught the gold.

"I want to give this to you, Maddie," he whispered, mindful of Woody sleeping in the next bedroom. "I want you to know how I feel."

Jace fingered the intricate chain, knowing what a treasure it was. He would never give it to just anyone. He hoped he wouldn't have to use a lot of words, but for him this was a gesture of love. If he only knew how Maddie felt about him.

Suddenly a small, breathless laugh escaped Jace, relief filling him. He knew exactly who he could ask. He would check with Cathy. The dilemma was solved; he was finally ready to sleep. Cathy would tell him how Maddie felt. Of this he was certain.

Eden arrived back in Tucker Mills seven weeks after she had left. Still angry, she had not written to her brother in that time but then realized she'd made only herself miserable. Jace had a new life, and probably a new love. His life was fresh and exciting, while she had only the day in, day out grind of the boarding-house. She didn't mind the work—most of the time she enjoyed it and prided herself on a clean establishment—but with Jace gone and not sharing his life with her, she felt cut off and lonely.

She didn't plan to apologize, but she hoped he had put their clash behind him and assumed that she had done the same. She was not a person who gave up easily, and getting Jace's affections back was the main goal of her visit. And she had a plan.

Since Jace and Woody were not expecting her, she didn't rush from the train station to the farm but took some time to look around town for a while. She and Jace hadn't really done this, and making a slow promenade, she walked around the green, taking in the houses and businesses. Nothing really struck her as noteworthy, but Eden planned to spend more time in town on this visit, and she wanted to get the lay of the land even before Jace showed her.

Not until she was completely satisfied that she'd seen every-thing did Eden begin the walk to the farm. She strode out pur-posefully, not willing to waste any more time, smiling a little when the farm came into view.

"Well, Eden," Woody said pleasantly when he opened the door to find her there. "Come in."

"Thank you, Uncle Woody. How are you?"

"Can't complain. Here, have a seat. I'm just having my tea, and you can join me."

"Thank you. Is Jace around?"

"No, he's in town."

"In town?" Eden asked, losing some of her calm control. "I didn't see him."

"Well, you wouldn't have from the train station," Woody said.

"But I was in town," Eden said before she thought, wishing she'd held her tongue when Woody's brows rose. "When do you expect him back?" Eden asked, changing tactics.

"I've no idea."

"Where did he go?"

Woody's look was longsuffering.

"I don't expect him to tell me, Eden, and I don't ask," Woody replied, uttering the half-truth. "I'm not his keeper."

"Oh, certainly." Eden backed down, her manner and tone changing to one of compliance. She had no desire to upset her uncle or be caught in her attempt to keep track of Jace.

Woody went ahead with his tea, and Eden did join him. The food was very good, and she was reminded of what a proficient housekeeper Clara was. Eden even thought about asking for her recipe for the scones they were eating.

But her contentment lasted only until she remembered that Jace was not home. Such a thing had never occurred to her. True, it was Friday evening, but Saturday was a workday, and she expected to find him working at the farm or settling in for the evening.

Well, no matter, she told herself. *I'm going to be up when he arrives, and he'll be so surprised to see me that he'll tell me exactly what I want to know.*

∞

"Cathy," Jace kept his voice low, aware that Maddie had slipped upstairs for only a moment.

"What?"

"Does Maddie ever tell you how she feels about me?"

"Not in so many words."

"What does that mean?"

But the question had to wait. They both heard Maddie returning, and Jace knew better than to get caught asking.

"I found it," she said, holding a small frame in her hand, one that showed a drawing of her parents.

"Let me see." Cathy reached for it and stared down into the faces. "I haven't seen this in years."

"You gave it to me when I was six."

"Do you keep it out or put away?"

"In Boston I kept it out, but when I arrived here I tucked it into a drawer and almost forgot about it."

Jace came to look over Cathy's shoulder. He didn't know if feelings would be tender, but in his estimation, Maddie looked more like Doyle and Cathy than her parents. Cathy was an attractive woman. Maddie's mother was not very eye-catching.

"I can sure see Doyle in Daniel, but I can't find you in your mother, Maddie," Cathy stated plainly.

"Paige used to say the same thing to me," Maddie said with a chuckle. "When she was very tiny, she would stand in front of the picture and come right out and ask why I was so pretty. Her mother heard her one time, and when Paige was scolded, she didn't say anything for a long time."

"Who is Paige?" Jace asked.

"Paige Nunley. My last child left in Boston," Maddie said fondly. "She's a character."

"But not so much of a character that she can't spot beauty," Jace complimented.

Cathy didn't comment, but for Maddie everything else in the room faded away. She smiled into Jace's eyes, asking herself how she'd been happy before they met.

It wasn't extremely late when Jace reached the barn, but he was ready for bed. He yawned all the way from town and was relieved to climb from the saddle. He went through the motions, glad the day was over. What he didn't expect was to find someone emerging from the shadows. For a moment Jace was startled, and then his uncle spoke.

"I snuck out to warn you," Woody began, sounding pleased.

"About what?"

"Eden's here."

Jace chuckled softly. "I take it you didn't tell her where I was."

"You didn't tell me where you were headed," Woody exaggerated. "How could I tell her?"

Jace laughed again.

"You could really drive her mad and sleep out here tonight," Woody suggested.

This time Jace's laugh wasn't so quiet. He had all he could do not to shout with mirth.

"I can finally see why you never married," Jace said when he could catch his breath.

"On the contrary, I would have been a model husband. I just wouldn't have married someone like Eden."

"Nor will I," Jace agreed.

The men went toward the house, but when Jace headed for the front door, Woody slipped around to go in by way of the kitchen.

As Jace expected, Eden was still up, handiwork in her lap, a candle burning on the table in the parlor. Jace heard the quiet sounds that Woody made coming in the side door and using the stairs, but he didn't think his sister noticed.

"Well, hello," Jace said, making an effort to sound surprised.

"Hello, Jace," Eden said with a smile.

"When did you get in?" Jace asked as he took a seat.

"About teatime. Where were you?"

"In town. Didn't Woody tell you?"

For a moment Eden hesitated. She knew she treated Jace like a child and needed to stop, but it had always been that way, and old habits are sometimes hard to get rid of. Right now she knew she was foolish to think that he would tell her anything he didn't want to share.

"I was just surprised," Eden started again. "Tomorrow is Saturday."

"How was the train ride?" Jace asked, choosing to ignore her probing even as he told himself he was ready to have Eden meet Maddie.

"It was fine. Not very crowded."

"I haven't heard from you much. I figured you were still angry."

"Oh, Jace," Eden dismissed him with a lie. "That was weeks ago."

"You have a long memory, Eden," Jace reminded her, but he didn't sound irritated.

Eden *was* irritated. She didn't want Jace to confront her in his way, and it frustrated her to no end.

"How long can you stay?" Jace asked.

"Until the Monday train," she replied, managing to keep her voice calm.

"Good," Jace said and meant it. He didn't hate his sister. He was just weary of her need to have the upper hand. "Well," he finished, coming to his feet. "I'm for bed. I hope you don't mind."

"Not at all." Eden's voice said otherwise, but Jace ignored it, believing she was impossible to please.

"Goodnight, Eden."

"Goodnight."

And for Jace it was a good night. He slept soundly. In a strange bed with strange sounds and her emotions out of control, Eden didn't sleep much at all.

∞

"Okay, boys," Douglas said, kneeling down to be on a level with his two older sons, Joshua and Peter. "What are you quarreling about?"

With tears threatening, Peter said, "Josh says I took some of his blocks from his town set, but I didn't."

Douglas' eyes swung to Joshua, who was the older of the two.

"First of all, Josh, I want you to tell me what is more important to you right now, your brother or your town blocks?"

Joshua's eyes dropped. He knew the answer he wanted to give was all wrong, but he just wanted his small missing blocks: the wood barn, church building, and schoolhouse. He looked at his brother, saw how upset he was, and relented some.

"He took some of the blocks one other time, and I just thought he did it again."

"Wasn't that about a year ago, when he hid them in his bed?" Douglas reasoned. "I spanked him for that, and it's never happened again that I know of."

Joshua nodded.

"Now, listen to me, Josh," Douglas went on. "If Pete has taken something of yours without asking, he will be punished, but by accusing him and then all but calling him a liar, you've made up your mind that he's guilty, and I don't think you know that for certain. Not to mention, you don't have to get that upset about some toys. No one was hurt; no one was killed. It's just a few toys."

Joshua nodded, his face calming.

"Okay, Pete," Douglas turned to his other son. "Rather than panic or defend yourself and start shouting, how about offering to help Josh look for the missing blocks?"

"But he said I took them."

"Yes, he did, but you just told me you didn't, so the best thing for you to do is stay calm and talk about it. Listen to what Josh has to say and help him any way you can."

While Douglas was working this out in his study, Alison was in the kitchen, well aware that the boys were in trouble for fighting. She was working over the table by the fire, putting some final touches on two loaves of bread to go into the oven, when Martin came in behind her.

"Mama," he said quietly. She turned.

"Oh, Marty," Alison said with compassion, seeing the pilfered blocks in his hands. "I'm very glad you showed me, but now you must go and tell Papa."

"Do I have to?"

"You know you do."

The little boy nodded, nearly breaking Alison's heart.

"Come on," she urged him. "I'll walk with you."

They were at the study door long before Martin was ready, but they had to wait anyway because Douglas was praying, asking God's blessing on his sons. When he looked up, his eyes met those of his wife.

"Marty has something to tell you."

Alison didn't linger, but as she moved away, she heard Douglas say, "You did the right thing by telling your mother, Marty. I'm proud of you."

"Maddie," Cathy gently knocked on her door and opened it a bit. The older woman peeked her head around and found a half-asleep niece on the side of the bed.

"Is something wrong?" Maddie slurred, thinking morning had come way too fast.

"I'm going to work in the store today," Cathy informed her. "Go back to sleep."

"You're going to the store?"

"Yes. You haven't had a day to sleep in since you arrived. Go back to bed."

"What about Doyle's breakfast?"

"I took care of that. You can eat when you get down there. Go on now."

"All right," Maddie said, too weary to even remember a word of thanks. She climbed back under the quilt, not hearing Cathy's descent down the stairs.

∞

"He looks mean," Eden said of the rooster that eyed Jace in the barn.

"He's not a pet, that's for certain."

"Have you been spurred?"

"Nearly. He doesn't trust me. He barely glances at Woody, but I haven't gained his trust."

"How do you get the eggs?"

"I shoo him off and go in there. The hens don't mind. He's the problem."

Eden lived in a city. She was not a farm woman and had no plans to be, but she had to admit that such a life fascinated her. She had not planned to shadow Jace to the barn, but he'd invited her out when he went to feed the livestock. She took her coffee with her, hoping it would wake her up, and trailed after him.

"Here come the chicks," Jace said, and Eden smiled. Six chicks followed their mother from inside the hen enclosure, coming close to get the feed Jace was tossing their way.

"They're so small." Eden voiced her pleasure and then remembered that these chickens would end up in the oven or a pot.

"What's the matter?" Jace asked as he happened to look up and see her face.

"Nothing." Eden knew she could not admit her thoughts or Jace would tease her. But in her mind she had established two things: She could live here at the farm because it was tranquil and beautiful, but she could never be a farm woman. It wasn't the life for her.

Eden had not been happy to learn that Jace had plans for the evening that didn't involve her, but he felt no guilt. He had invited her on every task and talked to her all day. He knew he deserved a break that night, and he was going to take it. When he got to the store and saw that Cathy was in attendance, he was even happier that he'd walked away from his sister's frowning face.

"How was your day?" he asked Cathy, leaning on the counter, completely at home.

"It was busy this morning but quiet this afternoon. How about yourself?"

"Well, my sister's in town and we talked all day, so it went fast."

"I didn't know she was coming."

"She doesn't usually tell me. She just shows up."

"You quarreled the last time she was here, didn't you?"

Jace nodded. "She can't get used to my having my own life. She didn't even want me to come to town tonight."

"You could have brought her."

Jace's look said otherwise.

"Well, Jace," Cathy reasoned. "We want to meet her."

"We'll be at services tomorrow."

"Why don't you plan on dinner?"

"We will, thank you."

"So now tell me," Cathy said, leaning a little closer. "What were you trying to ask me last night?"

"If Maddie shares with you? Do you know how she feels about me?"

"Not specifically, but she said she was all wrong about you."

Jace nodded, worrying his lower lip a bit.

"What's going on, Jace?"

"I want to give her something, but I don't know how she'll take it."

"How do you want her to take it?"

"I want her to know she's not some passing fancy."

"Can't you tell her that?"

Jace didn't answer. Maddie could be hard to talk to, at least for him. Jace didn't think he was good with words. In fact, it wasn't unusual for Maddie to be angry with him. In those situations he could usually talk her around, but he didn't know how to give her the bracelet and tell her how he felt.

"Were you here all day?" Jace suddenly asked.

"Yes, I thought Maddie needed a day at home."

"How is Doyle doing?"

"Very well. He'd like to come back, but for the most part he's been patient."

"Can I do anything to help you close up?"

"No." She waved a hand at him. "Head over to the house. Maddie and Doyle will be glad to see you."

Jace thanked her with a smile and went on his way.

Woody watched Eden for a full five minutes, but she never once looked his way. She was too busy knitting and watching the window and door. He wondered why keeping track of Jace was so important to her, but he doubted he would get a straight answer if he asked.

She was never idle. Indeed, the knitting needles in her hands flew through the wool. Woody thought she might be making a

sock and then shook his head. A sock made with worry and anxiety—no pleasure in the task at all. He thought if she rocked that
chair any harder, she might move across the room.

Eden chose that moment to glance his way and was visibly
startled to find his eyes on her.

"I'm sorry, Uncle," she said sincerely. "I thought you'd fallen
asleep."

"I think I did for a time. Tell me something, Eden. Why have
you never married?"

Eden set her work down. "What made you think of that?"

"A number of things" was all Woody would say.

"I know what you're thinking." Eden decided to be blunt,
her voice and face showing all the control she felt. "If Eden had
a family of her own, she'd let Jace go. But that's not true. I'll
always worry about Jace. I always see him as someone who needs
to be cared for."

"Then you're headed for a life of misery, Eden, because he
doesn't want or need that from you."

"He's told you this?"

"He's told *you* this, Eden, and you don't want to hear it."

Eden was forced to drop her eyes. She knew Woody was correct, but admitting it would take more than she could give.

"In the long run," she said, picking up the wool again, confidence exuding from her, "he'll see that I'm only looking out for
his best interests."

Woody shook his head, but Eden didn't see him. In her mind
the matter was closed, and she'd gone back to her knitting.

She was set in her ways, and Woody knew that no amount of
talking from him was going to change that. He reached for the
newspaper he had dropped and held it back to the light. If he'd
been tired, he would have gone to bed, but the nap must have
taken care of that. His lack of fatigue and a strange fascination to
see how long Eden would sit there kept Woody in his seat in the
parlor.

❈

"Wait a minute." Cathy caught Doyle's arm and tried to pull him back when he would have walked away.

"What's the matter?" he asked, turning to look at her in surprise.

"I think we should leave them alone," Cathy whispered, stealing over to close the door between the kitchen and the parlor.

"What do you know?" Doyle asked, sounding like an excited kid.

"Jace talked to me at the store this evening. He wants to give something to Maddie."

"What?"

"He didn't tell me that, but he did say that she was not a passing fancy."

"Well, of course she's not." Doyle frowned. "I've known that all along."

"Yes, but has he known it?"

"Of course he has. He's not like those other men."

Cathy smiled at him.

"Do you think he's asking her to marry him?" Doyle suddenly asked.

"No, I don't think it's to that point yet, but it has to be close."

A huge sigh lifted Doyle's chest. Nothing could make him happier than for Maddie to fall in love with Jace Randall. If such a thing happened, he knew she'd be well taken care of and living in town to boot.

Doyle was so pleased he thought he could shout. Instead, he grabbed Cathy and kissed her until they were both breathless.

Eleven

Jace did not let Maddie out of his arms for a long time. He saw the closed door as private enough and wasted no time in kissing her.

"Well, now," Maddie said, a bit breathless when contact was broken. "What was that about?"

"I just missed you," Jace said.

Maddie laughed. "You've been here all evening."

"But I didn't get to do that."

Maddie smiled at him, and Jace kissed her again.

"I like you, Jace Randall," she told him. "You're easy to have around."

"I rather like you too," Jace said, seeing the opportunity opening up to him. "In fact, I even thought about telling you that in a different way tonight."

Maddie's brows rose. "A surprise?"

Jace reached into his pocket and pulled out the small chain.

"Will you wear my mother's bracelet?"

"Oh, Jace," Maddie breathed, reaching for the delicate gold links. "It's so pretty."

"Well, then the two of you will get along just fine."

Maddie looked up at him. "I don't know what to say. What if I lose it or break it?"

"Just as long as you don't do that to my heart."

Maddie's eyes closed and she whispered, "We're both so afraid, aren't we?"

"At times, yes. I think you're headed back to Boston with little or no notice, and you think I'm going to lie to you."

Maddie looked up at him, truly believing for the first time that he would never lie to her. Wordlessly she handed him the bracelet and held out her wrist.

Jace found his hands suddenly shaking, but he still managed to secure the chain around her wrist, taking a moment to study it before looking into her eyes.

"I feel as though it's on loan," Maddie admitted, "because it was your mother's."

"I want you to enjoy it."

"And not take it off?" she teased him a little.

Jace felt his heart thunder but knew the words had to be said.

"You can take this off when I no longer love you."

Maddie put her arms around him and held on tight.

"I love you too," she murmured close to his ear, and found herself crushed in his embrace.

In the kitchen, Doyle listened at the door but found only silence. When Cathy came from the buttery and found him lurking by the closed door, she shooed him away. What he didn't see was the way she took his place once he'd gone upstairs.

Things fell so swiftly into place for Eden that she barely managed to keep her calm composure. The Shephards welcomed Jace like a member of the family, and there was no missing the eye contact between Jace and Maddie. And that was all before spotting her mother's bracelet on Maddie's wrist.

Eden had all she could do to smile kindly and speak without gritting her teeth. And her anger was not confined to Jace. Conversation told her that Woody and Jace joined the Shephards often, and yet Woody had behaved as though he didn't know where Jace was or what he was doing.

Feeling that she'd been conspired against, Eden was quiet during dinner, although her face gave nothing away. The only person she didn't fool was Jace. He knew she was angry, but he hadn't known how else to go about it. He could have told Eden about Maddie and the Shephards, but that wouldn't have done them justice.

Seeing that she was barely holding her rage, Jace inwardly sighed. He should have known that no woman or her family would have been good enough for Eden. He should have known she was too desperate to be right; there would be no pleasing her.

What he didn't see was Eden's desire to be around Maddie. When she offered to help Maddie with the dishes, Jace let his guard down. Not for a long time would he see that he'd missed a tactical move on Eden's part.

"So tell me, Maddie," Eden began, her voice as sweet as she could manage. "Have you always lived in Tucker Mills?"

"No, I've spent the last nine years in Boston."

"Doing what?"

"I've been with a family, first as a nanny and then a companion."

"You must miss it."

"The family, yes."

"No young men?"

Eden didn't miss the change in Maddie's eyes. They clouded for a moment.

"No," the younger woman said quietly.

"How about here? Lots of young men have fallen for you, I expect."

For some reason Maddie laughed a little. Eden's words brought to mind David Scales and how smitten he'd been at one time, only later to fall very much in love and marry another woman. Maddie couldn't have been happier for him.

"Tell me what made you laugh," Eden invited, her voice like that of a fun-loving big sister.

"Oh, I was thinking of someone named David. He thought he was so in love with me." Maddie stopped and shook her head.

"So Jace is just another conquest to you, isn't he?"

Maddie's hands stilled in the wash basin. She had heard it this time, the angry tone in Eden's voice. She turned her head slowly to look at the other woman but found only kindness in her face. Nevertheless, Maddie wanted to get away from her.

"I think we're all done here," Maddie nervously observed, reaching for the towel.

"Good," Eden said quietly, and again, Maddie felt she should read more into that word. "I'll just go join my brother."

"Okay," Maddie agreed. "I'll be out in a little bit."

"Don't hurry," Eden said this time, not bothering to cover the hatred in her eyes.

Eden turned away, her message very clear. Maddie took a chair next to the kitchen table when Eden had gone back to the parlor and shut the door in her wake.

The hand Maddie put to her face was shaking. She didn't understand what had just happened, but it frightened her. It scared her in a way she'd never experienced before.

She eventually did join the others in the parlor, but not until Cathy came looking for her.

"You're certainly in a good mood," Jace commented to his sister as soon as they arrived back at the house; Woody had already gone indoors.

"Am I?"

"Yes. After pouting through dinner all you've done is talk. What changed?"

"I don't know what you mean."

Jace's eyes rolled in his head. "You're obviously not going to tell me," he said and moved off to settle the horses.

Eden didn't follow. She was completely pleased over the way the afternoon had ended. Maddie Shephard appeared to be strained and upset. And it was only a matter of time before Eden would turn that to her advantage. She had to leave in the morning, but that was all right. It would give her more time to plan.

"You look tired," Cathy said on Monday morning.

"I didn't sleep that well."

"Why is that?"

Maddie shrugged, not wanting to tell Cathy that she could still see Eden Randall's eyes, eyes that continued to frighten Maddie.

"Everything all right with you and Jace?" Cathy asked.

"Yes, but I'm not sure his sister likes me."

"That's normal," Cathy said, surprising Maddie into staring at her.

"What's 'normal' exactly?"

"According to Jace, Eden all but raised him. She's bound to be overly attached. He's led me to believe that she's never approved of anyone he liked."

Maddie desperately wished Cathy had mentioned this at bedtime. She might have slept. If that's all it was—nothing personal—then Maddie could relax. Jace loved her and she loved him. Eden could hate her all she wanted. She lived in Pine

River, not Tucker Mills. And right now, Tucker Mills was where Maddie was planning to spend the rest of her life.

"What put your sister in such high spirits?" Woody asked of Jace when he arrived back from the train station. "She came home from Shephards in a good mood and just kept smiling. You two do a bunch of drinking?"

"No, nothing like that," Jace said thoughtfully. "I'm not sure what she's thinking."

Woody shook his head. "I feel terrible saying it about my own niece, but I don't trust your sister."

"She has a mind of her own. I'll say that much for her."

"Do you realize she's glad she isn't married so she can look after you? She told me you'll always be someone she needs to worry about and look after."

Jace stared at him. "She told you this?"

"Yep. I thought she would rock that chair right out the door when you went to town without her on Saturday night. We talked a little, and she feels she's completely correct in her thinking."

"That's no surprise," Jace said tiredly. "The word *wrong* is not in Eden's vocabulary unless it's directed at me."

"What will you do?" Woody asked, thinking he'd take some type of action.

"I won't *do* anything," Jace informed him, "except be thankful she doesn't live here."

"For now," Woody said, causing Jace's eyes to widen. The older Randall's head went back as he laughed and clapped Jace on the back.

"You'll work it out," he said confidently, and Jace knew it was his way of saying it was time to get back to work.

✌

"Did you have a good visit with your sister?" Maddie asked when she saw Jace again. It was midweek, and Maddie was a little tired. She had just put the kitchen to rights and now sat in the other chair adjacent to the kitchen table.

"About like last time," Jace said cryptically, more interested in Maddie than thinking about his sister.

"You're going to think I'm silly, but I was worried that she didn't like me."

"She doesn't like anyone," Jace sighed with a comical look, making Maddie laugh.

"That's what Cathy said, and not to worry about it."

"That's good advice." Jace smiled at her. "You should be worried only about my opinion of you."

"Which is?"

"I'm not sure I should say," Jace teased her gently.

"But you want to," Maddie coaxed, her fingers brushing softly along the back of his hand.

Jace had to look away. They didn't have great privacy tonight. Doyle and Cathy were in the parlor, but the door between the rooms was open. When Jace looked back, Maddie was watching him, her eyes shining with love and teasing.

"My opinion," he whispered slowly, his eyes caressing her face, "is that you're sweet and beautiful, and I think we're sitting much too far apart."

Maddie leaned toward him a little. "The door is open."

"I noticed that."

Maddie laughed softly, not because Jace had been funny, but with delight. Just being with Jace did that to her.

They looked at each other, able to hear the rustle of Doyle's newspaper in the next room and the occasional comments the older couple made to each other. They didn't kiss or do more than hold hands on the top of the table, but the longing was there, and they both knew it. They also knew there would be other times, and for those they could wait.

"I read the most astounding thing in my Bible this week," Douglas Muldoon told his small congregation on Sunday morning. "Look with me at Genesis 5. I've read these verses before but not really thought about what was here.

"I'll read starting in verse 21: 'Enoch lived sixty and five years, and begat Methuselah. And Enoch walked with God after he begat Methuselah three hundred years, and begat sons and daughters.' Now this is the part I want you to catch—verses 23 and 24: 'And all the days of Enoch were three hundred sixty and five years, and Enoch walked with God, and he was not, for God took him.'

"My friends," Douglas preached from the corner of the kitchen that allowed him to see into the parlor as well, because both rooms were full of worshipers. "We are called to faithfulness, are we not?

"Now, let's see." Douglas scanned the two rooms, his eyes lighting on one of the older men. "Doc MacKay," Douglas began with a smile, "would you mind sharing with us how old you are?"

To the sound of some laughter, the kind doctor smiled and admitted, "I'm 52."

"Did you hear that?" Douglas asked the group. "He's off to a great start, but he still has 313 more years to walk with God." There was more laughter as Douglas went on. "How about you, Alan, how old are you?"

"Almost 33."

"Great! You have 332 years to go. I have 328 years, and my wife has—" Douglas stopped and smiled in her direction, his grin widening when she wagged a finger at him. He then waited for everyone to stop laughing before he continued.

"I hope, dear friends, that you have caught my point, and that Enoch amazes you as he does me. He's a hero of the faith. I think I'm weary and can't go on after 37 years, but I'm a novice, a pup. Enoch was a master. Enoch knew what it meant to walk with God, and he did this all the days of his life."

Douglas went on and shared what it meant to him to have an example like Enoch. He explained that life was no easier or harder in the days of Enoch, but that man has always wrestled with sin, and God has always provided a way of salvation.

Alison listened to her husband and was filled with thankfulness for that man. He didn't get up on Sunday morning and try to be someone that he wasn't all week. She glanced at her children's faces just then and prayed with all her heart. She prayed that they would walk in their father's footsteps because he would lead them down the path that always led to God.

"Do you believe that the Bible is the Word of God?"

Sunday afternoon found Jace and Maddie on a walk. Maddie hadn't asked any questions of Mr. Sullins, but as usual, being in the service got her to thinking.

"I don't know," Jace admitted. "I've never thought too much about it."

"Can you think about it now?"

To please her, Jace did as she asked, but he wasn't overly successful.

"I guess I don't see it as all that important, Maddie. Why do you?"

"Well, only because if it is the Word of God, it should be taken seriously."

"True," Jace agreed with her and then shook his head. "Actually, I don't feel that way. I think the Bible could be God's Word, but it's an old book. I'm not sure it relates to anything today."

Maddie nodded, thinking about what he'd said. The problem with his statement, however, was that many things they already did were because of God's Word. Maddie said as much.

"What do you mean?" Jace asked.

"Well, I think we all know it's wrong to steal and kill, and that's mostly because of the Ten Commandments. We accept those commands as being right, but is it okay just to pick and choose what we want to follow or obey?"

"So you would want to become a religious zealot?" Jace asked, not unkindly.

"No, but a little direction would be nice."

"Direction for what?"

Maddie looked away. "You'll only be irritated with me."

"No, I won't."

But she still didn't share. She had been asking about death and heaven for so long that she knew it angered people. Doyle had grown flustered with her on more than one occasion.

"You can tell me," Jace encouraged, trying not to be distracted by the way her hair escaped in little curls from the braided bun she wore.

"I still have questions about heaven and death. I don't know why I find those concepts unsettling, but I do."

Jace stopped walking, and because they were holding hands, Maddie stopped as well.

"Do you fear death, Maddie?"

"Not death itself, but what happens afterward concerns me."

Jace stepped back a little and looked at her. He was much more concerned with life, working hard, and having money to show for it. What happened after death was not something he thought about at all. He knew he was not perfect, but he didn't think he deserved to be in hell. He didn't know what more he had to worry about.

"Are you angry?" Maddie asked when he was silent for so long.

"No, just thinking. Just trying to understand why it's so important to you."

Maddie looked almost embarrassed. She glanced away, wishing she'd kept her mouth shut. Jace's hand to her cheek brought her face back to him.

"I'm not angry."

"I know."

"Then why do you look upset?"

"I just wish I could talk to someone who understood why it's so important to me. In all these years there's only been one person who has."

"Who was that?"

"Mr. Muldoon."

"Who is that?"

"He's the other pastor in town. I think I told you about him."

"Yes, you did. Why don't you talk to him again?" Jace urged.

"He doesn't come into the store that often. In fact, I've only seen him once."

"You can't go to his house or meetinghouse?"

Maddie remembered that he had invited her to do that.

"I might do that," she said at last.

Jace began walking again, this time drawing Maddie's arm through his to have her closer. He fingered the bracelet at her wrist, pleased that she was wearing it every time he saw her.

"What are you thinking about?"

Jace's thought had strayed to an impure place, so he hesitated. Maddie misread this and stopped.

"You were touching the bracelet," she said, her voice quiet. "You want it back, don't you."

"No," Jace protested, trying to take her hand. "I just like the fact that you wear it."

"But you don't want to tell me what you were thinking?"

"It was nothing," he said, thinking she looked vulnerable. He wasn't sure that sharing his intimate thoughts of her was a wise idea. "Nothing's wrong, I assure you."

Maddie nodded, telling herself she was being foolish. Jace leaned down and kissed her gently—not the least bit worried about privacy but only glad to see her smile at him.

"Shall we go back or walk on?"

"It doesn't matter," Maddie told him, thinking that as long as he was with her, she didn't care where they were.

Jace tucked her close to him again and resumed the walk. He too was thinking that their location was only a detail. The company was everything.

Jace woke in the night to a dark and silent house. The days were long enough to keep him asleep all night, but tonight was an exception. Tonight he felt achy and sore, and as soon as his body woke, his mind came awake.

Not strangely, his first thoughts were of Maddie. He was ready to have her beside him all the time. He was ready to marry her. He knew they had things to work out, but he was confident their love would see them through anything.

It was in the midst of Jace's thoughts about Maddie that he noticed the quiet. The walls of the farmhouse were not so thick that noise was never heard, and it wasn't at all unusual to hear Woody snoring. Jace now listened for it but heard nothing.

Jace slipped quietly out of bed and into the hall. He didn't want to wake or alert his uncle, but it was too quiet for comfort. He was almost to Woody's bedroom door before soft snoring met his ears. Relief filling him, he returned to his room and slipped into bed, his mind now fully on Woody's health.

For the first time he could remember, he thought about Woody and the afterlife. Woody wasn't a religious man, but there were men much worse. He was moral, and a fair businessman and farmer. Was God more particular than that? Did God exact more from His children than to do their best with the few years they had? How often did He look down on Sunday and count heads in the meetinghouse, or was life weighed in the day-to-day grind and dealings with others?

Jace nearly laughed out loud. Maddie was rubbing off on him. A subject to which he'd given almost no thought now had him wondering in the night. And with no answers! This was why Maddie kept asking. This was what kept her unsettled. For answers about the newspaper you went to the printer. For information on dry goods, there was the general store. But when one had questioned the reverend about a biblical issue and gained no knowledge, to whom did one turn next?

Sleep didn't come for a long time. Jace was just drifting off when Clara let herself in the kitchen door.

I forgot to ask you about something before I left, Eden had ended her letter to Jace. Woody had actually wanted to head into town midweek and had brought home the mail. *Has Maddie talked to you about David? I guess he was a man she loved before. His name came up while we did the dishes, and I sensed some regret on her part. Is she all right now?*

Jace frowned down at the words. Was David the man from Boston? Jace was surprised to know that Maddie had discussed him with Eden, but then he knew from firsthand knowledge that Eden had a way of getting words out of a person. It took separation from her to learn what to avoid. Maddie would have been unaware.

At the same time his sister's words did make him wonder. Why had Maddie never spoken to him about David? A woman he'd been involved with in Pine River now came to mind. Jace had genuinely cared for her and had been hurt when she'd broken off with him. He'd not trusted women for a long time, at least not with his heart. He'd spent time with other women, but he'd not actually given his heart away until Maddie.

Jace all but shook his head because he was just now realizing that. And had he been wise? Yes, Maddie was the sweetest woman he'd ever known, and when he was with her, he could think of little else, but how much did he really know about her?

Jace made himself put Eden's letter and his wild thoughts aside. Maddie was the girl for him; he was sure of that. He was just tired and letting his imagination stray.

When Woody came looking for him a few minutes later, wanting help in the barn, Jace was very ready to get his mind onto farm and field work.

Twelve

"What are you doing?" Maddie asked her uncle, having come home from the store and caught him in the act.

"What do you mean?" Doyle tried for an innocent face, but Maddie wasn't buying it.

"You know exactly what I mean. You're working on something and not resting. Now, what are you up to?"

Doyle glanced around, his mind scrambling even as he continued to look innocent. Maddie put a hand to her mouth because she had an overwhelming urge to laugh. It was at that moment that Maddie thought she smelled paint. She came around to where he was standing in the kitchen and peered into the buttery. Her eyes widened when she found it empty and partially painted.

"Did you do this all this morning?" Maddie asked.

"I had to. It's the first time you and Cathy have left me alone for ages."

Maddie covered her mouth again, but it didn't work. This time she laughed out loud. He had sounded like a small, aggrieved child. And she knew that his confinement had been a long trial.

"You know she'll smell this," Maddie said, having composed herself, "as soon as she walks in the door."

"But it will be done by then," Doyle reasoned.

"She'll be angry," Maddie tried.

"That's okay. Her heart isn't in trouble."

Maddie's shoulders shook with mirth as she moved toward the door.

"I've got to get out of here. She's going to ask how you are, and I can't know too much or I'll be in as much trouble as you're going to be in."

"Just keep her in the store until closing."

Maddie could only roll her eyes, not about to give any guarantees. Keeping Cathy in the store and away from Doyle that many hours was quite probably impossible.

Douglas stood at the edge of the kitchen and watched his wife out the window. She didn't like anyone around when she was sick, but his heart was so hurt by the sight that he couldn't move.

And she was growing thin. The nausea had not lasted this long before. Nearly every meal came back, and Douglas was growing concerned. At first the main topic of conversation was whether she would carry the baby full term. Now it was about how long the sickness would last. It seemed that the pregnancy was a strong one, but that didn't change the fact that she had to find a way to survive it.

Douglas watched her come toward the door, and he went to pour her some water, greeting her with a cool glass and asking her to sit down.

"I'm fine, Douglas."

"But I'm not," he said, and Alison looked at him with compassion.

Douglas put a hand to her cheek.

"You're getting thin."

"I'm not very hungry these days."

Martin came looking for Alison just then and saw the glass of water.

"Mama, did you burp?" he asked, his word for something far worse.

"I'm afraid so."

"Does the baby know that she makes you sick?"

Alison laughed and put her arms around him, wondering at the way he always said "she."

"It might be a boy," she felt a need to remind him.

"But we want a girl," Douglas put in.

"Are you the one giving him ideas?" Alison asked, earning a huge smile.

Alison pulled Martin into her lap to talk to him, knowing that Douglas would figure out that it was all for him.

"Does God have a plan for everything, Marty?"

"He does."

"Yes, even when a woman has a baby, God knows just what He wants that baby to be."

Alison glanced up to find Douglas fighting laughter.

"So we will be thankful," Martin finished.

Alison hugged him closer. "It's good to know, Marty, that your father hasn't completely ruined you."

The little boy frowned up at her in confusion, which only intensified when both husband and wife began to laugh.

Maddie helped David Scales load some of the building supplies she'd been holding for him into the back of his wagon. He had parked at the side of the building, and Maddie had carried the lighter items.

"How will you get your wife out of the house for the surprise?"

"She left on the morning train. She's headed to Worcester to see her cousin's new baby. She'll be gone a week."

Maddie smiled. "You've planned this very well."

"I hope so. I'm just afraid that I won't get it done before she gets back."

"That doesn't matter."

"Why is that?"

"She'll see what you started and be surprised anyhow. My guess is she'll be delighted."

David stared at her. "Do all women think alike?"

"Not all, I guess, but probably most."

"I can't thank you enough, Maddie. Katie will be so surprised over this larger kitchen. She has so little space right now."

"I hope it's wonderful."

"I think it will be, and I couldn't have done it without you. I feel I should give you a hug."

"Of course you can give me a hug," Maddie told him warmly, and David bent down to give her a tight squeeze.

Maddie smiled and waved as he left, hoping the surprise would work, and hoping beyond that, that David's wife knew what a special guy she had married.

Jace could hardly believe Eden was standing on the doorstep just as he and Woody finished dinner on Friday at midday. He'd read her letter only two days before, and she'd visited just two weeks back, but she was there again—no mistake about that.

"Well, Eden," he said, welcoming her in a decidedly luke-warm manner.

"Hello, Jace. How are you?"

"Fine." Jace stepped back to let her in, just holding his tongue from asking why she had come. "Are you hungry?" he asked instead. "Dinner's still on the table."

"Thank you." She smiled as though nothing was amiss.

Jace led the way, able to watch Woody's face when Eden came through the door. The older man did not looked pleased.

"Eden's here," Jace announced unnecessarily.

"Well, Eden," Woody said, sounding just like Jace.

Eden was aware that they were not glad to see her, but she ignored their faces. She was here to do a job, and already things were going very well.

"Is Clara around?" Eden asked conversationally after a few bites. "I've got to tell her how good this cheese souffle is."

"In the kitchen," Woody said, some of the few words he had uttered since Eden's arrival.

Eden went that way, and Woody wasted no time in speaking to Jace.

"Is it me, or was she just here?"

"Two weeks ago."

Woody nodded, his face thoughtful. "I teased you before about her moving to Tucker Mills, Jace, but right now I would say you have a real problem on your hands. Eden's getting ready to move here, and she will if you don't stop her."

Eden returned to the parlor before Jace could speak, but he agreed with his uncle about Eden's plans. He couldn't actually stop his sister from doing something she wanted to do, but before she left to go home, he would make his own wishes very clear.

"Jace, I have something I need to tell you," Eden said, catching him just outside the kitchen door before he could follow Woody to the fields.

"Okay," Jace agreed, his voice calmer than he felt as he steeled himself to have Eden announce she was selling the boardinghouse and making a move.

"When I got into town, I realized I needed a few things, so I went to the store."

Surprised, Jace wondered where this was going, but Eden didn't finish.

"Well," he questioned a little impatiently, "did they have what you needed?"

"I never went in," Eden said, her voice full of regret. "I saw Maddie with a man, and I didn't know what to do, so I just turned around and came directly here."

"What are you talking about?"

"They were doing a lot of hugging, Jace, and they kissed. They were outside, on the side of the building, for the most part hidden by his wagon."

Jace stared at his sister. She had managed to take him completely by surprise.

"It wasn't Maddie," Jace said after a moment, even as suspicion filled him.

Eden looked helpless, playing it for all she was worth.

"It looked just like her, Jace, but you know the women in town better than I do. Maybe it wasn't her."

Jace stared at her, not really seeing her, imagining Maddie with someone else. Unfortunately for Maddie, he was able to picture it quite clearly. The man was a little vague, but Maddie's lovely eyes and smile as she looked up at another man were very clear in Jace's mind.

"I have to get to work," he said finally and turned to leave.

"Okay," Eden said, regret still filling every word. She watched Jace leave, careful not to look as triumphant as she felt. Clara was still in the house, and she knew that woman talked with Woody and Jace all the time.

Eden slipped back inside and quietly offered to help with the dinner dishes. Clara agreed in her indomitable fashion, and the women had a stilted conversation while they worked. But as soon as the kitchen was in order, Eden made herself scarce.

It was tempting to find Jace and ask what he was going to do about Maddie, but that might show her hand. Eden knew how hard it was going to be, but if she was going to interfere with this relationship, it would have to seem as though she were on Jace and Maddie's side and regretful about the whole episode. Even if she had to leave on Monday without knowing just what effect her words might have, she would do that in order to disguise the way she felt.

Jace had never been more torn. He walked along the rows of corn, checking heads along the way, Maddie constantly on his mind. He knew deep in his heart that Eden had seen Maddie; there could be no one else. All this time she feared that he would hurt her, and she was the one with someone else.

The name *David* raced through his mind. He knew if Maddie were here right now, he would be furious with her and demand to know who this David person was. As he worked, he realized that seeing her was the worst thing he could do. Working along, methodically hoeing between the rows, Jace made up his mind to go to town, but he'd steer clear of the Shephards. He needed a drink, probably several, and some companionship with people he knew he could trust: men.

Eden listened to Jace on the stairs, certain he had had too much to drink. When he'd announced he was going to town, she'd been discouraged but had not given up. Now listening to him mutter to himself and bang into things in the hallway, she knew her scheme had worked.

There were still Saturday and Sunday to get through, and even though her train left on Monday, somehow Eden knew that her trip to Tucker Mills had been a success.

First one week passed, and then two. Doyle and Cathy did a lot of talking behind closed doors, going to bed early to do just that, but neither one said a word to Maddie. It wasn't unusual for Jace to miss a Sunday dinner, but a full weekend was unheard of.

And in that time the light went out of Maddie's eyes. She went about the business of running the store and doing all she could at the house, but her face was pale and her eyes were sober. She joined in all conversations that were directed her way but initiated none.

Doyle had begun to feel significantly better. He thought his heart was just about right again, but suddenly it seemed as if the weight of the world had landed on his chest. He did all he could to hide that fact, but Jace's absence was beginning to weigh on all of them.

What Cathy and Doyle didn't know was that Maddie couldn't take it anymore. She had made a decision, and even if it landed her in trouble, she was going to follow through. She only hoped that both her aunt and uncle would want to turn in early, much as they'd been doing in the last two weeks.

"Are you expecting someone?" Jace asked of Woody from the upstairs hall; both men had just headed upstairs to go to bed.

"No, but I heard the knock too."

"I'll get it," Jace said, using the candle and heading back down. He opened the door to find Maddie on the step. The anger that had plagued him and been smoldering just below the surface for days now filled him.

"Jace," she wasted no time, "can I talk to you?"

Jace opened the door and let her in, and Maddie was struck by how bold she was being. Not until she stepped into this house did she realize this was all wrong. She had no business coming alone to this man's house after dark.

"Jace?" Woody called down the stairs.

"It's for me," Jace called back as he set the candle above the fireplace. He then turned to Maddie. "What are you doing here?"

"I missed you," she said quietly, deciding that she'd come too far not to have her say. "I haven't seen you in two weeks."

Jace turned back to the fireplace, staring down at the dark interior. His back was to Maddie in a way that made the room much colder than the actual temperature.

"I've been busy," Jace said shortly.

Maddie didn't know when she'd been so confused. "Jace, what have I done?" she finally asked, desperate to know what this change meant. "Did I say or do something?"

"My sister saw you," Jace said quietly.

"Your sister was here? I didn't see her."

"No, but she certainly saw you."

"Saw me? When?"

"With a man. I assume it was David."

"How do you know about David?" Maddie asked innocently.

With his back to Maddie, Jace closed his eyes in pain. Part of him still wanted Maddie to tell him she loved him and that there would never be anyone else.

"I want you to go," Jace finally said.

"Do you mean that?" Maddie asked, her voice telling of her hurt and shock.

This time Jace turned to face her. "Yes. It's time you leave."

Maddie could feel herself shaking, but there was nothing she could do about it. She started away but felt the bracelet fall down her wrist.

"Oh." She stopped and looked down at it. "You'll be wanting this back."

Jace felt as if his heart was being ripped from his chest. Even in the dim candlelight, he could see the way she shook, the way her hand kept losing the clasp before she could unhook it.

"I'll just put it on the desk here," she whispered, not able to look at him.

Jace was completely still as he heard the chain land on the desk and then watched as Maddie ducked her head and rushed for the door. Even after he heard the latch click, he couldn't move.

How did you know about David? Jace knew he would never forget those words.

Jace walked to the desk and took the bracelet in his hand. He closed his fist around it and went up the stairs.

"Jace?" Woody called from his room.

"I'm going to bed" was all Jace would say, but he was thinking, *I loved you, Maddie. I wanted you to be my wife.*

Jace blew the candle out and stood in the dark for a few minutes, fresh pain assailing him. He knew he couldn't let that happen or he'd never get past this. He felt his way to the small dresser and dropped the bracelet back inside. This time it would stay there, and he wouldn't think about it or her any longer.

"I did something last night that I shouldn't have," Maddie said at the breakfast table, causing Doyle and Cathy to stop everything and look at her. "I waited until after dark and went out to the farm and spoke with Jace. He doesn't want to be with me any longer. I hope you didn't hear me go and worry about me, but I wanted you to know why Jace won't be coming around."

"Did he say why, Maddie?" Doyle had to ask.

"He thinks I've been with David Scales," Maddie said quietly. "Without even asking, he just accused me." Maddie looked into her uncle's face and saw his poor color and the strain around his eyes. She knew this had to be the end of it. "I don't wish to speak of it anymore. We'll put it behind us, all right?"

"As you wish," Doyle told her, wishing his breathing to be a little easier.

Cathy, who hadn't cried in years, wanted nothing more than to go someplace and cry her eyes out. She managed an understanding smile when Maddie looked her way, but in truth, she was in shock.

"I'll go to the store today," Maddie offered, thinking it might rescue her.

"I'll check on you in a little while," Cathy offered.

Maddie hadn't touched her breakfast, but her aunt and uncle said nothing about this. They sat quietly as she left for the store, their meals untouched as well.

"Will you talk to Jace?" Doyle asked his wife.

"I doubt he'll come in," she said, and then shook her head. "Even if he did, I wouldn't want to speak to him."

Doyle knew that Cathy could be very protective and wondered whether she would ever welcome Jace to the store again. Oh, she would wait on him, but she would also see him on his way as swiftly as she could.

And what will I do? Doyle asked of himself. *One of these days I'll be back over there. Will I wait on Jace and put this behind me?* Doyle didn't know the answer to that, but he suddenly knew why Maddie said they would put this all behind them. To do anything else would not be something they could survive.

The days and weeks that followed built something of a buffer around Maddie's heart. She worked in the store as usual but with little anticipation of anything save her uncle being well enough to come back to his old life. And it seemed that he would. He was stronger lately, as though the recent hurt had forced him not to sit around any longer and wait to be well.

Cathy wanted him to keep sitting, but by the end of July, one month after Maddie had confronted Jace, Doyle was coming over to the store two mornings a week and doing everything but climbing the stairs and lifting.

But that wasn't the only change. Jace and Woody no longer went to services. Indeed, the Shephards never saw Jace in town at all. When Woody needed something, he would come on his own, without explanation or any mention of his nephew. If he had feelings one way or the other concerning Jace and Maddie, there was no sign of it while he was in the store. He was affable and seemed in good health.

Had Jace still been social with the Shephards, he could have told them this was not always the case. It hadn't taken Woody very long to figure out that Eden had had a hand in Jace and Maddie's breakup. Woody had tried to point this out to his nephew, but Jace would only say that Maddie had all but admitted that she had been with David.

The older man finally gave up, but not for a few weeks. At that time Jace had blown his top, telling his uncle he would hear no more, and Woody had quieted. That Jace was miserable was very easy to see, but Woody had heeded Jace's warning and was keeping his mouth shut. He would not have done so if Eden had been in town, but once she'd stirred things up, she'd left and not been back.

Woody knew that letters still arrived from her, but he noticed that they lay on the desk for days or a week before Jace touched them. But that wasn't Woody's main concern. Jace had stopped caring about himself. The farm and mill were handled with an impeccable touch, but it had become the norm for Jace not to shave for several days or care if his hair was combed or cut. And come the weekend, he could be expected to arrive home very drunk on Saturday night.

When Woody was in to the store for something, he half-hoped that Cathy or Maddie would question him about Jace, but it never came up. Jace had obviously been the one to cut things off, and it would seem that Maddie—Cathy too—was doing her best to get over it.

If Maddie's smile wasn't as bright and her eyes seemed a little sad, Woody thought he might be the only one to notice such things. But notice them he did, and it was hard to see her. It bothered his heart no small amount. The peace he'd felt about leaving the farm and mill to Jace had only heightened when he pictured Maddie there as well. Now Woody watched Jace each day and knew that whatever Eden had said or done, it had left a hole in Jace's heart as well as his world.

Watching all of this, Woody's heart developed a hole too. But his situation was different. He did not have time on his side and feared his life would be over before any mending could begin.

"I'm going on a buying trip," Doyle announced at the end of August. "I think it's time to get back on my feet, and that's how I'm going to start."

Cathy stared at her husband but didn't speak. She wanted to object, but in truth he was doing very well.

"Cathy?" Doyle pressed her.

"I'll worry, Doyle, but I can see you're ready to do this."

Doyle reached over and patted her hand before turning to Maddie. She was somewhat lost in thought but didn't take long to respond when her uncle's eyes turned to her.

"May I go with you?" she asked.

Doyle looked at her, clearly surprised.

"Go with me?" he questioned, having never thought of it.

"Yes. I'm sure you'll go to Boston, and I'd really like to. It's been a long time since I've seen the Nunleys, and I would enjoy it so much."

Doyle nodded slowly, his eyes not meeting Cathy's.

"I think that would be all right, Maddie. It's really your decision to make."

"Thank you, Doyle," Maddie said, rising to take care of her dishes and then to head upstairs.

Husband and wife finally looked at each other. They had watched her hurt and struggle for the past few months, bearing up like a soldier in war, uncomplaining and never giving up. How could they deny her such a thing? The question echoed in both of their minds even as they knew that if she accompanied Doyle to Boston, she would not make the return journey.

Thirteen

Boston

"Maddie," Paige said, having found her in the back hall. "Have you seen my dark blue coat?"

Paige hadn't really been looking at Maddie, and when she did, she found the other woman holding the garment out to her. Paige grinned.

"How did I find anything when you were gone?"

"According to your mother, you didn't."

Paige's eyes rolled. "She was most unhappy with me at times."

"Well, I'm here now."

"Until we leave," Paige put in.

"Oh, I'll still be here." Maddie would not be drawn. "It's you who will be gone."

"There's still time for you to come," Paige invited.

Maddie didn't comment, but Paige had come to accept her silence. She was the same Maddie, but then she wasn't. Something had happened in Tucker Mills, something she wasn't talking about, something so serious that she didn't even want to accompany them on their trip. Mrs. Nunley had coaxed and pleaded, but Maddie was staying in Boston for the months they would be gone.

Nevertheless, Paige had devised a plan. They weren't scheduled to leave for two more months, and she hoped she might be able to talk Maddie around. Deep in her heart, however, she knew they would be sailing for Europe without their companion and friend.

"All right, Paige," Maddie said, snapping the younger woman from her thoughts. "Head to the front door; your mother will be waiting."

"Oh, that's right, but when I get back I have something to show you."

"I'll be here," Maddie assured her, smiling when Paige looked so pleased. She walked behind her to the foyer and saw her and the missus off, glad to have the house quiet again. For a long time she stood just inside the front door, her thoughts wandering.

Maddie's head tipped back as she took in the beautiful crown molding that stretched from the foyer into the rest of the downstairs. It really was a lovely home, and Maddie had been happy here, but she now wondered whether a change might be in order.

Paige would not be home for many more years. Maddie would not rush away before then, and she would want to give the missus a chance to adjust, but in a few years, Maddie thought, it might be time to move on. She knew not to where or what, but beautiful as it was, she didn't think she wanted to live in this house forever.

Thoughts of Jace filled her mind without warning. She had been planning to live in Tucker Mills forever, happy to do so, happy to wait for Jace to ask that question and then become his wife.

Maddie shook her head a little and told herself to get to work. There was no point in crying over something she couldn't have. It was over, and the sooner she realized that, the better it would be.

Tucker Mills

Jace was nearing the one-year mark. He'd come to the farm in the midst of the harvest last year, and now he was here to meet the harvest head-on. Woody had lots of tricks up his sleeve to make things more efficient and productive, but there was no getting around the hard work involved. The men put in long hours each day, their backs aching and sore, but satisfaction over the harvest and fruits of their labor dulled their fatigue.

But what pleased Jace the most was knowing that the mill waited. Repairs to the equipment and even to the building, if needed, to ready the mill for cutting boards in the late winter, would start as soon as the harvest was done. Jace enjoyed the farm work and even the animals, but he loved the mill. The mill had gotten into his blood in a surprising way.

He didn't want to wish his life away, but looking forward to working in the mill, even knowing how cold some of those days could be, put some fire back into his blood and gave him something to look forward to, something that had been sadly lacking in his life of late.

The thought that things might have been different lingered in his mind from time to time. He asked himself what he could have done to make it so but always ended up frustrated or hurting worse. In the end, he tried not to look at the future at all but do his work and get through one day at a time.

"How is Maddie?" Clara asked Doyle when she was in the store; she was the only person from the farm who didn't seem afraid to voice the question.

"She's settled back in Boston and writes each week."

"Does she sound all right?"

"I'm not sure," Doyle admitted to the woman who had been shopping in his store for as long as he'd had the doors open.

"You can't always see between the words, if you know what I mean."

"I do know what you mean. I miss seeing her."

Doyle cleared his throat. "Stop in and see Cathy. She's missing her something terrible."

"I might do that, Doyle," Clara told him. She thanked him for his time, took her basket, and went out to visit the other shops on her list. Her errands took more time than she expected and she had to get home, but she told herself she would make a point to see Cathy Shephard the next week.

Clara drove the wagon out of town and down the road, spotting what seemed to be a familiar figure up ahead. As she drew abreast of Eden Randall, she stopped the wagon. She didn't like Eden and didn't trust her, but no one had asked her opinion, and she was Jace's sister, so she deserved at least some respect.

"Headed to the farm?" Clara asked.

"I am, yes."

"Climb in."

Eden did so, glad for the lift. The days were getting cooler, and since she had been too warm on the train, her body temperature was now headed the other way. She was swiftly becoming chilled.

"How are you?" Eden asked, her voice a little cautious.

"Fine."

"And the farm?"

"The farm's fine as well."

Eden's chin came up a bit even though she didn't speak. She knew that Woody and Clara didn't like her, but this was Jace's home now, and she had every right to visit. Until Jace told her to go away and not come back—something she knew would never happen—she would consider herself welcome.

It was a relief, however, to see the farm come into view. She only hoped that Jace wasn't so far into the fields that she couldn't see him. A familiar face would be nice, and somehow Eden was certain that as soon as she saw Jace, she would know for certain, one way or the other, whether Maddie Shephard was still in his life. She had stayed away all this time. She now deserved to know.

It was midafternoon. Dinner was over, and Eden had retired to the room she stayed in while at the farm to settle a few things on the dresser. She was glad for the time alone. Jace had not been as she expected. His jocular, easygoing manner was gone. He was subdued, thinner, and ill kept. Eden had never seen him like that, and it shook her.

She had tried to find some of the old Jace, but he was unresponsive and distant, even with Woody and Clara. Eden knew that Maddie was gone. No one had said it, but the sense of it hung around the farmhouse like a cloud. Eden began to doubt herself for the first time. She had been so certain that Maddie was a passing fancy.

A sudden vision of her mother's bracelet hanging from Maddie's wrist came to mind. For a moment she asked herself whether Jace may have truly lost his heart this time.

A strong shake of her head sent that notion away. Maddie was gone, and Jace would get over whatever infatuation he might have felt. Eden finished in the room and went downstairs. There was nothing else to worry about. She had done the right thing.

"What are you baking?" Hillary asked of her mother on the last Saturday in September.

"A few breads, muffins, cookies, and scones."

Hillary smiled at the parent whose likeness was so similar to her own.

"What are you grinning about?" Alison caught the look.

"Just you."

"Why?"

"Because it's always so fun when you feel better. The smell of flour made you sick until just recently, and now you're baking enough to share with all the village."

"Which reminds me," Alison replied, perking up. "I need you to take one of those pies over to Mrs. Carter."

"When did you bake pies?" Hillary asked with a laugh, but Alison only smiled.

Hillary did as she was told, however, and the next person through the kitchen was Peter.

"I can't remember which was created first, fish or animals," he told his mother.

"Day five for fish and birds, and day six for animals," Alison answered, stirring all the while. "It's all in the first chapter of Genesis."

"I was going to look it up," Peter explained, "but Papa's door is shut."

"You were wise not to disturb him. He might be praying."

Peter came close and laid his head on his mother's extended stomach.

"Have you been kicked today?"

"A little."

"She's going to be naughty," Peter predicted, and Alison smiled. They were still all so certain that it was a girl. She couldn't tell, and in truth thought that another girl would be wonderful, but she didn't have her heart set one way or the other.

"Where is Marty?" Alison suddenly asked, and Peter's eyes grew large.

"I forget to get him from Ben's house."

"Go," his mother ordered and shook her head when he made a run for the door. "Some days," she said quietly to the Lord, "I can't keep track of four. I'll certainly need Your help with five."

ॐॐॐ

"Have a good trip," Jace told Eden at the train station on Monday. His voice carried little inflection and even less expression.

"Thank you. I hope the harvest continues to go well for you."

"It should," Jace said noncommittally, still thinking about the mill work.

And with that they waited in silence. Eden shot glances from the corner of her eye, taking in Jace's thin cheeks and unshaved chin but also noticing his eyes.

Jace had always had an eye for the ladies, but not today. Several attractive women walked by, all looking his way, but he did nothing. His eyes did not meet theirs or follow them when they walked past. He looked straight ahead at the side of the train, seeming dead inside to his sister.

"I'd better board," Eden finally said, knowing she couldn't stand to watch him any longer.

"Take care," Jace said with a small wave and moved off the platform.

Eden found a seat on the train and stared ahead, willing herself to be in control. She was always in control. It was best that way.

I got my way, she said to herself. *I planned and I worked and I got my way, and I'm happy about it.*

Eden felt herself begin to shake and thought she might be cold, but deep in her heart she knew better. She was a woman who had lied to herself often; she just never admitted it or faced that fact. Right now her heart wouldn't allow her to do anything else, and that knowledge made her cold all over.

Boston

"Maddie, did you pack my light blue cloak?" the missus asked Maddie for the second time.

"I'm sure I did, but I'll check," she had learned to say.

With plans to be gone for several months, the family was leaving in just one week, quite possibly not returning until after the first of the year.

Maddie had mixed feelings about this. There was always a small amount of chaos with the missus and Paige at home, but there was also plenty to do, plenty to occupy her mind. When they were out, Maddie would breathe a sigh of relief—as would the rest of the staff—and feel free for a time. But this was early October. The first of the year was weeks and weeks away, and Maddie worried that she would have too much time on her hands.

In any other year, she would have jumped at the chance to make plans for an extended stay at Doyle and Cathy's, but not this year. Right now Tucker Mills was the last place she wanted to be. She toyed with the idea of asking them to come to Boston but knew that Cathy would not come without Doyle, and Doyle would not leave the store so soon after returning. If his letters were any indiction, he was still having the time of his life, feeling almost the way he did in the days when he'd first opened.

"There's still time," the missus suddenly said, and Maddie was jolted back to the moment.

"Thank you, Mrs. Nunley," Maddie said to her, coming close to touch her arm. "Your wanting me to come means a lot to me, but I need to stay here."

The older woman looked into her eyes, not wanting to be separated so soon, but mostly not wanting Maddie to be hurt ever again.

"Will you ever want to talk about it?"

"I don't know," Maddie said honestly. "I guess I don't see much point."

Mrs. Nunley nodded, but secretly she didn't agree. She felt that talking about something could be a great help, and in her opinion was the only real help. For now, however, she let the matter drop. The sadness in Maddie's eyes was almost too much for her, but she wouldn't press her, not on any subject. Much as she wanted Maddie to join them on the voyage and to talk to her about her pain, she was wise enough to know when to listen to the younger woman's wishes.

Tucker Mills

"How are you, Doyle?" Doc MacKay stopped in at the store to ask. "I see you up and around and assume you're doing well."

"I am feeling well, thank you."

"Did you hear about Woody?"

"Yes," Doyle replied, his voice sober.

"I got the news this morning but haven't heard details on the funeral."

"It's this afternoon," Doyle answered. The townspeople expected the general store owner to be the keeper of important information.

Doc MacKay nodded, his mind thoughtful. He'd known Woody for years, but they'd never had a deep discussion of any kind. He knew this day was coming and now wondered how Jace would deal with it. Tucker Mills' doctor almost mentioned that younger man but then remembered the rumors he'd heard about why Maddie had returned to Boston.

Beyond asking how Cathy was doing, he didn't linger in the store but took himself off, making a mental note to be at the funeral in a few hours.

Jace could hardly believe what he was seeing. The coffin was done; Woody's body had been prepared and wrapped in a white shroud; and he was lying in the parlor. Jace's eyes went around that room. How many nights had they sat by the fire in this room in companionable silence or with Woody explaining some aspect of the farm or mill to Jace? And now it was over. Jace could barely take it in. He thought he was prepared for this time but now knew he wasn't.

Yesterday morning Woody had not gotten up. The three of them had been through this several times—Jace arriving in the kitchen to find Clara on her own, and then the two of them heading up to check on him only to learn that he just needed more rest or that his chest hurt.

Yesterday had been different. Yesterday Woody had not answered them or moved. And for the first time since Jace had known her, Clara cried. Her apron had come to her face, and she had sobbed like a child. She had cried the way Jace wanted to, feeling suddenly bereft and utterly alone.

But when the tears were done, she set to work. Doing as he was told, Jace helped Clara prepare the body. He'd never been involved in something like that before, and even now couldn't repeat what happened. Everything was in a fog, a fog of unreality that this man, this uncle who had taken him in, was gone.

And then word had gone out. Clara had been the one to walk to the neighbor's and ask them to tell Mr. Sullins. Clara told Jace that Mr. Sullins would spread the news and come and read over the body. Jace didn't know what he would have done without her. He wanted to cry when he looked at her, but just having her nearby was a comfort.

Amid these musings, the first mourners began to arrive. Jace and Clara sat stiffly side by side in chairs to the right of the coffin as the townsfolk filed through the house. His world became almost artificial. Folks approached and recited rehearsed words to him. Jace answered them, but he remembered little of it. And then Mr. Sullins was speaking, and Jace had to fight away Maddie's questions concerning death and heaven.

Before Jace was ready, the coffin was being loaded into the back of a wagon, and they all followed the wagon to the cemetery. Mr. Sullins said a few more words but kept it mercifully brief. As the grave was being filled in, folks began to depart, stopping to see Jace and Clara on their way. To his utter amazement, some of the last ones were the Shephards.

"I'm surprised to see you here," Jace said, and then wished he could take it back.

"We considered Woody a friend, Jace," Doyle told him, his tone quiet but also quite formal.

Jace nodded, unable to miss the fact that Cathy would not even look at him.

"How's Maddie?" Jace asked, not sure where this had come from.

"Now is a fine time to wonder that," Cathy said. She'd spoken with no heat, but still she turned on her heel and left the men.

Doyle looked at Jace with sadness, but he wasn't ready to let him back into his life.

"Goodbye, Jace," was all Doyle said, slowly moving after his wife.

Jace stared after them, asking himself not for the first time how things could have gone so wrong. They had been his friends. Had Maddie's crimes really been so bad that he had to lose everything?

"Come on, Jace," Clara urged him, having heard the exchange. She wasn't angry with the Shephards for having their say, but she was angry that they chose this day to say it.

She took Jace home and tried to get him to eat, but Jace was interested in only one thing: drink. By evening he was asleep in the chair by the fire, having consumed enough alcohol to blur the pain.

Jace did not remember to write Eden for several days. He knew he should have thought of that immediately but made up for lost time by walking the letter to town as soon as it was done.

Having done this, he was not surprised to see her the weekend after she should have received it.

He had enough to do that he'd not been wallowing in self-pity for days, and in truth was glad for her company. He was missing Woody something awful, and having Eden around for the weekend suited him quite well. What he hadn't expected was the amount of planning Eden had been doing since his letter arrived. She waited to speak of it to Jace until Sunday afternoon when Clara was at home and they had the house to themselves.

"I've been thinking about moving to Tucker Mills," she began.

Jace looked up from his plate to find her watching him.

"Sell the boardinghouse?" he asked.

"Yes. I think it would work."

"You like Tucker Mills that much?"

"I do like it, yes," Eden answered, trying to gauge what he thought.

"So would you try to find a house in town to set up as a boardinghouse, or build one?"

For a moment his question stunned her. It took a moment for her to see the joke and laugh a little.

"I would live here with you," she finally said, a pleased smile on her face.

"No, you wouldn't."

"Of course I would. Don't be silly, Jace."

Jace sat back, his food forgotten for the moment.

"No, Eden." Jace's voice was more than serious. "You're not living here."

"Why ever not?"

"Because you're not," Jace said, picking up his fork. In his mind, that was the end of it.

"I want an answer."

"I gave you one."

"Jace Randall, I think you owe me an explanation."

"Fine," Jace agreed. "Eden, you're not living here because I don't want you to."

Eden was stunned. This was his idea of an explanation? She decided that he was deliberately being rude and would call him on it.

"What's the matter with you?"

"I could ask you the same thing."

"What do you mean by that?"

"Only that you're not happy unless you're in my business and my life. Why can't you be happy with your own life in Pine River, or even Tucker Mills, but not in this house?" Jace stared at her, waiting.

Eden couldn't speak. To deny what he said would be a bald-faced lie, and Jace would know it. She had never been forced to answer that question before, not to herself or anyone else, and she found her tongue strangely quiet.

"I think you need more time to think about it," Eden said at last.

"Don't you try that with me, Eden." Jace was angry now, hating the guilt she could so easily lay at his door. "When you get on that train tomorrow, you remind yourself that you are not welcome to live here with me. Don't go back to Pine River and persuade yourself that I said otherwise. If you up and sell and try to move in here, you'll find yourself without a home."

Eden was speechless. Jace's eyes had been steely. She knew he would not bend on this issue.

Not surprisingly, little was said the rest of the day. And in the morning, Eden was still so hurt that she told Jace she would walk to the train station. She was even more hurt when he didn't argue with her.

The shaking began again as soon as she found her seat on the train. It was unsettling and familiar all at the same time. As the train pulled away, Eden felt almost desperate to jump off and somehow turn back the hands of time.

I've gotten everything I wanted. I chased Maddie Shephard away, and Jace doesn't even blame me. Woody is gone and no longer standing in my way. But it wasn't them. Jace really wanted this change, and not because he was under the influence of his uncle or some woman.

This realization for Eden was almost more than she could take. She nearly broke down on the spot. Jace's rejection of her and her need to control him was so complete that she wanted to sob.

And she did sob, completely losing control, but she waited until she was back in Pine River. She took a long walk in the woods and cried for the first time in years, knowing she was completely alone.

Fourteen

"Listen to this," Doyle said when Cathy came to the store to bring his dinner. He'd just opened a letter from Maddie and now pulled Cathy close to read it to her.

"'I'm not missing the Nunleys just yet. The staff is turning the house out, cleaning everything in sight, and I'm categorizing all of the missus' collections. It keeps my days very full. And the treasures I've found!—things that Mrs. Nunley has probably forgotten she owns.'

"'I'll probably do Mr. Nunley's books next and then start on the missus' letters. She wrote and asked me to do this, and that's what got me started on the collections. I thought I would be lonely, but the days are rushing by, and I look forward to all I'll get done before they arrive back.'"

There was more, but Doyle stopped reading. Just the night before, Cathy had cried, missing Maddie and worrying about her welfare. Now her head lay against her husband's chest, and she thought that this was the first encouraging letter they had received from Maddie since she'd gone back to Boston. This letter sounded hopeful, as if she were finally moving on in her life.

"Sit here with me a while," Doyle invited, and the two took the chairs by the stove that sat in the middle of the store. Doyle ate and Cathy talked to him. It was almost an hour before a customer interrupted their time, but even then Cathy didn't rush away. She wanted to finish the letter, but not until they could be alone. Such good news needed to be shared, and who more perfect than Doyle.

It was happening again. Eden was back after just two weeks had passed. Considering the way their last visit had ended, Jace was not thrilled, but he didn't verbally attack his sister or leave her in the cold. He was, however, mentally steeled for the worst.

"I need to talk to you, Jace," Eden began, having asked her brother into the parlor and shut the doors.

"You're back awfully soon," Jace mentioned, his tone guarded.

"I am, yes, but it's not what you think."

"You're not moving to Tucker Mills?" Jace had to know.

"No, I'm not," Eden said, able to be at peace about this for the first time. "I came to apologize. I realize I could have written, but this was too important."

Jace could only stare at her. Eden had never apologized for anything in her life. He didn't know what to say.

"I've been wrong," Eden began, but Jace cut her off.

"You're saying you're wrong?"

"Yes, I've been very wrong. I did something terrible."

Jace could not believe what he was hearing. He stared at Eden in amazement and then realized how pale she was. This was costing her dearly, and Jace told himself to listen.

"You were right, Jace. I did want to be in control of you and your life. I see that now. In fact, I wanted it so much that I lied to you."

Jace kept listening, trying to find his sister amid the words.

"I never saw Maddie kiss a man," Eden admitted, feeling sick about what she'd done. "All she did was help a man with his load, and he gave her a quick hug."

Jace blinked at her several times, his mind racing.

"Did you hear me?" Eden asked.

"Yes, but what about David? You said she talked to you about David."

Eden shook her head. "All she did was mention that a man named David had once been in love with her. I lied about that too."

Jace's eyes grew round and his face flushed. He stared at his sister as though she'd sprouted horns. Eden read the look and wanted to be sick, but she knew this had to be done. She knew she had to repent to her brother, even if he never forgave her.

Jace came to his feet. He paced around a bit and then spotted the desk. He could see her. He could see Maddie that night she came to see him. He could see the way her hands trembled and the way she left the bracelet on the desk. Jace turned to his sister, his rage nearly choking him.

"Do you know what you've done?" he asked her, all but shouting.

"I ruined everything," Eden said, tears coming to her eyes. "I'm so sorry, Jace; truly I am."

"I sent her away." Jace hadn't heard her. "I told her to get out. I cut her off and wouldn't even listen to her."

Eden looked miserable, but Jace finally saw his role in all of this. He had never even asked Maddie about David. Based on Eden's words, he assumed the worst of her, but he'd been assuming things about her before Eden even spoke to him.

Jace sat back down, dropping heavily into a chair. Eden watched him, waiting for another blast of his temper and praying as she'd never prayed before. It took some time, but Jace finally looked her way.

"Why, Eden? Why did you do this?"

Eden shook her head in misery. "I was certain that I was the only one who could truly care for you, Jace. I was so full of pride and wanting my own way, I couldn't see anything else."

"You've changed," he finally said. "What's happened to you?"

Eden sighed. "I want to tell you, Jace. I want to tell you more than anything, but first I want to help you fix this with Maddie and her family. I want you to find her, so I can apologize to her too."

Jace came to his feet. Such a thing had never occurred to him. Maybe it didn't have to be over. Maybe he could explain and apologize as well. Maybe he could have her back. Jace went to his sister and took her by the shoulders and brought her gently to her feet.

"I've got to go and see Doyle and Cathy. I've got to talk to them."

"Will they be home right now or at the store?"

"Oh, right." Jace hadn't thought that far. "I guess I'd better wait until this evening."

"Do you want me to come?" Eden asked.

Jace looked down into her face. Even her features were softer. "No," he said quietly, "but thank you."

"Jace," Eden whispered, "I'm so sorry."

Jace nodded. "Thank you for telling me, Eden."

The desire to hug him was so strong that Eden almost acted on it, but Jace turned away, and Eden had to let it go. She watched Jace pace around some, thinking out loud as to when he would leave for town. She hoped he would ask her again about the changes he saw but reminded herself to be patient. At some time she would tell him, maybe not today or this weekend, but at some time she would explain that she wasn't the same person anymore. She would tell him all about the miracle that had happened in her life.

Both Doyle and Cathy heard the knock on the front door. They were in the middle of tea, but there was plenty, so company would certainly be welcome. What Doyle didn't expect was to see Jace Randall, hat in hand, standing humbly on the step.

"May I talk to you, Doyle? To you and Cathy? It's important."

Doyle nodded, his face not welcoming, but he stood back to let Jace enter. Cathy had come to her feet but frowned in confusion when she saw Jace.

"I'm sorry to disturb your tea," Jace began when both Shephards stood in the parlor and faced him. "I have something to tell you and something to apologize about. If you'll let me."

"Sit down, Jace," Doyle invited, and Jace pulled a chair a little ways from the table; he didn't feel overly welcome but couldn't blame his hosts for that fact.

"Have you had tea?" Cathy asked, old habits of hospitality dying hard.

"I'm fine, thank you."

Neither Shephard returned to the meal, so Jace knew he was expected to speak. Rubbing his damp palms on the tops of his pant legs, he tried to begin.

"Eden is here," Jace said. "She came, but not to move here." Having said this, Jace remembered that they knew nothing of this and started again. "I think I told you about Eden and the way she wants to be a part of my life. I mean, too much so. And well, she's here now and told me that she lied to me about Maddie."

"What does Eden have to do with Maddie?" Cathy asked. Jace noticed that she did not sound upset.

"I was a fool," Jace admitted. "I condemned Maddie on only Eden's words. She told me that Maddie had been kissing another man, and I believed her."

"Does Maddie know about this?" Doyle asked, realizing how little they knew.

"Some of it, maybe. She was probably very confused over the way I treated her. I knew I couldn't trust Eden, but for some reason I did, and then I sent Maddie away."

Cathy's mouth thinned. The memory of saying goodbye to her girl was still fresh. She missed her so much she ached.

"What exactly do you want us to know, Jace?" Doyle pressed him. "That Eden lied and you were unfair?"

"Yes, that and the fact that I sent her away without cause. I wouldn't even listen to her or ask her. I just accused."

"She told us that. She didn't tell us much, but she said you didn't ask her about David; you just blamed her."

"Who is David?" Jace finally asked. "My sister seems to know, but Maddie never mentioned him. Is he the man from Boston?"

"No," Doyle supplied. "He's a man who once loved Maddie, but she didn't love him back. There's nothing more to it than that."

Jace fell quiet. He was so drained from all of this but also desperate to make it right and to find out where Maddie could be located. He hadn't thought it completely through, but he wasn't going to let Maddie go on thinking he didn't love her.

"She's finally doing well," Cathy said. "Her last letter said she was doing well."

"I'm glad. I was rather hoping I could get her address."

"Why?" Cathy asked, suspicion rising instantly.

Jace looked at her and then to Doyle.

"I've never stopped loving Maddie, and I wonder, even with the way I hurt her, if she might still love me. I was a fool and drove her away, and she may not want anything to do with me, but I've got to talk to her. I've got to explain that I'm sorry I listened to Eden and not to her."

"No," Cathy said, no longer calm but coming to her feet. "You can't see her. She's been hurt enough."

"Please, Cathy," Jace begged, not caring how he sounded. "Please tell me where she is. I've got to explain to her."

"No," Cathy began, but Doyle spoke up.

"What do you hope to accomplish, Jace?"

Jace took a deep breath. "I guess I'm mostly hoping for her forgiveness, but I also want to know if her feelings have changed.

Mine haven't. I hid behind anger and drink, but my feelings are the same."

Doyle looked at his wife.

"Don't you do it, Doyle Shephard," she warned. "I won't have it."

"Cathy." His voice was gentle. "You know she still loves him. You saw her face. Jace should have given her a chance, but this is Eden's doing. Otherwise, Jace would never have sent her away."

Cathy shook her head, not wanting to hear it, but Doyle was making sense. She thought that if Jace hurt Maddie again, she would become violent, but to not give him a chance to fix this was a fight she was losing in her heart.

Making herself calm down, Cathy went back to her chair. She even picked up her cup and took a sip of the now-cool tea.

Jace watched her, looking to Doyle now and again, but Doyle was watching his wife.

"I'll give you the address," Doyle finally said, "but I need to know what you have planned."

Jace nodded, thinking fast. "First I need to find someone to look after the farm animals. The harvest is done, and Clara will mind the house. I have to find someone, and if I can accomplish that, I'll leave on the Monday train and head to Boston."

"And then what?" Doyle wished to know.

"I'll find where she lives and talk to her."

"To what end?" Doyle was not satisfied yet.

Jace looked at the two people he'd thrown away with Maddie and knew nothing but regret. At one point they had trusted him completely. He'd given all of that up.

"At the very least," Jace explained quietly, "I'll leave Boston knowing that Maddie has forgiven me. But if I have my way, I'll leave Boston with Maddie by my side."

Doyle leaned close now, his voice dropping.

"If you hurt her, Jace Randall, after gaining our trust again, you'll never know another day's peace in all of your life. If you use our girl or go to see her just to assuage your conscience, you'll have to live with that forever. You've been totally selfish in all of this. You have to go for her, not just for yourself."

Jace swallowed hard. Doyle's words and tone made Jace doubt his own motive, but only for a moment. He knew why he was going to Boston. He was going to Boston for a second chance with the woman he loved. If there was a woman in all the world sweet enough to offer him such a thing, it was Maddie Shephard. If Jace could just speak with her, he had a tremendous sense that all was going to turn out.

Jace and Eden parted ways at the train station in Worcester. They had ridden the train that far together, but Eden's train home went in another direction. At the beginning of the journey, Jace had questioned her about the changes he saw—not just on Friday when she arrived in Tucker Mills, but the whole weekend. She had been genuinely kind to Clara, not defensive or underhanded. And on Sunday morning, she had gone into town to services even though Jace had not wanted to go.

Eden had done her best to explain. Jace sat in quiet horror as he learned that his sister had arrived back in Pine River with the intent of taking her own life. She had even gone so far as to find a sturdy branch in a large tree, and she was trying to figure out where she could get a rope when a child interrupted her.

"She was so little," Eden explained, "but she could talk. She said she couldn't find her house. She was very brave, not crying or carrying on, but she looked so frightened, and for a moment I forgot about myself.

"I walked her back in the direction I thought she might have come, and her family was looking for her. They were so happy to see her—just a man, a woman, and an older boy—that they wouldn't allow me to leave. They brought me in out of the cold and fed me, wrapped a warm blanket around me, and gave me something hot to drink. I couldn't remember the last time anyone had taken care of me.

"But then the most amazing thing happened: The man asked if he could pray. I didn't like it. I was uncomfortable, but I didn't feel I could say no. He sat in a nearby chair, his wife and son on the sofa, and his little daughter in his lap. He bowed his head and thanked God for bringing his child home, but that wasn't the hardest part. He then thanked God for me, Jace. I've never been so touched. By the time he was finished, I was crying and I couldn't stop.

"His wife came and put her arms around me, and I only cried more. I was so embarrassed, but they didn't seem the least surprised. He waited for me to calm down a little and then began to ask me about myself. And I told him! I don't know what came over me, but I told him what a selfish person I am, and how my own brother didn't even want me.

"But that's not all," Eden had told Jace, the story pouring out of her as the train rocked along the tracks. "He said he understood, and what's more, he said God understood. He said God understood about my sin so well that He sent His Son. He said that I could be forgiven if I only believed what God had said about the Lord Jesus Christ, and that He was the way to life eternal.

"I have to tell you, Jace, I wasn't thinking about life at that point, eternal or otherwise. I just wanted forgiveness. I was desperate for it. I had driven Maddie away from you, and Woody was gone, but you still didn't need me the way you used to. I was losing control and ready to do anything I could to get it back. I hated what I saw in myself. It was so ugly and awful that I wanted to die. I thought if I could be forgiven, maybe I wouldn't feel so bad."

She stopped then, seeming to be out of words, but Jace was still trying to understand.

"So what happened, Eden? This man said a prayer, and you were forgiven?"

"His name is Mr. Engler, by the way," she said quietly, sounding tired. "He's a pastor. And no, he didn't pray. I prayed. I told God I believed in His Son and wanted the salvation He offered." Eden sighed a little. "As soon as I told God that I was a sinner and needed His forgiveness, I knew a peace that I can't describe to you.

"Mr. Engler and his wife, Lissa, talked to me for hours. They brought their Bibles out and showed me things that I never knew. I told them more about what I'd done, especially with you and Maddie, and they showed me where Scripture says I had to repent to you." Eden looked into his eyes. "That's why I came, Jace. I don't exactly know what this new life will look like, but lies are not part of it."

"Eden, how do you know you can trust these strangers? Weren't you afraid of that?"

"I was too upset to think about it, but if they have some hidden agenda, they have an odd way of going about it. All they do is give to me. They offer me meals and times with their family, and they introduce me to others who attend their meetinghouse. They come by the boardinghouse just to say hello. Quite frankly, they're the kindest folks I've ever known."

Jace didn't know what to say. He wanted to be afraid for his sister—this sounded so radical—but there was no denying the change in her.

"You're sure?" he had to ask. "You're sure they're safe?"

"If they're not, Jace, I at least have known some days of peace—something I've never had. There's so much I don't know. That doesn't scare me, but even if I find out it's a lie and they have misrepresented themselves in some way, I'll at least know that I made an effort toward God, and that it was the right thing to repent to you."

Jace looked at her, honestly wondering how she could be the same person. Eden caught his stare and smiled.

"I wish you could know how changed I am on the inside, Jace. That's where it really matters."

"I'm happy for you, Eden," Jace found himself saying. "Maddie has lots of questions about death and heaven. Maybe you'll have answers for her."

"I don't know about that, Jace, but I'm glad you mentioned Maddie. Do I write to her at this address in Boston?"

"Not yet, Eden. I hope to bring her back to Tucker Mills."

"Will you let me know what happens?"

"Yes," Jace was able to answer with assurance. "I'll write this time, no matter how this comes out."

They looked at each other for a few minutes, and then Eden looked away. "I love you, Jace," she said quietly, hoping that he heard.

Jace reached over and briefly squeezed her hand before moving in the seat and trying to get more comfortable. It had been an emotional time, and both Randalls fell asleep. When they woke, they were nearly to Worcester and had to say their goodbyes. Again Eden wanted to hug her brother but held back. Instead, she boarded her next train, asking God to work the same miracle in Jace's heart that He'd performed in her own.

Boston

"Maddie," Beth said, having finally found her in the kitchen. Her voice was oddly low as she spoke. "There's someone here to see you. I put him in the front parlor."

"Oh." Maddie was unconcerned. "Is it that man I contacted about cleaning those portraits in the hall?"

"I don't think so."

Maddie frowned at the maid, thinking she was acting odd, but she left her apron on the kitchen counter and headed toward the parlor. The door was shut, and Maddie almost laughed. They were never overly formal with the servicemen that came. She didn't know what had gotten into Beth.

"Hello, Maddie," Jace said as soon as the door opened and she stepped in.

"Jace," Maddie whispered, forgetting herself for a moment and almost moving toward him. She stopped in time, however, and turned with deliberate movements to shut the door.

"Why have you come?" Maddie asked him, her stance and voice formal.

"I have something to tell you."

"You could have written."

"No, this had to be said in person."

Maddie nodded, the pounding of her heart belying the sedate way she looked. Why had she not remembered how wonderful he was to look at? Why had she thought that all feelings for him had been carefully put away?

"Please, sit down," she invited, and waited to take a chair some ways from his. Jace noticed this but didn't comment.

"How are you?" he asked, drinking in the sight of her and hoping not to get caught doing it.

"I'm well. And you?"

"I'm glad to be in Boston," he said, sidestepping the question. "It's my first time."

"I'm sure you'll enjoy it."

"Thank you."

Maddie hated herself for making small talk, especially when a silence fell. She determined to let Jace speak next. He said he had something to tell her, and with what his presence was doing to her heart, he needed to say it and go.

"My sister came to see me recently. She told me some awful things."

Maddie didn't want to be interested but found herself more than a little curious.

"She lied to me, Maddie. She never saw you kissing someone else. She made that up."

"She told you I was kissing someone?" This was news to the small blonde.

"Yes."

"And that's why you stopped seeing me?"

Jace nodded. She was getting angry, and he couldn't blame her. He watched her come to her feet.

"Let me get this straight. You know that your sister doesn't like anyone, but when she tells you I've been kissing someone, you believe her?"

"I'm sorry, Maddie."

"You're sorry?" Maddie demanded. "You asked me to leave, Jace Randall. I walked alone to the farm in the dark, and you told me to *leave!*"

"Maddie," Jace made the mistake of saying, "you never told me about David. I didn't realize."

"David is a happily married man, whose wife does *not* need to be reminded that he was once in love with me!"

Jace could only stare at her. He'd never seen her so angry. She was beautiful too, but he knew this was the last thing he could mention.

"I think you need to leave," Maddie finally said.

"My uncle died," Jace added quietly, not sure why he mentioned it and surprised at the change in her.

"Oh, Jace." Her voice was as soft and sweet as he remembered. "I don't think Cathy wrote me about that. I'm so sorry."

"Thank you. I don't know why I told you just now, but I thought you would want to know."

"I'm glad you mentioned it. I truly am sorry."

The silence that fell between them in the next few seconds was uncomfortable. Maddie wanted Jace to leave, and Jace wanted anything but. When Maddie couldn't take the quiet any longer, she sat back down and looked at Jace. She had realized this was not settled, and she wanted some answers.

Fifteen

"I guess I still don't understand why you came," Maddie stated plainly. "Why was it so important that I know?"

"After the way I treated you, I couldn't handle it any other way. The last thing I deserve is your forgiveness, but I'll admit that I'm desperate for that very thing."

His words touched her in a way she didn't expect. Jace should have asked her about what he'd heard, and not just assumed, but he'd been lied to as well. And he'd come all the way to Boston to tell her.

"I do forgive you, Jace. Indeed, I feel sorry that your own sister is so horrid."

"As a matter of fact, she seems to be a different person now, but you're right, she has been horrid."

Maddie nodded and then watched Jace look around the room.

"You said one time that you couldn't begin to describe the differences between Boston and Tucker Mills. I think I can see what you mean."

Maddie smiled. "It's quite a house," she said, her own head turning to take in the grandiose furniture, high ceilings, and lovely trappings in every direction.

"I don't suppose you want to show me around," Jace invited, and Maddie looked at him in surprise. "No matter what else I see in Boston," he went on, "I won't be allowed into any more houses like this."

Maddie couldn't stop her smile. He could certainly be charming when he wanted to be.

"If it will get you into trouble, Maddie, just forget I asked."

"No, it's nothing like that. The family isn't even here. They're traveling in Europe."

"That sounds fun."

"They were looking forward to it," Maddie said, standing at the same time and beginning the tour without further ado. She showed Jace the entire downstairs, watching his look of awe while in the library, and then took him into the servants' quarters and the kitchen. They went upstairs but confined themselves to the hallway and only peeked into rooms; that is, until she reached her own room, where she felt free to enter and show him.

Jace was more affected by this room than he let on. It was feminine in every way and smelled fresh and clean. And on top of that, Maddie's nearness worked like a drug. She was telling him about something outside the window, the curtain pulled back so she could point, and he was trying to listen but ended up watching her instead. When she finally looked at him, their eyes caught. Maddie told herself to look away, and Jace mentally begged her not to.

"Have dinner with me tonight," Jace invited softly, working hard to hide his deep feelings. He let Maddie see his interest but not the ache he felt inside to have her love again.

"I can't," Maddie found herself whispering, not having been prepared to see interest in his eyes.

"Why?"

"Well," Maddie improvised quickly, "the man I'm seeing won't like it."

Had Jace not counted the cost of such an action, he would have laughed. She was a terrible liar, but he didn't blame her for trying.

"Well," Jace replied, his voice calm and deep. "Can't you tell him we're old friends? He could even join us," he added, quite certain there was no such man.

"He's not in town right now." The lies grew, and again Jace had to keep from laughing.

"Then you can explain to him when he gets back that you went to dinner with an old friend."

Maddie opened her mouth and then shut it. She wanted to say yes—she wanted it more than anything—but she was scared. Terrified, to be exact.

"Come with me," Jace invited again. He read her hesitation but just waited, his eyes dipping to her mouth in a way that used to distract her no end.

"All right," Maddie agreed, nearly shaking her head over what had just happened.

"I'll pick you up at 6:00," Jace said.

Maddie could only nod.

"Whoever the guy is, Maddie," he added, reaching up to stroke her cheek with a single finger, "he's one lucky man."

Maddie couldn't move from her spot. She turned her head to watch Jace leave the room and even heard the front door open and shut in the distance, but not until both Beth and Sherry came looking for her did she move from her spot by the window.

They wanted to know who he was and hear every detail. Maddie kept the information vague until she admitted that they were going out that evening. The two other women went into action as though they had a date of their own. They dragged Maddie down the hall, where they insisted that she bathe and wash her hair. Beth was not happy until Maddie agreed to let her style the long blonde locks, and throughout the process Maddie was in a state of shock.

Jace Randall had come to Boston today. After being four-and-a-half months apart, he'd been right here at the house and touched her cheek the way he once did. His eyes had looked at her with caring and desire. Maddie shook her head a little and was told by Beth to hold still. It didn't matter that the man she lied about might be real, Jace was as interested as he'd always been. She'd be a fool to believe anything else.

"Oh, my," Maddie said when she came to the foyer and found Jace dressed very formally.

"Will I do?" he asked, having spent an outrageous amount of time and money on one outfit.

"Yes, Jace, you look very nice."

"As do you," Jace said, trying to pretend that she was someone else's girl in an effort to keep his heart in check. "Quite beautiful, and I hope it's all right to tell you."

"Thank you," Maddie said with a smile.

"Shall we go?"

"Yes. Let me tell Sherry that I'm leaving."

Jace waited where he was, but from the whispers and soft laughter he heard a short time later, he thought that Sherry and at least one other woman must be very near.

Maddie came back to the foyer, the small smile on her face telling Jace that she and these other women were friends. Jace opened the door for her and stood back while she slipped outside. A small coach was parked at the street, driver and all, and Maddie couldn't help but be impressed.

They were not very talkative in the coach. Maddie was telling herself to behave like a woman in love with another man and thought that the less talking she did, the easier it might be.

She didn't plan on how much she would enjoy the restaurant in the hotel. Jace took them to the Seaside Hotel. Maddie looked around at the quiet elegance and forgot who she was supposed to be.

"Have you seen my aunt and uncle lately?" she asked as soon as they'd been served their meals.

"Just before I left. I went there to apologize to them and tell them how much I wanted to be in touch with you."

"They gave you the address?"

"Yes. I hope you're not angry with them."

"I'm not," Maddie said with a small shake of her head, but she could tell that his visit was going to affect her for a long time. She still had feelings for this man. She'd be lying to say other-wise. But she also feared being hurt again, and she knew that fear would keep her from doing anything rash ever again.

"How is your meat?" Jace asked, hoping all he'd heard that day about the meals at this hotel proved to be true.

"It's very good. How is yours?"

"I'm enjoying it."

"How is Clara?" Maddie thought to ask, but before Jace could answer, the waiter arrived with a bottle of champagne. He asked Jace whether he could pour some for the two of them. Maddie shook her head no, but the waiter didn't notice. She found her-self with a glassful she knew she wouldn't touch.

"Did you ask about Clara?" Jace asked after taking a sip from his glass.

"Yes."

"She's doing well. She misses Woody, but then we both do."

"It must be a little strange. I mean, you've never known the farm without him, have you?"

"No. I've been busy, but the winter months might get a little long without him."

Jace barely managed the sentence. Maddie looked so lovely to him right now that he wanted to beg her for another chance. He took another sip of champagne, trying to calm down, and then realized how mild the flavor was.

"Did you tell me once you don't drink because you don't like the taste?"

"Yes, I never have."

"Try that," he pointed to her glass. "It's very mild."

Maddie looked skeptical but still picked up her wine glass. Her nose wrinkled a bit, and Jace laughed.

"Clearly you're not going to drink it. You look like a five-year-old being forced to eat boiled spinach. Here, give it to me."

Maddie's brows lifted over the challenge, and she put the glass to her mouth. At first she didn't like the taste, but the after-taste was intriguing. She took another sip and then another.

"I like this," Maddie said, taking a larger swallow before going back to her meal.

"You should always listen to me," Jace teased.

The look Maddie gave him made him laugh. He knew he'd been forgiven but that she still had reservations. Not for several more bites of food did the memory of the picnic come flooding back to him. He watched when she reached to taste her third glass of champagne, but his hand was there to stop her. Maddie looked at him in confusion.

"I don't want this night to be cloudy in your mind, and the champagne might do that."

"Oh, all right," Maddie agreed after just a moment, smiling at him in a warm way. "Jace," she suddenly leaned a little across the table as she spoke. "I've missed you."

"I missed you too," Jace said, his heart pounding with emotions.

"I'm so glad you came."

"Maddie, I need to ask you something," Jace made himself voice the question.

"What is it?"

"Are you seeing a man right now?"

"No," she admitted sheepishly.

"Oh, Maddie," Jace said. He still loved her, and nothing in the world would convince him that he wasn't loved in return.

They finished their meals with pleasure, knowing their love couldn't be disguised any longer.

"Did you need anything, sir?"

"Maddie?" Jace asked her.

"No, I'm fine," she said, her eyes clinging to his face.

"We'll be going," Jace told the waiter, and waited only until they were back in the coach to kiss her. Indeed, they kissed and made plans all the way back to the Nunley's house. When they arrived, Sherry and Beth were waiting in the small sitting room off the kitchen, the one that belonged to the staff come evening time.

"Well, you two have had a good time," Sherry said, seeing Jace's and Maddie's dreamy faces.

Maddie grinned at her and asked, "How would you like to go to a wedding?"

The other women took no time to catch her meaning. They came to their feet in a rush, hugging Maddie, and both talking at once. When order was restored, the two ran about in a flurry of excitement and gaiety to get the reverend to do Maddie's bidding.

Maddie's whole body felt weighted, especially her head. There was light coming in the window, she was almost certain, but she didn't want to open her eyes to find out. She rubbed her face in the pillow and told herself she had to wake up.

Just then she heard the door open and what sounded like Jace's voice in the hall. Maddie froze, not sure what to think, before peeking out to see him slipping inside her room.

"Jace?" Maddie muttered in confusion.

"Right here," he said, taking a seat on the edge of the bed. "Sherry made you some coffee. It's here on the table."

"What time is it?" she asked as she rolled over, her brain still not working.

"Almost 8:00."

"Jace," Maddie finally managed. "You can't be in here."

"What was that?" Jace asked, not sure he'd heard her.

He waited a moment, but Maddie said nothing and only stared at him. Jace wanted to pay attention to what she might say, but the covers had slipped down her chest a bit. Jace's gaze went that way.

When Maddie realized it, she tugged them up in a hurry. Gathering all blankets and sheets around her, she scooted against the headboard and frowned a little.

"Jace," Maddie whispered. "Did something happen last night?"

"A lot of things happened last night. Why are you whispering?"

"Jace, do Sherry and Beth know you're in here?"

"Of course."

"You have to get out," she wanted to tell him urgently, but her head ached.

"It's all right, Maddie." He smiled a little and reminded her, "They were at the wedding."

"What wedding?"

Jace stared at her, waiting for her to smile back or throw a pillow his way, but she did neither. Jace was starting to feel as confused as she.

Maddie looked back at him, certain she had misunderstood, her mind still on the other women. She knew that having Jace in here at this time of the morning meant that Sherry and Beth would assume the worst. She had to clear her head and figure out how to explain to them.

"You said there's coffee?"

"Right here."

Jace handed it to her and moved to lean against the foot-board. Since Maddie looked so sleepy, he was keeping his distance, but it was no easy feat. If this is what waking up next to her would be like every morning, he couldn't believe he'd wasted a moment in asking for her hand. Her hair was a delightful mess, spilling around her face and shoulders. Bare shoulders. And her face, a little flushed from sleep, looked as soft as he knew it to be, her eyes very blue in the morning light.

"Now tell me," Maddie suddenly said, half the coffee gone, "did I hear you talking to Beth or Sherry?"

"I was talking to both of them. What is bothering you about that?"

"Jace," Maddie shook her head a little. Something wasn't right. "What are *you* talking about?"

Jace began to put it together. He forced himself to stay calm, knowing he didn't have all the facts, but things were not looking good. He took a breath and started with a question.

"What do you remember about last night?"

"Last night?"

"Yes. We went to dinner at the Seaside Hotel."

"I remember. I had the beef and you had chicken."

"Right. What else do you remember?"

Maddie closed her eyes and rubbed her head.

"I tried the champagne," she said before her brow creased in thought.

"What about the ride back to the house?" For Jace, this was when the evening truly began. "We talked and made plans. Do you remember?"

"After dinner?" Maddie asked, and Jace felt anger rising inside of him.

"This couldn't have happened again," he said sternly. "You didn't drink that much. You were completely lucid."

"What are you saying?"

"We got married last night. You have to remember, Maddie."

Maddie searched her mind but found nothing. It was so frustrating, so maddening. She wanted more of the night to be there, but it was gone.

"I would remember if we had gotten married," she finally said. "I know I would."

Jace didn't say anything. She had been normal. A little giggly, but not staggering like that day on the picnic. He was sure she had been herself. Even Sherry and Beth had been all for it. If Maddie had been that drunk, wouldn't they have seen?

Maddie wished she knew what to think. She wished Jace would say something, but he looked a little upset. Not until Maddie reached again for her forehead did she realize the bracelet was back in place. Having no memory of receiving it, she looked at it and knew in a heartbeat that Jace had been telling the truth.

"Was I drunk?" she asked, her heart sinking.

"Evidently." Jace's voice was tight.

"Were you drunk?"

"Not in the least."

Maddie glared at him.

"Do not get angry with me, Madalyn. You did not seem drunk to me, and last night you were all for this."

"I still hold you responsible. You know from last time what happened."

"How was I to know that you can't handle a drop of alcohol?"

Maddie glared at him and Jace glared back.

Maddie stared at him until she realized his attention had been drawn. The sheet had slipped a little more. He wasn't used to seeing that much skin on any woman, and certainly not on his wife. Every other man he knew would understand. Maddie did not.

Maddie looked to where Jace's eyes had landed and then yanked the sheet into place. Her voice was little more than a hiss when she spoke.

"Get out."

Dragging his attention back to her face, he said, "We need to talk about this." But Maddie only shook her head.

"Out." She pointed at the door, clearly furious.

Jace—no more happy than she was—saw no help for it. He rose from the bed and looked at her, but Maddie would not look his way. Jace let himself out the door, not sure what he was supposed to do. He was in the hall before he realized that his warm welcome in this home was probably going to be short lived. He headed toward the kitchen for some breakfast and coffee of his own. As soon as Sherry and Beth discovered that Maddie knew nothing of last night's events, he'd be in trouble with all three of them.

"All right," Maddie began, having come from her room dressed and ready for battle. After talking to Sherry and finding out with a few subtle questions what had gone on the night before, she'd found Jace and asked him to join her in the library. "I think I have this figured out."

"You have what figured out?" Jace asked, not liking her tone very much, but having calmed down quite a bit.

"What we're going to do."

Jace already knew what they would do, but he said nothing. Maddie walked around a bit before facing him, feeling very much in charge.

"We're just going to forget about last night. I mean, nothing really happened, and no one needs to know. Sherry and Beth will be very discreet. You can just head back to Tucker Mills, and I'll stay here in Boston."

"I see," Jace said quietly, wanting to stay calmer than he had earlier. "So you never want to see me again?"

Maddie hadn't expected this. She looked away, not wanting to admit that nothing could be further from the truth. Yes, she was upset, but she didn't hate Jace. She could never hate Jace.

"I think this is for the best," she tried this time, but her voice lacked courage, and she steadfastly refused to look at him.

Jace rose and went to stand before her.

"Tell me something, Maddie," he asked. "Do you know that I love you?"

Maddie made herself look up at him; she had no choice but to nod in the affirmative.

"I'm glad you know," Jace said, realizing that being gentle was all he wanted to do. "But there's something else you need to understand. I know you love me. You might be angry right now. I was angry too until I realized you couldn't help what happened. But you nevertheless love me."

"What makes you so sure?" Maddie was ready to argue just to maintain control.

Jace brushed gently at the hair on her temple. "I remember last night."

It was the most potent thing he could have said to her. Last night was shrouded in mystery. Maddie could attest to nothing. It had been her wedding night, and she remembered not a thing.

"So something did happen?" she asked, sounding very young and uncertain.

Jace nodded, feeling as cheated as she did.

"None of this would have happened if I had realized you'd had too much to drink, and I'm sorry I didn't see it, but I'm not sorry you're my wife. And you can fight me, Maddie, but I won't let you go. I won't leave Boston without you."

His words were a comfort and a concern all in the same breath. She knew what was waiting for her in Tucker Mills, and she knew what life in Boston had been without him. Neither place could boast of perfection.

"What if I do refuse?" Maddie had to get in one more blow.

"You won't have to refuse," Jace surprised her by saying, having changed tactics just that fast. "All you have to do is tell me you don't love me, and I'll leave you alone forever."

Maddie couldn't do it. She would never lie about such a thing, and Jace obviously knew that. She still had a little fight left in her, however.

"I won't be able to leave for several days, quite possibly a week."

Jace bent to make his point, his eyes direct.

"Much as I'd like to stay here in the lap of luxury, Madalyn, we leave tomorrow," he told her. "I have a farm to run."

Maddie looked like she would argue, but she caught Jace's eye. He meant it. Maddie still frowned at him, and Jace frowned right back.

"Are you going to ask Beth or Sherry to help you pack your things, or do you want my help?"

His kindness disarmed her, and she wondered if he would always be the one to defuse the situation.

"I think I can do it on my own. I have to leave a letter for the family too."

"Do I need to write one as well?"

Maddie shook her head no. "I'll explain."

Maddie was ready to turn away, but Jace's hand to her waist stopped her.

"Never forget my feelings for you, no matter how rough a start this might be."

Maddie nodded and allowed Jace to pull her into his arms. She relaxed against him, feeling cherished and secure.

"Have you considered the fact that you might be carrying our child, Mrs. Randall?" Jace asked softly.

It was the worst thing he could have said. It only reminded Maddie of the hours missing from her mind. She left the library and didn't speak a single word to Jace until well into the afternoon.

Sixteen

Tucker Mills

Clara heard the commotion on the kitchen side of the house, but Maddie had walked in before she could get out there.

"Well, Maddie," Clara said with surprise, not unhappy to see her.

"Hello, Clara."

"Is Jace with you?"

"Yes," she said quietly. "We were married in Boston."

Clara wanted to smile and hug her, but she looked so young and pale right now that Clara stuck to business.

"What business does he have marrying you without the family and then dragging you across the country like a sack of feed? Sit down right here while I make you a cup of tea."

"I am a little tired."

"Of course you are," Clara consoled, secretly delighted at the news. "Where is Jace?"

"I think he's talking to the man who fed the stock."

"Oh, that would be Delmont. He did an okay job, but it was time for Jace to come home."

"I heard about Woody, Clara. I'm sorry."

"Well, he's better off I 'spect. He was only going to get sicker, his heart hurting and all."

210

Maddie suddenly wanted to cry. She glanced around the room, realizing she'd never been beyond the parlor of this home and had seen that room with only one candle burning. It looked like a nice kitchen with a large buttery, but it wasn't her Aunt Cathy's and it wasn't Sherry's. And because she'd been cold to Jace for most of the trip back, she didn't even have him to console her.

Clara talked to herself, muttering under her breath in a way that Maddie did not feel she was required to answer. She had only just received her tea when Jace arrived inside. She looked up at him, but he had eyes for Clara only.

"What have you gone and done, Jace Randall?"

"I expect you already know."

"Was her family there, or your sister?"

"No, I'm afraid not."

Hands on her hips, Clara shook her head.

"Maddie's being the sweetest girl in the county is the only reason I'm not running you out of this kitchen."

Jace had to smile at that.

"Is Delmont bringing your things in?"

"Yes. He'll get it all upstairs."

"I'd better go and see that he doesn't drop anything."

As soon as they had the kitchen to themselves, Jace brought a chair up close to the table. He sat across from Maddie.

"Are you all right?"

"Yes."

"Did Clara fix this for you?"

Maddie nodded.

"I never explained to you that Woody made provision to take care of Clara for as long as she lives. But that doesn't mean she has to be here all the time. She'll give you your space or be here every day. She's just that way. So you can tell her what you want."

"It might be nice to have her show me how she does things here."

"Would you like me to show you upstairs?"

"Please."

Jace led her through the parlor, toward the front door, and up the stairs to show her the house's three bedrooms. He didn't specify that one was his, one was Woody's, and the last was the spare room. He let her peek into each one before walking back to his own. Maddie followed. As he expected from Clara, everything was in apple-pie order, but things were not fancy. It had been a bachelor's home for many years, and that was more than obvious.

"Maybe you'll want to decorate a bit," Jace mentioned.

"You won't mind?"

"No. Your room in Boston certainly was nice. Do what you like."

Maddie nodded.

"Will you go see Doyle and Cathy tonight?"

"I think I'll wait for morning."

"I'll take you in."

Maddie nodded, more than a little amazed to be in Tucker Mills but not in town. And the man next to her was her husband! How many nights had she dreamed of that very thing, only to find herself confused and almost lonely now that it was reality.

Jace saw the look on her face and misread it.

"I'm sorry about the house. I know you're used to better."

"No, Jace." Maddie was swift to stop him. "It's a fine house, but I didn't expect to be here in this way. I'm still not used to—" Maddie hesitated, looking for words. "I'm not used to us, I guess."

"That might take some time."

They looked at each other, and Maddie thought Jace might reach for her, but noise in the downstairs reminded them they were not alone. And on top of that, Maddie wasn't sure if she wanted intimacy yet. She was frightened of the physical side of marriage but didn't know how to tell Jace.

"Jace?" Clara called from the bottom of the stairs, and he went that way. "Where do you want things?"

"In the spare room for now. I don't want Maddie tripping over her trunks in the room she's sleeping in."

Maddie heard this from the other bedroom and had one question answered. Hers was not the spare room.

"How many times are you going to adjust your pillow?" Doyle asked of Cathy, feeling her move for the fifth time.

"I can't sleep. I thought we would have heard from Jace or Maddie by now."

Doyle didn't comment. He hadn't taken time to figure out how long it would take for Jace to arrive back but now wished that he had.

"I can't believe you're not thinking about them," Cathy said next.

"I am thinking about them; I'm just not worried."

Cathy didn't believe that for a second, but she didn't comment. Neither one did. Sleep finally came, but it took much longer than usual.

Not until Maddie took a candle and carried it upstairs to retire did she think about how accustomed she was to oil and Argand lamps. Even Doyle and Cathy used oil lamps. Maddie was used to candles as well, but one had to be slightly more careful with hair and clothing.

Maddie took herself into Jace's room where she had laid out some of her things earlier. She was extremely tired, emotionally and physically, and wanted nothing more than to sleep. She had just climbed beneath the covers and settled on the pillow when Jace walked in.

"What are you doing?"

"I'm coming to bed," Jace told her.

"In here?"

"Yes." His voice was patient. He did not want to fight with her tonight. "What's the matter?"

"I don't know if I want you in here."

"Maddie, we shared a bed in Boston," he pointed out.

"I didn't want Sherry and Beth to talk."

"We're not going to start out in separate beds, Maddie. Not here."

"I just thought you would sleep in your own room tonight."

"This is my room."

"I thought this was your uncle's room."

"No," he said, his voice showing how weary he was.

"Fine." Her voice wasn't angry, but she still wanted the last word. "You just keep to your own side."

Jace didn't comment. He readied for bed, Maddie's back to him, and climbed beneath the covers. It was odd having someone in the bed with him, but he didn't mind. He knew he just had to be patient and Maddie would move toward him. It had happened every other night; he was sure it would happen tonight.

A full ten minutes passed before she fell asleep. Jace was relieved that his willingness to wait paid off when he felt her shift. As on the other nights, she rolled toward him, seeking his warmth. Jace pulled her close while she slept, his head pillowed near her own. Only when she was warm and soft against him did Jace relax enough to fall asleep. He certainly hoped things would not be this strained every night, but for now he would take whatever closeness he could get.

꒰◌꒱

Dear Eden... Jace had risen very early to write the letter she was watching for. *I found Maddie, and we were married in Boston. It's a rather long story that I won't try to explain right now. I hope this finds you well. Thank you again for coming and telling me the truth. It means more than you know.*

Jace read the letter over, debating whether he should tell her to visit soon, but he didn't write the words. He wasn't angry with Eden anymore, just sorry for her, but the main reason he did not invite her was his current relationship with Maddie. It was on thin ice, and he figured that the last thing they needed was a visitor.

Feeling as if he'd done the right thing, Jace sealed the letter and readied it for mailing. He and Maddie would be going to see the Shephards right after breakfast.

It was a quiet couple who headed into town a few hours later. Maddie had no idea how her aunt would react to the news, and Jace knew he would have to face Doyle at the store. Jace had gone to Boston to see Maddie. There had been no talk of marriage.

"I'll put the team in the barn," Jace said, heading that way.

"I'm going right over to see Cathy," she explained. "Should I look for you in the store?"

"I'll come to you unless Cathy doesn't want to see me."

Maddie realized then that she'd been much too involved in her own feelings. The look on Jace's face was hard on her heart. He looked vulnerable, dread filling his features. She had wanted to stay angry, but that wasn't fair to him. Maddie put her hand on his arm.

"Come over when you want. Cathy won't send you away."

"She will if that's what you want."

"I don't want that," Maddie told him. "I wish I knew what I wanted, but I don't want you to be hurt or cast off."

Hoping it was true, Jace nodded and moved toward the store. He stepped inside the rear door and came through the back room to see Doyle talking to a man who looked as though he was only seeking information. By the time Doyle turned and shut the door, Jace was standing by the stove.

"I have to talk to you," Jace said. "Maddie's at the house with Cathy."

"All right," Doyle agreed, feeling more relieved than he let on. The older man was ready to give Jace the benefit of the doubt, so he motioned him to a seat by the stove and took one himself.

"Did Maddie ever tell you about the picnic we went on last summer?"

"Nothing specific."

Jace sat back a little, his eyes on the hot stove, wondering how this was going to go over, but he still began, telling himself to keep to the facts.

"I was nervous that day so I grabbed a flask of liquor. Maddie got cold and drank some of it, not knowing what it was." Jace couldn't look at Doyle. "Your niece is a very loving drunk."

"Are you trying to tell me…" Doyle began.

"No. All we did was kiss, but that's not the worst of it. She remembered nothing. When I tried to kiss her later, she was furious with me because she didn't remember a thing from the picnic."

Doyle waited, knowing more was coming.

"I didn't think wine or champagne would affect her in the same way. We were at dinner in Boston, and we had a bottle of champagne brought to the table. The stuff in that flask had been the real thing, but after the champagne, Maddie seemed fine…" Jace paused, knowing he had to finish. "I married her, Doyle, but she can't remember a thing."

Jace's eyes flew to the older man when a small laugh escaped Doyle.

"You think it's funny?"

"I guess I do. It wouldn't be if you didn't love each other, but it is rather amusing."

"I wish Maddie thought so," Jace grumbled.

This really caused Doyle to laugh. The older man knew all about unhappy women. He waited on them weekly and at times was married to one. It delighted him to no end to learn that Jace was having a taste of that very thing.

"I still can't believe you're laughing."

Doyle made himself calm down.

"Is she all right?"

"I think so. She naturally feels cheated, and I can't say that I blame her. *I* feel cheated! I just hope she'll get over it sooner than later."

"You'd better hope Cathy does too," Doyle decided to add.

Jace's head fell back. He didn't even want to think about what was going on over at the house.

"If you can't remember a thing, how do you know you're married?" Cathy demanded, hoping with all her heart that Jace was not playing games with all of them.

"I talked with Sherry—both she and Beth were there. Evidently we got back to the house right after dinner and told them we wanted to be married. Beth went for her reverend, and we were married in the main parlor."

"And your wedding night?" Cathy wasn't done. "Did you have a wedding night?"

"In my bedroom," Maddie said quietly, her sober eyes causing Cathy to calm a bit.

"Do you remember it, Maddie? Were you able to enjoy it at all?"

"I don't remember. Jace has apologized again and again, and I'm still a little angry with him, but I can't remember a thing."

The question was in Cathy's mind, but she debated asking it. It really wasn't her business, but she wanted to know whether there was a night Maddie did remember. After all, they'd been married for five days.

"I don't want you to be angry with him," Maddie suddenly said. "I feel guilty about the way I've treated him, and he feared that you would not even welcome him here after I told you what happened."

"I'll not hold it against him, Maddie. If you're upset with him, that's punishment enough."

"What do you mean?"

"You're newlyweds, honey. The last thing a man wants is for his bride to be angry with him."

Maddie felt terrible. Jace was as hurt in all of this as she was. Maddie thought about how cold she had been to him. She thought now that that might have been wrong but wasn't sure how to fix it.

"I'm going to head to the store," Cathy said. "I assume Jace is there."

"Yes." Maddie rose as well. "I'll go with you."

Maddie woke to a quiet room Monday morning, the other side of the bed empty. Most of Saturday had been spent with her uncle and aunt, and even part of Sunday. Jace had been a complete gentleman, kind and solicitous. Nevertheless, there was a wall between them that only Maddie could take down—something she had not done just yet.

For a time Maddie lay there and then remembered that Cathy was not downstairs taking care of things. It was her job now. Maddie was up and out the bedroom door a short time later. It was time to get to work.

"Clara, do we have any ginger?" Maddie asked midmorning, studying the recipe for pumpkin pie in front of her.

"In the spice chest on the wall. Try the top left drawer."

Maddie actually found the spice in the next drawer down. She had cooked the pumpkin already, careful not to scrape the inside, since the sweetest part was closest to the seeds, or so the recipe said. The crusts were ready, and the batter was almost ready to fill them.

Jace had gone to the mill, and Clara had arrived to work. It had taken Maddie a moment to get her bearings, but she kept reminding herself that these jobs were hers now. She had set to work in the kitchen, in the mood to bake. Sometimes Clara was next to her and sometimes she was off doing something else.

"Maddie," Clara said, suddenly arriving back, her voice thoughtful. "Are you and Jace going to stay in Jace's room?"

"I think so. Why?"

"Have you looked at Woody's room? It's much larger."

Maddie stopped mixing and stared at the other woman.

"I was trying to be respectful," she admitted.

"Death is a part of life, Maddie." Clara's words were matter-of-fact, but her voice was serious. "It makes no sense for the two of you to stay in the smaller room when you have a larger one available."

Maddie liked the idea, and Jace said she could redecorate. She assumed he wouldn't mind. She had brought some things from Boston. A number of things, in fact. Even without touching the walls or painting, she could make some very nice changes.

"Let me get these pies in the oven," Maddie told Clara, "and we'll go to work."

Jace came in around dinnertime and found the downstairs quiet. Food was ready in the kitchen, but not on the table. Jace was moving to the stairs to find Clara or Maddie when he noticed the furniture stacked in the small room off the kitchen. His heart sank as he saw it was furniture from his bedroom.

What type of statement was Maddie trying to make now? He knew he was still in trouble, but at least they were sharing a room. He realized all was not going well, but why was their bedroom furniture down here? That room was too small to hold it.

Jace was at the bottom of the stairs, headed up to look for answers, when both women came down.

"There you are," Clara said as if he were late. She planted herself on the bottom step and said, "Dinner's on. You should wash up."

"Dinner's not on. It's still in the kitchen."

"But it will be on by the time you wash."

Maddie peeked around Clara, her look much too innocent.

"What are the two of you doing?"

"We're trying to get dinner on," Clara stated, "but you won't wash up."

Jace gave up. With a shake of his head, he went back to the kitchen. Obviously they didn't want him to know something, but nothing in Maddie's speech or demeanor said that she was more angry or upset than she had been.

Jace left it alone. He had to get back to the mill right after dinner anyway. Whatever they were doing would have to wait until evening.

"Jace Randall got married," Hillary told her mother after school on Monday.

"Do I know Jace Randall?"

"You might not, but you know his new wife, Maddie Shephard."

Alison looked as surprised as she felt.

"I didn't realize there was even a wedding," she commented.

"They were married in Boston. At least that's what Greta and Mercy have heard."

"Well, we'll have to make them a gift."

"I think they're having a party, so maybe we should wait."

Had Jace and Maddie heard the conversation at the Muldoon house, they would have been confused. Doyle and Cathy had just decided that a Tucker Mills reception was in order. They had begun to spread the word from the store but not seen the couple to tell them.

Indeed, word would be all over town before they were informed.

When Jace came in that evening, he washed in a quiet kitchen. It smelled as though someone had been baking, but tea was not on the table. He wasn't irritated by this, just intrigued. It wasn't until that moment that he remembered how odd the women had been acting earlier when he came home for dinner.

Without calling for Maddie, Jace started toward the stairs again. This time there was no one there to stop him. At the top, he went toward his own room. The bed was nearly torn apart, and the furniture had all been moved. Indeed, there was little to recognize about it, but then he heard movement next door.

He walked to Woody's doorway and just stood there. Maddie's back was to him. She was fixing lace curtains at the window, curtains he'd never seen before. She adjusted the valance just the way she wanted it and then turned.

"I didn't hear you," she said after she started, a hand going to her pounding heart.

"You must have been preoccupied because I wasn't very quiet."

This said, Jace went inside. Woody's room had been transformed. The quilt on the bed was full of color, both elegant and inviting. Little lacy cloths lay on the dressers, and beautiful pictures hung on the walls. Jace was very pleased, but the effect was far beyond simple pleasure. He was certain Maddie didn't realize.

"You said I could redecorate," Maddie said, sounding nervous and wringing her hands a bit. "So I didn't think you would mind."

"I don't mind," Jace said, still looking around and then at her.

"So you think it looks all right?"

"It looks beautiful."

Maddie nodded, looking relieved.

"In fact," Jace said, eyes still on her. "It gives a man ideas."

A hush fell between the couple. Jace's gaze spoke volumes that Maddie couldn't help but read. It was too bad for both of them that she wasn't ready.

"I think I'd better get tea on," she said softly and watched as he nodded. "Is it all right if I do that?"

"It's fine," he said, having tempered his reaction to hers.

"I'll go and do that now," she explained unnecessarily, scooting past him in a bit of a hurry.

"I'll be right behind you," Jace said, moving much slower. He hoped she would forgive him soon; either that, or stop being so inviting. If one didn't happen, he didn't know how long he could survive.

Seventeen

Jace looked out the window and noticed Maddie at the water pump. She pumped water into her mug and then stood outside to drink it. She drank three full mugs before she was done, and then Jace watched her hide the tin cup under the wooden partition that covered the mechanism.

Jace darted away from the window when she turned to come back inside. He didn't know why, but he was reluctant to be caught watching her. Clearly she had thought she was on her own.

Jace went so far as to go to the desk in the corner of the parlor and pull out his account book. He had some thinking to do and figured the best way to accomplish that was to appear to be busy. And it worked. Maddie came back inside, peeking around the corner at him, and left him on his own. Jace said nothing, but he did continue to think.

"A party?" Jace questioned.

Doyle and Cathy were sitting in the Randalls' parlor, and Cathy answered.

"Yes, a reception for the folks here in Tucker Mills. We spread the word."

Both the bride and groom looked at her and then at each other.

"Are you all right with this, Jace?" Maddie asked.

"I was going to ask you the same thing."

"It's fine," Maddie said, hoping Jace wouldn't see how worried she was. They had things to work out. They were not a normal married couple right now. Would everyone at the party see that? Tucker Mills was famous for its nosy life on the green. Maddie did not want their marriage to be fodder for the gossipmongers.

"When were you thinking we would have this?" Jace asked, still wondering what he'd seen in Maddie's eyes.

"This Saturday night," Cathy was pleased to announce.

"As in four days from now?" Maddie asked.

"Yes! We'll have it right at the house. We'll dance and eat for hours."

Maddie was not overly thrilled with her aunt. Why had they not checked with them before telling everyone? She thought that if anyone would be sympathetic to the way they had been married, it would be her aunt, but clearly even Cathy thought things were rosier than they actually were. But what could she do? Word had gotten out, and folks would be coming.

Doyle changed the subject just then, and Maddie was somewhat pleased. There was no sense in fretting about the coming weekend. They would get through it one way or the other.

Maddie's gasp sounded in the room, and she almost sat up in bed. In the dream she'd fallen on the road, and a team of horses had been running out of control in her direction.

"Maddie?" Jace called to her, his voice rough with sleep.

"It was just a dream." She had figured it out by then and turned on her side to go back to sleep. Jace was instantly asleep again, but Maddie lay there for a time, thoughts of death and heaven coming to her mind all over again.

Clara was still coming every day, and Maddie was suddenly glad of that fact. She especially wanted her to come tomorrow, because there was something important she needed to go into town and do.

∞

"Well, Maddie," Alison said with pleasure, opening the front door to her knock. "Come on in."

"Thank you, Mrs. Muldoon. I hope I'm not catching you at a bad time."

"Not at all. We heard that congratulations are in order."

"Thank you," Maddie said, hoping she didn't look as strained as she felt, but she was determined to see the only pastor who had enjoyed her questions. "Would Mr. Muldoon be available by any chance?"

"He certainly is. Let me get him from the office. You go right ahead to the parlor, Maddie."

Maddie watched the woman walk away, realizing she was a good way along in her pregnancy. Maddie had not been aware of the Muldoons' pending arrival and then remembered she was new back in town.

"Hello, Maddie," Douglas greeted, coming to shake her hand. "How are you?"

"I'm not sure," Maddie admitted. "I was hoping to ask you some questions."

"Certainly. Get comfortable and ask away."

"I can't exactly remember what you said about heaven." They faced each other across the room in their chairs. "Do you believe it's there?"

"Yes, I do," Douglas answered.

"Why do you?"

"I'm glad you asked me that," Douglas said, just like before. "I believe in heaven, Maddie, because I put such stock in what Jesus had to say. You see, I believe He's God's Son."

I think so too, Maddie thought to herself, just now realizing it.

"And Jesus Himself tells us that He came from heaven."

"Where did He say that?" Maddie asked.

"In John 6:38. The verse says, 'For I came down from heaven, not to do mine own will, but the will of him that sent me.' Now tell me, Maddie, why would Jesus make such a thing up? There would be no reason for Him to do so."

Maddie thought for a moment and then admitted quietly, "He wouldn't. As you said, there would be no reason."

"That's right. If you recall, I urged you to figure out what to do with Scripture. If you don't believe the Bible to be the very writings of God, why would you believe a word of it? Because I believe the Bible is God's Word without error, I can read those words said by Jesus Himself and know that they're true."

Maddie nodded thoughtfully, feeling peaceful about the existence of heaven for the first time. Her face cleared, and she glanced around a bit. She seemed through with her queries, but Douglas was hoping for more information.

"Tell me something, Maddie. Are you afraid of dying? Is that why this subject troubles you?"

"No. I was baptized as a baby. I know I'll go to heaven, I just wanted to know for sure that it was there."

Douglas felt his heart sink.

"I never baptized my children when they were infants," Douglas told her gently, not surprised to see Maddie's eyes widen.

"You didn't?"

"No."

"What about this new baby?"

Douglas shook his head no. "I can't find in Scripture where we're commanded to do so. The people we see being baptized in Scripture have made a decision for Jesus Christ. Jesus was baptized as an example to us, to show others that John's words about Him were true. Jesus was not baptized as an infant."

Maddie looked at him a moment. "He wasn't, was He? I never thought about that until now, but He was baptized as a grown man by John."

"That's right, and His example to us is huge. My three older children came to understand the death, burial, and resurrection of Jesus Christ, and repented to Him for salvation. Once that change occurred in their lives, they each desired to be baptized. They wanted to show others what they believed."

Maddie nodded, but her look became distant. Douglas watched her, waiting for more questions to come, but she surprised him.

"Is this where you meet?" She was looking down the length of the parlor now. Most of the furniture was against the walls, and it struck her as odd.

"Yes, here and in the kitchen."

"How do you handle pew rental?"

Douglas was reluctant for this change in topic but knew he needed to explain. "Actually, we don't have pew rental. Scripture teaches us to give of what God has given to us, so we leave all the giving to the hearts of the folks who worship with us. We don't charge people for coming to worship."

Maddie had never heard of such a thing, but she thought to admit it might sound insulting. Instead, she decided to leave. After all, he'd been a great help.

"Thank you for your time, Mr. Muldoon."

"You're welcome, Maddie. I hope we can talk again. I'd like to."

Maddie was gone just seconds later, and Douglas stood in the middle of the parlor. Alison came to the door from the kitchen.

"I heard a little of it," she said. "She's not ready."

"No, she's not. I hope she won't be able to rest on the knowledge of heaven's existence, Alison. I hope she thinks more about where she's put her faith."

"I'll pray with you, Dooner," Alison told him, starting the moment he thanked her and went back to his study.

Jace could not have been more pleased to see his wife stopping at the mill. He watched her park the buggy and climb down to come inside, knowing he would never grow weary of the sight of her.

"Are you very busy?" she asked from just inside the wide double doors, not sure she should have stopped.

"Just getting things ready for the season. How were things in town?"

"Fine. I stopped and got the mail."

Jace waited. There was something on her mind, and he wanted to know what it was.

"Jace, were you baptized as an infant?"

"Sure. Eden's told me all about it."

"Did you know that Jesus wasn't baptized as an infant but as a grown man?" Maddie asked, still rather amazed.

Jace shrugged, "Maybe they did things differently back then."

"But when did it change?"

"I don't know. I figure it's not that big of a deal."

"But what if it is?"

Jace tried to remain tolerant. First it was heaven and death, and now she was worried about baptism.

"I don't know, Maddie. My sister has been studying the Bible lately. Maybe she would know something."

"I got a letter from her," Maddie remembered.

"What did she have to say?"

"I haven't read it."

Jace nodded, not sure what else to add. He didn't have answers for her, and there was little he could do about that.

"I guess I'd better let you get back to work."

Jace didn't try to detain her. He walked her to the buggy and helped her into the seat.

"Thank you."

"Always a pleasure," Jace surprised her by saying.

"What is?"

"Touching you."

Maddie stared down at him, her heart squeezing.

"I think you might have made a terrible mistake in marrying me," she found herself saying, but Jace only shook his head.

"I'll never feel that way," he said, not breaking eye contact for a second, "and I'm sorry you do."

"I don't. I was just afraid you did."

"Come here," Jace beckoned to her with one finger, and Maddie leaned toward him. He kissed her softly, cupping her cheek. "I'll see you at home with no more talk of regrets."

"All right," Maddie agreed, thinking he was much better than she deserved. One of these days she had to take down the physical wall between them. She drove the buggy away from the mill, wishing she had more courage to get the job done.

Dear Maddie, or should I say Mrs. Randall?

I don't know whether Jace told you that I planned to write. I came in person to apologize to him, but the last thing you need right now is company, so I will do my best in a letter.

I'm so sorry for what I did, Maddie. There is no excuse, and I will offer none, except to say that I have, just lately, learned how to treat people better. I never had anything against you—not really—I just didn't want Jace to care for anyone for fear that he might forget all about the sister who raised him.

It was a foolish need and want in my life, and I no longer feel that way. I ask for your forgiveness. I don't

*deserve it. But again, I wish to tell you how wrong I
was, and if you can ever think of a way for me to show
you, I hope you will let me know.*

    Hoping we can someday be friends,

                  Eden Randall

Jace had ridden one of the horses down to the mill. It was good to be done for the day, and as he stabled Robby, he took his time, savoring the warmth of the barn as well as its sounds.

The other stock also needed his attention, and Jace went through the jobs, liking the fact that some things didn't change. Tonight, however, there was something new. As Jace took down the bag of feed for the chickens, ready to spread some in the corner of their pen, he spotted Maddie in the yard by the pump.

Staying in the shadows of the barn, he was able to watch her pull the tin cup from beneath the board and pump the handle for water. Much as before, she filled it several times before returning the cup and going back inside.

Jace was not a fool, nor was he blind. When evidence was presented to him, he was fairly swift at deduction. His wife feared that he would give her alcohol again.

No wonder she doesn't want me to touch her. She doesn't think she can trust me—not even for this small thing.

Even as Jace thought it, he realized it was not a small thing to her. Jace went inside, cleaned up, and joined his wife for tea, his eyes still watchful. Maddie's cup sat untouched throughout the meal. In fact, she drank nothing all evening.

Jace said not a word concerning this. Planning to be up even earlier than usual, he lay in bed waiting for his wife to sleep and curl up against him. He had something he needed to do, and tomorrow was not soon enough.

Maddie heard Jace on the stairs but didn't assume he was headed back to their room. She was still standing in her shift, however, when he opened the door and came in.

"I need to show you something downstairs," he said, not seeming to notice the way she grabbed her dress from the bed and held it in front of her.

"Is something wrong?"

"No, but come out the kitchen door as soon as you're down."

Maddie stood for a few seconds after he left. Eventually curiosity got the best of her. She rushed into her clothes and threw a bonnet on her head. It was all too mysterious, and Maddie wanted to know what was going on.

As soon as Maddie stepped out the door, Jace was there to take her hand. He led her toward the barn, not speaking.

"Where are we going?" Maddie asked.

"Just over here" was all Jace would say.

Jace didn't rush, but he moved with a purpose. He led her through the barn and out the far door. At the corner by the fence he stopped, and Maddie saw what lay at his feet: broken and overturned jugs, empty flasks, and one open but empty barrel.

"This is all the alcohol from the house. There isn't a drop left in there, not even hard cider."

Maddie stared at the mess. "Why did you do this?"

"Because my wife shouldn't have to fear. My wife shouldn't have to drink only from the pump for fear that her husband will give her alcohol."

"I didn't know you knew about that."

Jace didn't answer. He watched her for a moment, debating whether or not to tell her the rest.

"I want you to understand the full import here, Maddie." Jace knew it might get him into trouble, but he was going to tell all. "This is larger than you might think; this is a huge act for me."

"I know you enjoy your drink."

"That's not it. I've never planned on it, I swear to you about that, but eventually I might have decided to get you drunk again. Since it didn't come to mind until after I was done breaking everything up, I don't know if I could have fought the urge or not. I hope I would have."

Maddie was instantly angry and wasted no time in letting Jace know it.

"You know how I feel! How could you even think of such a thing?"

"It would have been selfish, Maddie—I admit that—but I wanted you to know what this might have cost me."

"What are you talking about?"

Jace drew a little close, anger in his voice as well. "Let's just put it this way; you're a very loving drunk."

Maddie didn't get it. She frowned at him, still angry, her hands coming to her hips. "You're talking in riddles, and I'm not amused."

Jace put it plainly, working to stay calm and keeping his voice quiet. "You don't have any trouble with my getting close when you've had some alcohol."

This was the last thing Maddie expected. She wanted to be angry about the reminder, but curiosity got the better of her.

"What do I do?" she whispered back at him.

"Are you sure you want to know?"

Maddie nodded.

"You smile at me a lot, tell me how much you care, and let me kiss you all I want."

Maddie felt vulnerable and exposed, as though a secret part of her had been revealed to everyone but herself.

"Is that who I really am, Jace, or is that person just around when there's alcohol involved?"

"I don't believe it's just there when there's alcohol." His voice was calm now. "I think when you feel you can trust me, our time in the bedroom will be wonderful."

"Why do you think that?"

"Because we did enjoy each other before I sent you away. At some point between the picnic and the lies, we could barely keep our hands off of each other."

Maddie wondered how she could have forgotten that. Images of the kisses they shared, things coming dangerously close to too far, flitted through her mind. She looked down at the spilled alcohol and back at Jace.

"I'm afraid of a lot of things lately."

"Well, this is one less thing to fear. If you drink alcohol, it will be of your own choosing."

Maddie thanked him, her eyes going back to the mess.

"It smells terrible, doesn't it?"

"There was some powerful brew in there."

"And you won't miss it?"

Jace smiled. Lately the only thing on his mind was getting his wife into his arms.

"No," he said quietly. "One of these days my wife might want to kiss me, and I want my head for that."

Maddie looked up at him, knowing she was far from immune. She wasn't buying this morning, however.

"Clara will be coming soon."

"And we *mustn't* let her see us kiss," Jace said with exaggerated sarcasm.

Maddie almost smiled but refused to be baited.

"I'm going into the house now."

"That's fine," Jace agreed. "You look good going in either direction."

Maddie put her chin in the air and went on her way. She knew she was being watched every step of the way but refused to turn and give Jace the satisfaction. When she got into the house, however, she went to the window and did her best to catch sight of him without being caught.

"Have you thought about painting this house?" Clara surprised Maddie by asking later that same day.

"I hadn't," Maddie looked at her. "Have you, Clara?"

"Lots of times."

"Why didn't you?"

"It wasn't my house, and Woody didn't care how it looked."

Maddie nodded, "I suppose it's too cold right now."

"For the outside, yes."

Maddie smiled. In that instant she knew Clara had been wanting to do something with the house for years.

"You have something in mind," Maddie challenged.

"Wallpaper," Clara whispered, as though it were the greatest secret in the known universe.

Maddie laughed until tears came to her eyes, but when she could concentrate, she listened with huge eyes to every idea Clara Teckam had in mind.

"Well, now," Jace said when he came from the downstairs, having washed in the kitchen. He found his wife in a beautiful dress, even prettier than the one she was married in.

"Is it all right?"

"It's beautiful. You'll put us all to shame."

"I doubt that," Maddie said, knowing that Jace would wear the new set of clothes he'd purchased in Boston.

The look he gave her told her he believed that with all his heart. The next look he gave her was enough to make her flush from head to foot. Jace watched her intently, and Maddie knew it was time to make an exit.

"I'll wait for you downstairs."

Jace nodded, watching her exit. He would have to be careful not to overwhelm her, but if she knew how much he was looking forward to dancing with her tonight, she might not let him near her.

The space was a bit tight on the wagon seat as Jace, Maddie, and Clara headed into town on Saturday night, but it was cold enough that no one would have suggested anything else.

For two days now, it had felt as though snow could arrive at any minute, and tonight was no exception. Maddie loved the snow and Clara hated it, so the banter on the way to the party mostly came from one woman trying to persuade the other that she was right.

A few times Jace laughed out loud, which eventually dragged him into the discussion. He tried not to comment, but Clara would have none of it.

"Tell the truth," she dared him. "You hate it on those days down at the mill."

"Not the snow," he argued. "Just the cold."

"Well!" She was disgusted. "You don't get one without the other."

"Not that kind of cold," Jace corrected her. "The chilled-to-the-bone cold that hits in January—that I *don't* love."

Maddie sat in the middle of this, hearing what she and Clara must have sounded like. It never occurred to her before, but Jace and Clara were good friends. Probably much the way Clara and Woody had been.

"Well, it's time to go to the party," Clara said, a note of finality in her voice. They had stopped before the Shephard house. "And I for one still think you're wrong."

"Now you sound like Eden," Jace accused, even as he helped both women from the wagon.

On the ground now, Clara rounded on him, waving her basket in his face.

"If I could return this wedding gift, Jace Randall!"

But Jace only laughed and ushered them inside. It was a delightful start to a fun-filled evening.

Eighteen

Maddie woke up to an empty bed. She could tell it was not early; they'd been out rather late. The house was quiet, and for a long while she didn't want to move. Her mind was too full of her husband.

Jace Randall had been wonderful at the party. Without a hint that any part of their marriage was amiss, he held her hand, put his arm around her often, and danced with her like a man in love.

Maddie's eyes closed, but not in sleep. Jace *was* a man in love; she had known that for some time. She loved him too, and right now she was tired of keeping him at arm's length. She thought she might curl up against him if he were here right now, but he wasn't.

Suddenly glad it was Sunday and they had the house to themselves, Maddie got up and took extra pains with her appearance. Today was the day. She was going to let her husband know he was forgiven and that she loved him. Making vows to herself as she tucked in a final piece of hair, Maddie went downstairs with a mission.

She ate her breakfast, finished a pot of tea, and put the kitchen in order, and still Maddie had not seen anything of Jace. She had called out to the barn, but all was quiet outside as well. She sat at the table in the kitchen and wondered how her plans could have gone so far awry.

She thought about writing a letter to Paige before remembering that she was still in Europe. She spent some time thinking about how different life would have been had she gone with the Nunleys to Europe and then being very glad that she had not. She was still in the midst of all these speculations when Jace walked in.

"Good morning," he said, heading over to warm the front of himself by the fire.

"Good morning. Are you frozen?"

"A little. Clara's stovepipe fell apart."

"That must have made a huge mess."

"It did, but I was more concerned that she had heat."

"Does she need to come here? Should I go get her?"

"No. She had almost everything cleaned up by the time I left."

Jace turned then, the fire to his back, and glanced down at his clothes.

"I guess I'd better get changed. You won't want this all over the house."

Maddie was about to tell him it was all right, but he'd slipped into the small room behind the buttery to get rid of his dirty clothes. She didn't want to be caught sitting at the table looking as lost as she felt. Suddenly feeling misplaced in her own house, Maddie made for the stairs, hoping she could find some of her needlework amid the trunks she'd packed in Boston.

Not for the first time, Jace thought he was being watched. He wasn't actually working but had come out to putter with a drain that was sitting wrong and might break when a hard frost hit and all water turned to ice. He glanced up, looking first toward the barn and then to the windows of the house before deciding he was being imaginative.

The drain didn't take anywhere near as long as he expected, and that was too bad. Jace wanted to stay free of the house for a while. Maddie was not herself today. She had been acting strangely since he'd come back from Clara's. Every attempt during dinner to ask how she was was met with an uncertain face and an unconvincing answer.

Jace thought if this went on much longer, he would lose his temper. That was when he'd known it was time to head outside. But it was only getting colder, and try as he might, Jace didn't want to spend his Sunday afternoon in the barn. Seeing no help for it, he gave up and went inside, seeing right away he shouldn't have worried. Maddie was nowhere to be seen.

The whole day had passed. Maddie couldn't believe how badly her plans had failed. She had spent almost the entire day tucked up in Jace's old bedroom where she'd set up a large tapestry frame, trying to enjoy the scene she'd started before Doyle's heart gave him trouble. Just that morning she had been so brave, ready to say whatever needed to be said, and now after a wasted day of watching her husband out the window, they were sitting down to tea.

Across from her, Jace watched the emotions chase across Maddie's face. She had been acting oddly all day, but no amount of questioning had worked. She said nothing was wrong, but he didn't believe it.

They'd been married almost two weeks. Jace wondered how long he was going to have to pay for the mistake he'd made in

Boston. He didn't want to start an argument, but he wanted an answer.

"How long are you going to be mad at me for mentioning a baby?" he asked when the meal was coming to an end.

Maddie looked at him, her face giving nothing away.

"I won't say it again," Jace promised. "I won't even say it when your waist expands and your pains begin. I promise you, Maddie."

His tone made Maddie laugh a little, but Jace only watched her.

"I'm not upset about that anymore."

"But you are upset," Jace stated.

"I don't know how to explain it," Maddie said, looking helpless, remembering things she had wanted to say for days. "What woman wants to miss all I've missed?"

"It won't be the same," Jace responded, his tone compassionate. "But I can tell you anything you want to know. I can give as much detail as you want. And I can even give you something to remember."

Maddie frowned in confusion over this last statement until she read the warmth in Jace's eyes. She would have left the table, all bravado deserting her, but he caught her hand.

"What are you afraid of, Maddie?"

"That!"

"What exactly? That you'll be hurt? That you won't know what to do?"

"Yes, all of that and more," Maddie said, not looking at him, still trying to pull away. Jace would not allow it. He stood, still holding her hand captive, and came around the table to her chair. He moved it so that he could kneel in front of her, and then he did something Maddie did not expect.

"Okay, Maddie." They were almost at eye level. "You touch me."

"Touch you?" her voice rose a bit.

"Yes," he took her hands and put them on his shoulders. "You touch me."

For a long time Maddie didn't move, but then she realized how firm the muscles were under his shirt. She rubbed his shoulders gently, liking the feel. But that didn't last long. Maddie had always loved Jace's hair, and soon her fingers reached for the locks that fell across his forehead.

"I've always loved the way this hair falls over your brow," she told him softly, and Jace had all he could do to keep his hands to himself. "Your hair is soft."

Jace smiled at her when Maddie looked into his eyes, and then she bent to kiss him.

"Don't you want to touch me?" she asked shyly.

"Very much."

"Why haven't you?"

"I wanted you to want that."

Maddie took his face in her hands now, so drawn to him and in love that she didn't have words to explain her feelings.

"We might have to go slow," she felt a need to say. Desire was crowding in, but the fear still lingered.

"We can do that," Jace promised.

When Maddie bent again to kiss him, Jace felt free to wrap his arms tightly around her. He didn't think anything had ever felt so wonderful.

For the first time Maddie woke up with Jace in the bed. Every other morning he was not to be seen, but this morning she was pressed against his back, an arm over his waist.

"Are you awake over there?" she heard him ask.

"I think so. Why are you facing that way?"

"The other hip hurt, so I had to move."

Jace rolled to his back, Maddie scooting over to give him room. They lay on the pillows and smiled at each other.

"You're usually up by now," Maddie noted.

"I didn't have a good reason to stay before," he said, slipping an arm around her and pulling her close. Maddie lay her head on his chest, thinking the room would be very cold after having cuddled with Jace.

"I don't suppose you want to get up and make us some coffee?" Jace asked.

"I was hoping you did," Maddie replied. She smiled but then shifted to look at him. "Should we invite your sister to visit?"

"Why would we do that?"

"Well, she is family, and she did write to apologize."

"Did you write back to her?"

"I haven't because I want to be able to say that she's welcome, but I'm afraid she'll come between us again."

"I don't think that will happen, Maddie. She's very different."

"Do you think she's all right? Is someone taking advantage of her?"

"It didn't sound like it when we talked," Jace said, but then realized he was not sure. "Go ahead and write. Tell her to come anytime."

Maddie put her head back on his chest, her mind going without permission to her conversation with Mr. Muldoon. Maddie had not completely understood some of the things he said, but she could tell that he'd been sincere in his beliefs. For a time Maddie wondered if that's what God was looking for: a sincere heart.

Before she could make up her mind, Jace kissed her and said he had to get moving. Maddie followed him out of bed, ready to start the day but not thrilled to dress in such a cold room.

Maddie wasn't cold for long. Jace gave her a lingering kiss before going downstairs, one that kept her warm all the way to the kitchen.

ↄ৽৸

"Well, Maddie," Doyle said with surprised pleasure on Tuesday morning when she and Clara arrived in high spirits. "Doing some shopping?"

"As a matter of fact, we are here to look at wallpaper."

"Well, now," Doyle teased. "You must be trying to turn that old bachelor's house into a home."

"It's needed it for years," Clara wasn't afraid to add.

Doyle grinned at her tone, and even though Maddie knew the way, he led the women to the shelf where rolls of wallpaper could be found. Clara had a recipe for paste, and they would buy some extra supplies to make that.

"Look at this blue," Maddie exclaimed, pulling a roll down, wasting no time in her excitement.

"With little bits of green," Clara added as she touched it. "That would look good in the spare room or Jace's old room."

"What about the parlor?"

"It's not a huge room; you might want to pick something lighter." Clara looked back to the shelf. "How about this one?"

"Oh," Maddie touched the pale yellow stripe. "That's perfect."

"That tapestry you have started would be perfect on this. Maybe over the mantle."

"Clara," Maddie looked at her in amazement, and not for the first time, "you have an eye for this. You would do very well in Boston."

"Oh, go on," she said, waving her away, but Maddie was serious.

"Have you wallpapered your own house?"

Clara grinned. "Every room."

Maddie's mouth opened. "And why haven't I been invited down to see it?"

"Consider yourself invited. Anytime you wish."

Maddie knew she would take her up on that before the week was out. Acting like little girls on an outing, they ended up choosing wallpaper for four rooms. The only room they skipped was Jace and Maddie's bedroom. Maddie told Clara she liked it the way it was, which was true, but the main reason she held off was she wanted Jace's opinion about the print.

Maddie was still growing used to the idea of having a husband she didn't keep at arm's length. It was a wonderful new experience, but one she didn't feel she deserved. At any moment she feared it would all be taken from her. Superstitious as it might seem, changing the bedroom when things where going so well felt like courting disaster.

"What's the matter?" Clara asked, watching the emotions chase across the younger woman's face.

"Nothing. Just thinking about wallpaper."

"Don't worry," Clara said, misreading the true reason. "I'll help you put it up."

They didn't leave town without stopping to greet Cathy, but she wouldn't let them stay for more that a quick cup of tea. She said snow was coming, and they had to get home.

And she was right. They weren't even out of town when the first flakes began to fall.

Jace stepped out of the mill when he noticed the snowflakes. There was nothing heavy or threatening about the sky, but he wished that Maddie and Clara had already come past. He didn't have much more to do—things were ready for the next cutting season—but he was hesitant to leave before knowing they were on their way home.

Then another thought struck him. What if they'd gone by and he hadn't noticed? Trying to decide where he wanted to be, Jace paced around a bit and then gave up. He closed things down at the mill and started for home. He knew that all he would do was worry, but he decided to do that where a wagon or sleigh was readily available.

Just seeing his face, Clara knew that Jace had worried about them, but she'd not said a word. Maddie didn't seem to notice anything more than the fact that he came from the kitchen the moment they pulled into the yard.

"It's snowing!" Maddie called to him.

"I'm sure Clara is thrilled," Jace teased to cover the relief he felt. He hadn't foreseen this. Having a wife, someone to share his life with, had been the goal. But she hadn't come with any instructions. He didn't know when she would cry or get upset with him, and he certainly hadn't banked on his own feelings when she might be in trouble. He'd done nothing but pace and worry until he spotted them up the road. He'd gone to the kitchen to calm down some but also in an effort not to give himself away. Meeting them at the barn was his normal routine. If he'd gone out the front door, they would have known he was worried.

As it was, he suspected Clara was on to him, but she said nothing, scooting inside only to get out of the snow. And she didn't stay long. It was coming down hard now, and she wanted to get home. Jace sent her on her way with instructions not to come in the morning if the weather was at all unpredictable. Clara waved and went on her way, leaving Maddie alone with her husband.

"How did you do?" Jace asked, having brought in the packages.

"We found wallpaper for four rooms."

"Four? I thought you were doing one."

"You don't want me to do four?"

"Four is fine; I just didn't realize."

Maddie looked uncertain. "Maybe four is too many."

"Madalyn, it's fine," Jace said, wanting her to listen to him, his tone growing firm.

"Are you angry?"

Jace stared at her, asking himself what went on in town that would make her so uncertain over this. He didn't understand that she struggled with feelings of uncertainty all too often.

"I'm not angry," Jace told her, smiling to reinforce the point. "Not at all. Why don't you show me what you bought?"

Maddie did this, watching her husband's face for signs of upset, but he liked everything they had selected. He even won Maddie's heart again when he asked about their bedroom.

"Well," she explained, "I thought you might want to have some say."

"That was sweet of you," he said, bending to kiss the end of her nose. "You're still cold," he said sweetly. "Come over by the fire."

Wrapped in her husband's embrace in front of the fire, Maddie told herself she had been silly. It wasn't too good to be true. Jace really was hers. She still didn't think she deserved him, but for now, she ordered her fears to stop plaguing her.

A letter had come thanking Maddie for the invitation but also saying that Eden would not be visiting until December, weather permitting. Maddie had written back to say they would be there no matter when Eden arrived and then not given it any more thought. So when Eden trudged up the snow-covered road on a sunny day in the middle of December, she was the last person on Maddie's mind.

Clara had not come that day. She'd begun to take Tuesdays and Fridays as days at home. So when the knock sounded at the door, Maddie had no choice but to answer it herself. She swiftly wiped her hands, knowing whoever was outside had to be cold.

"Eden," Maddie exclaimed, feeling her heart lurch.

"Hello, Maddie," she said quietly. "Is this a bad time?"

"No, come in out of the cold. I was just doing some baking."

"Is there something I can do to help?"

"Come and get warm, Eden," Maddie offered, trying to work out who this really was. She hadn't had more than a few hours with Eden in the past, but the memory was a strong one. This looked like Eden, but nothing else was the same. There was a softness to her eyes and a gentleness to her speech and mannerisms that Maddie didn't recognize.

"Sit here by the fire. I'll make you a cup of tea," Maddie offered, and Eden glanced around.

"Everything looks wonderful."

"Thank you."

"You've done some wallpapering," Eden said, glancing back into the parlor they'd just walked through. "Oh, and in the small room too. Does your uncle carry those prints?"

"Yes, he has a good selection."

"Thank you." Eden smiled when Maddie set the tea in front of her. Maddie took a seat with her own tea, wondering what they would talk about.

"How is Jace?" Eden asked.

"Oh, Eden," Maddie said as she rose. "He's in the barn. I'll tell him you're here."

"It's all right if he's busy."

"Not at all. I'll just run and get him."

Maddie's brain raced all the way to the barn, so befuddled by Eden's presence she almost tripped on the threshold.

"Maddie?" Jace was suddenly behind her; she had walked right past him.

"Oh, there you are."

"What's the matter?"

"Eden's here."

"What did she say?"

"Nothing—it's not like that. She's just so changed."

Jace's racing heart slowed. For a moment he thought they had gone backward in time, a place he did not wish to be.

"Are you all right?"

"Yes, I just needed you to know she was here."

"I'll be right in."

"Don't hurry. We're just talking in the kitchen."

Jace watched her leave, understanding her plight. The Eden he'd talked to that weekend and then on the train was not the woman he'd known for 25 years. Maddie's only interaction with Eden had been completely negative. He could understand that she would be very confused.

Jace hurried to put away his tools. He was anxious to see his sister, and not because he couldn't trust her. He found the change in her utterly fascinating.

"I've never asked about the folks in the boardinghouse," Maddie mentioned over tea that Saturday night. The three of them had done a lot of talking, but this hadn't come up. "Have the same people been there for long?"

Both Jace and Eden laughed.

"What did I miss?" Maddie questioned.

"It's terrible of us," Eden admitted, "but I have one gentleman who looked to be 80 when he moved in, but he's been with me for over 15 years. I still have no idea how old he is."

"Is he ailing at all?" Jace wished to know.

"Not in the least. He's as strong as ever. May, she helps me in the kitchen," Eden explained to Maddie. "She determined to learn his age a few years ago, but no amount of probing or questions would do it."

"It doesn't help that he's half deaf," Jace put in.

"He hears what he wants to hear," Eden said. "Like a certain younger brother I know."

Jace tried to look innocent, but Maddie did not fall for it.

"What was Jace like as a child?" she had to ask.

"As a rule, he did very well, but there were times when I knew he was up to something, and it took some dragging to find out."

"What would you do?" Maddie asked her spouse.

"Nothing. I don't know what Eden's talking about."

Eden rolled her eyes.

"I won't tell all, Maddie, but Jace and a friend of his liked to torment the blacksmith. They never thought I would figure it out, but they always came home covered in soot. It was so obvious."

"Is that how you knew?" Jace asked, causing both women to laugh hysterically.

He was teased about that for the rest of the evening, but it didn't detract from their fun. Indeed, Jace and Maddie went to bed amazed over how much they were enjoying Eden.

Having to talk to herself about worrying, Eden also prepared to retire. The morning was on her mind in a huge way, and if she wasn't careful not to fall into old controlling habits, she would not sleep at all.

"Maddie?" Eden was the first in the kitchen on Sunday morning and spoke to her host as soon as she arrived. "Would it be all right if I went into town for services? Would you and Jace mind?"

"Not at all. I'd like to go with you. Jace thinks he's getting a cough, so he's going to stay in bed, but I would enjoy going to the meetinghouse."

"Maddie, I was going to go to services at Mr. Muldoon's. Do you mind if we go there?"

"How do you know Mr. Muldoon?" Maddie asked in surprise.

"His brother is a friend of my pastor in Pine River."

"What an interesting coincidence."

"So, do you mind?" Eden repeated.

The first thing Maddie wanted to say was yes, she did mind, but then she realized what an opportunity it was. However, she remembered some things Mr. Muldoon had said.

"Eden, I don't usually go there, and I don't know what it costs."

"It doesn't cost anything."

"Well, I know there's no pew rental, but I think Mr. Muldoon said something about giving. And I don't know how much to give."

"It's not like that, Maddie. I'm quite certain that Mr. Muldoon was talking about when the Bible tells us to consider the money we have and to give as cheerfully and generously as we can. You would be a visitor, Maddie. I don't think anyone would expect you to give."

"You're sure?"

"Very sure."

"And the Muldoons don't mind if others come?"

"They would enjoy it."

Maddie found Eden's expression so sincere that she agreed. She went back upstairs to put on one of her better dresses and tell Jace of her plans. As she expected, he was staying where he was, but the women left for town not long after breakfast.

Nineteen

"Eden?" Maddie asked when the sleigh was in motion. The service was over, and they were headed out of town. "What happened to you?"

"What happened to me?" Puzzled, Eden questioned her right back, not sure what she meant.

"Well," Maddie hesitated, afraid of offending. "You're different."

"I *am* different," Eden replied, relieved to tell her. "But I can't give myself any of the credit, Maddie. God has made the changes in me."

"How is that possible?"

"Oh, Maddie." Eden searched for the right words. Some of this was still so new for her, but she remembered Mr. Engler had advised that she simply tell her own story. "What you have to understand, Maddie, is that I was very flippant about God. I had no fear of Him at all. I just lived my life as I pleased until I wanted to die. I didn't understand what a sinner I was, or how holy God is. When that was explained to me, I chose to repent to Jesus Christ, who saved me from my sin. The Bible says that when we trust in Jesus Christ, the Holy Spirit of God comes to live inside of us. He made the changes you see in me."

Maddie was driving the sleigh but was barely watching where they were headed. Eden assumed the team knew the way and tried not to worry.

"But I believe in God," Maddie told her.

"I did too, but I didn't understand that He wanted a personal relationship with me. That was the reason Jesus came to earth. I was miserable and desperate, but it never occurred to me that I didn't have to be until a pastor told me that I could choose to do things God's way. When I understood that, I trusted Him for salvation."

Maddie had turned to the front now, so Eden stopped speaking. After a moment, Maddie thanked her.

"I appreciate your telling me what happened, Eden."

"I'm glad to do it, but I'm now wondering if I confused things for you."

"I don't know," Maddie said, not willing to tell Eden that she often felt desperate and miserable. "It's a lot to think about."

"Do you mind if I pray for you, Maddie?" Eden asked, not mentioning how often she already did this.

"No, I don't mind, Eden. Thank you."

This took them back to the farm. Jace was on hand, bundled to the nose, to see to the team and sleigh, so the women headed inside out of the cold. Eden was on her way to hang her coat in the room off the buttery but stopped before leaving the kitchen. She faced Maddie, putting her hand out to give her arm a squeeze.

"I'm so glad Jace has you, Maddie. I can't tell you how much."

Maddie stood very still, even after Eden moved away. It was nothing like she expected. She was having her questions answered, but she was as confused as ever. She wanted more than anything to find a warm place and have a good cry. However, she could hear Jace coming in and made a swift decision.

She would not let him know how unsettling she'd found the morning service or Eden's words on the ride home. Jace would think that Eden had said something to deliberately upset her. In having her with them for the weekend, Maddie had come to appreciate Eden in a whole new way. She thought Jace was enjoying her too and didn't want to take the chance of unsettling this newfound relationship.

"Thank you for putting the sleigh away," she said, greeting her husband with a kiss. "How are you feeling?"

"Not too bad. How are things in town?"

"Fine," Maddie said, not even thinking to mention that she hadn't gone to the meetinghouse with Doyle and Cathy.

Maddie set to work on dinner, Jace giving her a hand. Neither one of them noticed that Eden did not join them for some minutes. She was taking extra time in putting away her coat and scarf, using those few minutes to pray for her brother and sister-in-law.

"Are you warm enough?" Maddie asked Eden at the train station Monday morning. "Are you sure you have the lunch I packed?"

"Yes, thank you for everything, Maddie. I had a wonderful time."

Before she could talk herself out of it, Eden hugged Maddie. Maddie hugged her right back, nearly causing Eden's eyes to fill. Eden then turned to her brother.

"Thank you for a wonderful weekend."

"You're welcome. Come back and see us."

"I'll do that. You take good care of Maddie. She's a treasure."

"Yes, she is," Jace agreed, initiating the hug this time, having been oddly touched to see Eden hug his wife.

"I love you, Jace," Eden whispered just before she broke contact and hurried onto the train. She had wanted to cry again and thought she was going to fall to pieces if she didn't get herself out

of there. She climbed aboard, waved from the window, and settled back for the ride.

Outside, Jace and Maddie returned to the sleigh. Jace needed
something from the livery, but Maddie stayed snuggled under
the mound of quilts and blankets they had brought for the ride.
Her nose was cold by the time they left for home, but she didn't
mind. The sun was shining off the snow, and it was a decidedly
gorgeous morning.

Clara was working over the kitchen table when they arrived
back. She had a beef roast in the oven and was putting the final
touches on a pie. Maddie simply joined her in the work while
Jace went to his desk in the parlor.

"Did Miss Randall get off?"

"Yes."

"She seems friendlier these days," Clara commented.

"She *is* friendly," Maddie agreed, thinking the word seemed
somewhat inadequate. "She's done a lot of changing recently."

"Must mean she wants something," Clara said, and Maddie
was glad she didn't feel that negative about the situation.

Maddie went upstairs to take the sheets from Eden's room,
and that was when she found it: Eden had left a beautiful quilt
for a wedding gift. It was done in yellows and greens, and her
handwork was perfect. Maddie touched it, fingering the stitches,
very glad that she hadn't argued with Clara even though she
knew that woman was wrong. There was much she didn't understand about her sister-in-law, but of one thing she was certain:
Eden was not being kind in order to get something. And even if
Maddie had been tempted to feel that way, one look at the quilt
would allay such notions.

"Are you all right?" Jace asked over breakfast. It was Tuesday,
and they had the house to themselves.

"Yes," Maddie told him, smiling in an effort to be convincing. She had lain awake for a long time, questions swirling around in her mind, and not one of them had an answer. "How are you feeling?" She hoped to divert his thoughts about her.

"I feel good. If I was getting sick, I must have changed my mind."

Maddie laughed and said, "I'm glad. It's so cold out. Do you have much work in the barn today?"

"Nothing that can't wait if I start to freeze. What are you doing today?"

"I need to write a thank-you to your sister, and then I want to finish decorating in your old room."

"What will Clara say?" Jace teased.

"I'm hoping she'll be *very* impressed when she sees what I've done."

Jace went on his way a short time later, allowing Maddie to let her guard down. She could not get Eden's words about being desperate and miserable from her mind, and when she did manage to forget them, Mr. Muldoon's words about being ready for eternity crowded in.

"If I'm ready for eternity," Maddie said to herself as she cleaned up in the kitchen, "why am I so fearful? What do I really think is going to happen to me?"

But these were just more questions without answers, and for a moment Maddie's anger spiked. She wanted to stop thinking about it, and right now she was finally angry enough to accomplish that. Knowing she needed to occupy her thoughts, she put together a bread dough to rise for dinner and then went upstairs, stomping all the way. She would lick this thing if it was the last thing she did.

Looking for the ax he'd set down on Saturday, Jace stepped out of the barn wondering what had so distracted him that he would leave it outside. He was ready to get back in out of the wind, but he glanced up at the house and found Maddie at the window.

Jace smiled at the sight, but she didn't see him. Her gaze had traveled to the distance, out over the fields of snow all around them. Jace watched her with pleasure until he thought he saw her wipe a tear from her face. He squinted to see if his eyes were playing tricks on him, but just then Maddie spotted him. With a huge smile and wave, she grinned down at him, and Jace figured he'd been imagining things. He went back to work and put it out of his mind, giving Maddie the very thing she was hoping for as she turned from the window and continued to wipe the tears from her face.

"Good morning, Clara," Doyle greeted when she came in from the cold. "What did you and Maddie come in for today?"

"I don't work at the farm on Tuesdays or Fridays, so I'm not with Maddie."

"How did you get here?" Doyle knew she did not have horses or a sleigh.

"Mrs. Davis was coming in, and I came with her."

"A day off," Doyle teased a little. "You're turning into a woman of leisure."

Clara laughed, thinking that if he could see the work she was doing in her small kitchen, he wouldn't say that. She had decided to hang a spice cabinet of her own, much like Maddie's, and she was thinking about putting in another window on the east side of the room.

"What can we get for you today?" Doyle offered.

Clara was ready with her list but took her time because Mrs. Davis had several other stops. Doyle was busy, but Clara didn't mind. She let him be interrupted twice, even going so far as to sit by the stove for a time.

"How are Jace and Maddie doing?" Doyle asked when he joined Clara by the stove.

"Fine. As you know, Jace's sister was here over the weekend. She was actually decent to be around this time. Almost human."

"We didn't see them this weekend," Doyle told her, not the least offended but concerned about Eden. "What's going on with his sister?"

"I've wondered that myself, but Jace and Maddie seemed to enjoy her."

"Do you think she wants something?"

"I mentioned that to Maddie, but she didn't comment." Clara shrugged. "She's Jace's sister. I figure he can do with her what he likes."

"But how did she treat Maddie?"

"Real fine. They got along just great, and Eden even made a quilt and left it for them as a wedding gift." Clara shook her head. "Maddie already has it on the bed. It's beautiful."

Doyle worried some about Eden's presence and the fact that they didn't see them all weekend. He listened to Clara talk about the amount of snow in the fields, but only half of his mind attended. Not until Clara said she had to finish her list did Doyle come completely back to the present.

He had many unanswered questions in his mind, but the one at the top of the list was how much to tell his wife. She would worry twice as much as he would, and maybe the whole episode was innocent. Doyle still had no answer when Clara left, and that bothered him. He only hoped that he would have it figured out before Cathy brought his dinner.

Maddie had pulled it off for the better part of a week, but it was no longer working. She was clearly distraught, and Jace had stopped believing her when she said nothing was wrong. They had quarreled twice over nothing at all, and Jace was finished.

He came in for dinner on Friday, telling himself he wasn't leaving the house until Maddie told him why she was barely eating and pretending to be all right in his presence.

"This ham is good," Jace said, trying to find the words that would get the truth from his wife.

"Is it?" she was forced to ask. She was still working on her tea and hadn't touched her plate. Watching her, Jace suddenly knew how he must handle this.

"Have I done something that's made you afraid?"

Maddie looked surprised. "I don't know what you mean."

"Do you think I've brought liquor back into the house?"

"No, Jace. Such a thing never occurred to me."

"Have I been harsh with you, or do you think I'm angry?"

"No," Maddie answered soberly, sure she knew where he was headed with this.

"Then why can't you tell me what's bothering you? And please don't insult me anymore by saying nothing is wrong."

Maddie set her saucer down, seeing how she'd hurt her husband. She wasn't upset or angry with him, but neither did she think he would understand.

"It's not your fault that I haven't talked to you, Jace," Maddie admitted humbly. "But at the same time, you don't have tormented feelings about things like I do, so I assumed you wouldn't understand, or at the very least be weary of hearing from me on the subject."

Jace stared at her for a moment, knowing this had to stem back to Sunday. He suddenly wished he had gone with the women so he could have heard what Mr. Sullins had to say. At least then he might have had a fighting chance to follow her logic now.

"I know it hasn't worked in the past, but did you try talking to Mr. Sullins after the service?"

Maddie's mouth opened in surprise.

"Jace, I didn't realize I never told you. We went to Mr. Muldoon's house. That was where your sister wanted to go, and I saw no reason not to."

"What did Mr. Muldoon say that was so upsetting?" Jace asked, "or was it Eden?"

"It was both," Maddie admitted. "Mr. Muldoon talked about being so sure of your destination that you never have to fear death or anything else. That made me remember what he said about baptism coming after a decision, and now I'm all confused. And then your sister said she had been miserable, and I find that I'm tormented over all the questions in my mind that never get answered."

Maddie's voice had become agitated, and Jace knew he would have to step very carefully. Maddie was right: He was sick to death of this subject. He wished she could just relax and understand that everything was all right. *They* were all right. If Eden or Mr. Muldoon didn't like the way they lived their lives, it was their problem, not his and Maddie's.

"Have you considered talking to Mr. Muldoon?" Jace asked, unable to think of another thing to say.

"No, I'm afraid I'll misunderstand him or get more confused. Each time I leave there, I end up in worse shape."

"What if I go with you?" Jace offered, dreading the very thought.

Tears filled Maddie's eyes, something Jace hadn't seen before.

"Would you do that?" she whispered. "Would you go with me?"

"Yes, Maddie," he said gently, his heart touched by how upset she was.

Maddie was out of her chair a moment later, coming to throw her arms around his neck. Jace stood to hold her, not sure what he was getting into but certain he'd said the right thing. His wife was without words, and for the first time since he'd met her, she sobbed against his chest.

❧

Alison shifted in her seat during dinner, trying to get comfortable. She had just picked up her fork again when she realized that her family was staring intently at her.

"All right, all of you," she scolded with a laugh, "I have six weeks to go. You can't stare at me for all that time."

"You look so uncomfortable these days," Hillary said, her voice full of compassion.

"Well, it might be a long six weeks, but we'll just have to wait it out."

"Mama?" Joshua called her name to ask for the salt, but it had been left in the kitchen.

"I'll get it," Douglas offered, not wanting his wife to get up.

"Thank you." Alison smiled at him when he went past, and Douglas touched her shoulder.

He was trying to remember whether Alison had been so uncomfortable with Martin, but the details had slipped his mind. He asked when he got back to the table.

"Not quite this early, I don't think. It was a warm time of the year with Marty, and this time maybe I'm stiff because of the cold."

"I wonder why we don't remember the details," Douglas commented. "It's so big at the time, and then the memory fades."

"There's too much life to be lived after the baby's born," Alison said. "And it's such a comfort to finally meet the little guy."

"Little girl," two of her children said in unison, causing her to laugh. The meal didn't last much longer. Joshua and Peter had to get back to school, and Hillary was taking Martin to visit Mr. Sager.

Alison was not unhappy about any of this. She planned to put her feet up and do a little handwork. She had enough old things for the baby to wear but wanted a few items that were brand new, made especially for him.

When there was a knock on the door, however, she put her work aside and forced herself from the chair. As always, she was surprised to see it was Maddie, and this time the surprise was doubled because Jace had accompanied her.

"Come in," she welcomed. "Come in and get warm."

"Thank you," Maddie told her sincerely. "I'm sorry to bother you, Mrs. Muldoon, but could I please see Mr. Muldoon?"

"It's no bother at all. Go ahead to the parlor, and I'll get Douglas."

Jace kept his eyes on Maddie. She was nervous and close to tears again. What he couldn't gauge was whether the emotion was fear or relief. Did she finally think her questions would be answered or dread that they never would be?

Douglas joined them in the midst of these speculations, a smile of welcome on his face.

"Hi, Jace. Hi, Maddie. Good to see you."

"Is this a bad time, Mr. Muldoon?"

"Not at all. Sit right down."

Maddie did sit down, Jace beside her on the sofa, but she found her mind strangely blank. Jace waited for her to speak, and when she didn't, he tried to help.

"I think Maddie had some questions about eternity and being certain of such things."

Maddie nodded.

"Are you thinking about what I said on Sunday morning, Maddie?"

"Yes. You said we would have nothing to fear, but I feel like I can't find that place. I am afraid and don't know what to do about it."

"God does offer peace with Him, Maddie," Douglas explained to her. "And I think that's what you lack. Am I right?"

"Yes. I rarely feel like I have peace. I have so much else, but I can't even see it."

"You make a good point, Maddie. We're often blind to all of the blessings in our lives. Clearly you have much to be thankful for. I could even name things for you."

"Like what?" Maddie was all at once fascinated.

"Your husband, for one. I don't know very many men who would accompany their wives to the pastor's house when she wants to dialog about eternal issues. I have had many women come to me over the years, but not very often with their husbands."

"I am thankful that Jace came with me," Maddie admitted, not able to look at the man in question for fear she would cry again.

"And who are you thankful to?" Douglas asked, and then waited.

Maddie had to think about this. She knew he was waiting for her to say God, and she understood why, but it just wouldn't come.

"Do you see what I mean, Maddie? God is so kind and gracious. He gives us life, and others to love us, and every possible thing we can imagine, and much of the time we aren't even aware of all His goodness.

"And if that wasn't enough, He sent His Son to offer us life for all of eternity. But it's not without sacrifice on our parts, Maddie. It's God's way or not at all. We can't choose how we come to Him. He's told us the way."

"In the Bible."

"That's right. And I want to tell you that you can have peace with God, but there is a choice to be made here. You must decide what you want more, life your own way, or life God's way."

"What if life God's way is more than I can bear? What if I do it His way and I'm still upset and afraid?"

"Being upset or afraid is sin, Maddie, and God tells those who have trusted in Him to confess their sins, and He forgives them every time. So even if old habits enter in, there is a way to deal with those."

"But they might still be there?" Maddie questioned, clearly not happy. "I might still be afraid and have no peace?"

"Maddie," Douglas tried again to make it clear, "God might choose to take all fear and doubt away the moment you trust in His Son, but He might not. What He does promise is to never give us more than we can bear or leave us alone in any struggle."

"Why doesn't Mr. Sullins tell us these things?" Jace suddenly asked.

"I'm not sure what Mr. Sullins is teaching, Jace. I will say this, however. God has given you an amazing mind, and you must use it to think on all you've heard, to think and evaluate the things I've said to you," Douglas stated, wanting very much for Jace to feel responsibility in this matter. "If in your times of thinking you find you have more questions, I would be happy to answer them."

"Thank you for your time," Maddie said, and once again Douglas knew the conversation was at an end. He wondered whether Maddie would ever humble herself before God and believe, and for a moment he wrestled with a tactful way to ask.

"Before you go, Maddie, may I ask you something?"

"Yes."

"What do you think about what I've said? Do you think it's foolish or just not for you?"

"I don't know right now. I can't understand how we can know all of this. I don't know how you can be so sure."

"We all choose to believe in something, Maddie. We all have faith of some kind in something, and I choose to put my trust in the Word of God. That's how I can know."

Maddie nodded but was already on her feet. Douglas could see that it was over. He looked to Jace, whose face was thoughtful, but that man had no questions either. Douglas saw them to the front door, invited them back anytime, and prayed all the while. He then made his way to the kitchen to ask if Alison had heard.

Douglas had no choice but to assume she'd heard nothing. She was sound asleep by the fire, her knitting forgotten in her lap. Douglas tucked a quilt close around her, knowing she needed her sleep even more than he needed her prayers.

Twenty

Jace waited until they were home to have his say. He was not angry but firm, and Maddie listened as she'd never done before. "I'll say this for the man, Maddie, Mr. Muldoon is sincere about what he believes, but I've had it with pastors. They never answer your questions, and they run back to the Bible every time.

"Well, when are we supposed to use our brains?" he nearly demanded of his wife. "You're a smart woman, Maddie, and you can figure this out. Everything is fine. You're fine. I'm fine. Mr. and Mrs. Muldoon are fine. It's time you stop listening to your doubts.

"I love you. I love the life we have together. Why would we waste a moment worrying when we love each other and we plan to make a life together for the next 40 years? I don't want you to worry anymore. If you don't know the answer to something, don't let it upset you. Keep on as you're doing, and everything will work out fine."

"Do you really believe that, Jace? Do you really think I'll be all right?"

Jace put his arms around her. "I think you're going to be more than all right. I think you're going to be wonderful." Jace lowered his head at that point and kissed her for all he was worth. He squeezed her tightly against him, trying to show her that he believed in them. He agreed with Mr. Muldoon: He was choosing to believe in Maddie and the life they were living.

"Better?" he asked, looking down into her flushed face.

"Yes."

"Just answer this question, Maddie: What's wrong with our life? I like it the way it is. I wish you could too."

Maddie nodded, relief filling her. Why was she putting them through this? She didn't know that answer but wanted it all to stop. After all, Jace worked hard to make a home for them and gave her anything she wanted. It was time to stop worrying and enjoy it all.

"I love you," she told him, reaching to kiss him again.

Jace would not pass on such an offer. They held each other for a long time by the fire, both convinced for the first time that all would be well.

January brought lots of snow to Tucker Mills. Jace was nearing the end of the slow season, and it wasn't at all unusual for Maddie to join him in the barn while he worked, especially on days when Clara remained at home. She was now home three days a week, not counting Sundays, and Jace and Maddie enjoyed their time together as never before.

What Jace hadn't seen coming was that his wife could be a bit of a prankster. On one sunny January day past the middle of the month, Jace took for granted that Maddie was in the house. When his tools didn't seem to be in the places he'd left them, he assumed he was tired and forgetful. Not until he heard a small shuffling sound did he begin to wonder.

Maddie's hiding place in the barn was perfect. It was a dark corner where the feed was kept, and by bending low she could look through the slats in the wooden walls and see Jace working. She knew exactly when he would walk outside or to the shed.

For the better part of an hour, she'd been stealing out to move his tools and then scooting back to hide, sometimes with seconds to spare.

However, it was getting colder, and Maddie had begun to feel a little stiff. She thought she would just be done with the game and slip back inside the house, leaving him to wonder, but he must have changed his mind. He'd no more stepped outside than he was right back in, catching Maddie coming from her hiding place.

"Maddie!" she heard him exclaim softly. She bolted for the door. By the time she got out of the barn, it was to the sound of, "Madalyn Randall, you get back here!"

She ran around the barn, sliding in the snow and just barely keeping her feet. Trying not to laugh, Jace ran outside. Maddie's goal was the kitchen door. If she could just make that, she could lock him out and go to the window to laugh. She hadn't banked on slipping. A second later Jace had her.

"I've got you!" He fell on her without mercy, and Maddie could not stop laughing. "Move my tools will you! I thought I was losing my mind."

"I'm sorry," Maddie begged, but her laughter didn't help.

"You sound terribly sorry," Jace said sarcastically.

"You're crushing me, Jace."

"You deserve to be crushed."

Maddie could only laugh, but she was running out of air. Jace took pity on her red face and shifted enough to let her sit up. He lay beside her, looking up.

"There's going to be payback," Jace warned. "You have been very naughty."

"I don't know what you mean," Maddie said, deciding to feign innocence and coming to her feet to put a bit of distance between them. "I just came out to say hello to my husband and found myself yelled at and chased."

Still in the snow, Jace made a lunge for his wife's legs, but she anticipated him. Before he could get to his feet, she was back on the run. She circled the barn again, hoping to make the kitchen door this time, but Jace caught her almost in the same place. They didn't fall this time, but he wrapped his arms around her and pulled her close. They were both covered with snow, and Maddie's cold cheeks and shining blue eyes were too much to resist.

Jace dipped his head and kissed her. She was going to think this was the reward for teasing him while he was working, but right now he didn't care. They kissed for a time, Maddie laughing when she reminded Jace how confused his face had looked. Jace tried to be outraged but couldn't quite manage it.

For a while they stood in their own little world. Indeed, the man who stood at the end of the yard watching them finally had to clear his throat to be noticed. Both Jace and Maddie started, turning toward the sound.

Jace didn't know the man, but Maddie certainly did. With a delighted cry of pleasure, she called out, "Mr. Nunley!"

Cathy slipped into the rear door of the store, a few fresh muffins on a plate for Doyle. She went to the stove for warmth and watched as he worked with two customers before sending them on their way.

When Doyle turned to give his attention to Cathy, he knew with just one glance at her face that something was on her mind.

"Are you going to tell me?" he wasted no time in asking.

"Tell you what?"

"What's bothering you."

Cathy frowned at him. She didn't like to be caught in a mood, but he was right, she was a little upset.

Doyle didn't press her because he'd remembered that it was that time of the year for her: Cathy tended to battle with discouragement about midwinter when the snow had been deep for weeks on end and there wasn't a single hint of spring.

"I'm just worried about Maddie," Cathy finally admitted. Doyle was glad he'd remembered the season, or she would have him worried as well. He was also glad he hadn't told her about Eden's last visit.

"What in particular? Did you have words?"

"No, nothing like that, but Clara is coming less and less all the time, and I don't know if Maddie can do it all."

"What part of homemaking don't you think she's capable of?"

"I know she's capable," Cathy said testily. "It's doing it all. It's keeping track of everything."

"But she's done that with you off and on for years."

"But not on her own—not having it all on her shoulders!"

"Cathy," Doyle's voice stayed kind, but he'd heard enough. "They'll manage. If they run out of candles or dinner's not on time, they'll have to figure it out together. Jace isn't an impossible husband. He'll give Maddie all the time she needs to make this work. You know he will. He'll be making mistakes too, and Maddie will have to be patient with him."

Knowing he was right, Cathy nodded, but she was quite willing to worry about everything right now.

"And what about Clara?" Cathy changed her focus to another person. "What is she going to do on her own all these days?"

Doyle didn't let himself laugh, but it was close.

"I would think after working for Woody all those years, she'd be happy for some time on her own. Don't you think?"

"Yes," Cathy agreed, her voice weary.

Doyle hoped for a customer, but no rescue came. Cathy continued to sit and be sad by the fire, and Doyle gave up trying to cheer her but simply munched on the muffins and nodded sympathetically.

"I'm headed home," Cathy said after a time. "I've got some clothes to wash."

"Thank you for the muffins," Doyle told her but was only waved at.

Doyle watched her leave, confident that it would pass. Their Maddie and Jace were doing just fine, and as soon as spring made an arrival, his Cathy would be fine as well.

๛

"I can't believe you're here," Maddie said to her former employer, having given him a hug. "This is my husband, Jace. Jace, this is Mr. Nunley."

"It's a pleasure to meet you, sir," Jace said respectfully, hoping he'd not given the wrong impression in the time before they noticed him. "How was your train ride?"

"It was fine. You have a good line and a comfortable station."

"Come inside," Maddie invited, and the three trooped indoors. Maddie took Mr. Nunley's coat and hat and invited him into the parlor.

"I can't believe you're here," she repeated.

"Adele would have it no other way. She was quite upset over your letter."

"I'm sorry, Mr. Nunley. I never meant for Paige and the missus to hear of my marriage in that way, but we had to get back here to Tucker Mills. We couldn't leave the farm that long."

"But Jace is not a stranger to you, is he?"

"No, we knew each other before I returned to Boston. The decision to marry was rather sudden, but Sherry and Beth were both there."

"They told us all about that night."

"I'm glad. I hope you'll stay with us, Mr. Nunley. We have plenty of room."

"I'd like that. The train goes out on Monday?"

"Yes, and you're welcome for the whole weekend."

"Thank you."

"So tell me," Mr. Nunley began, but Jace caught little of it. He was still hearing his wife protect him to this businessman from Boston. At a time when she could have told all, no matter how damaging it might have been to Jace, she had stood up for him.

"Jace." Maddie finally got his attention.

"Yes?"

"Mr. Nunley has some things at the train station. Can you take him back to get them?"

"Certainly, or I can just go on my own. Someone will know which bags are yours, won't they?"

"I think so. I have a large trunk and two smaller cases. They're all marked."

"I'll go right now." Jace came to his feet. "Maddie, may I see you for just a moment?"

"Certainly."

Maddie excused herself and followed Jace all the way to the room where they kept their warm gear. They had no more passed out of sight when she found herself grabbed and kissed, kissed hard and long.

"What was that for?" she asked when she could breathe once again.

"I'll tell you later," Jace said, kissing her again before slipping into his coat and heading out the door.

"So what countries did you visit in Europe?" Jace asked over Sunday dinner; they had joined Doyle and Cathy. Mr. Nunley had spoken of his trip several times over the weekend, but Jace had not been in on any of the specifics.

"We spent most of our time in France, Italy, and Spain."

"What was your favorite?" Cathy wished to know.

"Spain. It was warm, and I think I could have stayed indefinitely."

"Tell them about Paige," Maddie encouraged.

Mr. Nunley shook his head in amazement. "She picked up on the language immediately. She ended up taking us all around and translating everywhere we went. The folks in the house where we stayed begged to keep her a while longer, but even with knowing the language so well, Paige was a little homesick. We all were."

"And worried about Maddie?" Doyle posed it as a question.

"My wife and daughter were not worried about Maddie, but they certainly missed her. After reading her letter, we had nothing but tears for a while."

"Are you still going to worry about me?" Maddie asked.

"No, I'll be able to go home and tell Adele everything she wants to know."

"But you can't tell her how thankful I am for the gifts," Maddie teased, "because you won't let me open them."

Mr. Nunley's eyes sparkled. "I'm your present right now. The gifts are for when I'm gone."

The two smiled fondly at each other, and Jace hoped that before Mr. Nunley left, he would invite them, or Maddie at the very least, to visit in Boston. He wanted his wife to keep ties with these folks who clearly cared so much.

Jace would have been pleased to know that Cathy agreed with him. Having forgotten that she'd worried about Maddie so recently, Cathy watched the two of them interact and wanted Mr. and Mrs. Nunley to know what a capable, fine woman Maddie had grown into. They were probably aware, but her pride wanted them to know just how special she was.

The five of them and Mr. Nunley had a nice, long visit, and then Jace took the sleigh the long way home to show their visitor the area. He was animated in his praise, and both Maddie and Jace knew a keen sense of satisfaction over his approval.

"So tell me," Maddie asked him that night, "what will you tell Paige and the missus when you get back to Boston?"

Mr. Nunley smiled the special smile he always had for Maddie, who still felt like one of his own.

"I'll tell them that Maddie could not have done better for herself. I'll tell them she has a very nice home that she's decorated herself. But most importantly, I'll tell them that Maddie has a husband who loves her and sees to her every comfort."

Maddie smiled, overwhelmingly pleased with the report and wishing there was some way to be there when he gave it.

Mr. Nunley rose to turn in a short time later, and when he did, Jace came to his feet, his hand extended. The men shook.

"Goodnight, Mr. Nunley, and thank you."

"It's no less than you deserve, Jace—no less than you deserve."

Alone in the parlor just moments later, husband and wife sat close on the sofa. Maddie rested her head on Jace's shoulder when his arm came around her. No words were said; no words were needed.

Like children at a birthday party, Maddie and Jace waited only to take Mr. Nunley to the station before looking to see what he had brought them.

Maddie recognized some things from the Nunley home, things she must have left behind, but almost everything in the cases and trunk were wedding gifts. All had little notes of explanation.

The table scarf in dark reds and black was from Spain. The candlesticks of silver were from Italy. And there was so much more. Maddie and Jace stared in wonder at the lovely things, Maddie's heart overflowing with love for this family in Boston. She missed them so much that she ached.

"There's a letter." Jace handed it to her, and Maddie read out loud.

> *My dearest Maddie,*
>   *I can't tell you how fearful and excited I am for you all in the same breath. Sherry and Beth told us every*

*detail, and I know you are in love. It never occurred to
me that I would lose you so suddenly, but I trust that
you will visit as often as you can. Paige is working on a
letter as well, but she's very tearful, so it's taking longer
and will have to come by post.*

*I can't thank you enough for all you did for Paige.
You gave her the confidence to write her stories down,
and while in France, she shared them with us. Sometimes we laughed, and sometimes we looked at her in
amazement. She has a true talent.*

Maddie stopped reading. It was harder than she thought. Jace
watched her, regret filling him again about the way their life had
started.

"Maybe you could visit in the spring," he suggested.

"Would you come?"

"It would depend on the work here. You could take your aunt.
Doyle and I would get along. We could always call on Clara."

Maddie smiled and put a hand out to him. Jace took it,
hoping she was going to be all right. He was learning that emotions were tenuous things. It wasn't that difficult to upset the balance.

"Maybe I will," Maddie said, not sure what she wanted to do.
She wasn't afraid of going there alone, but she didn't want to
leave Jace behind, not when there was so much in the city that
she would like to share with him.

Maddie looked over at Jace as he picked up a candlestick
and studied it. It occurred to her for the first time that sharing
her life with someone was exactly what she wanted to do. It
wasn't a life without mishap, but it was a life she loved.

When Jace looked up and saw her face, his brow wrinkled in
question. Maddie didn't answer—she only leaned close and gave
him a kiss.

∞

Not many days after the first of February, the Muldoon family celebrated a new arrival. Maddie didn't hear that a little boy had joined the family for a few days, but she had already been planning ahead. Not wanting Mr. Muldoon to think she had hard feelings toward him in any way, she had been working on a small blanket, knitting along at a smooth pace, hoping to have it done in time.

She had some finishing touches to make but overall thought it was in good shape. She waited another few days to make her visit, and then went into town, blanket in hand. Hillary met her at the door, a big smile on her face.

"Please come in, Mrs. Randall."

"I thought you called me Maddie."

"Well, you're married now, and I didn't want to assume."

"I'm still Maddie," she told the young woman, once again finding her resemblance to Paige rather uncanny.

What she also found uncanny was how well Mrs. Muldoon seemed to be doing. Her color was good, and she was moving comfortably around the kitchen, not looking as though she'd spent a moment in bed.

Alison welcomed Maddie and then took her to the cradle in the corner of the kitchen. Maddie looked down on the new baby boy, instantly taken with his small, dark head and tiny features.

"Would you like to hold him?" Alison offered.

"Please," Maddie told her sincerely.

Not until he was safely tucked into her arms did Maddie remember that he would not be baptized. For a moment, Maddie was quiet, trying to work this out in her mind. She realized swiftly that it was only going to upset her and did her best not to think about it.

They visited for a time, and Maddie noticed how joyful Alison Muldoon was. She seemed to take everything in stride and love her life. Maddie was drawn to her in a way she'd not been before. She might have even questioned her, but the baby began to cry and Martin came in looking for something, causing Maddie to hold her tongue.

When Maddie did take her leave, she couldn't help but wonder about a faith that had no fear of a baby dying without baptism. It stayed with her all the way to Cathy's house. There was no need to go to the store—she had no list to work with—and she was anxious to see her aunt. Jace was working long hours at the mill these days, and the last thing she wanted to do was bother him with what was on her mind.

"Cathy?" Maddie called as she stepped through the front door.

"In the kitchen, Maddie," that woman called to her.

"Um, it smells wonderful in here," Maddie said, coming to kiss her cheek.

"Scones. Would you like one?"

"Yes, please. I was just over at Muldoons seeing the baby."

"I went yesterday. Isn't he precious?"

"His skin is so soft. It makes me want one of my own."

"I'm sure it won't be long now," Cathy said encouragingly. "You started with a trauma, but things are settled down now." Cathy put a plate in front of her, a warm scone and butter nearby tantalizing with its aroma. "I'm a strong supporter of relaxing and letting things take their course. The couples who are desperate to make it happen only make it take longer."

"I never thought about that," Maddie admitted, even as she hesitated telling her aunt that relaxing did not come easily to her. She tended to worry about everything. Not about having a baby, but about everything else.

"What are you thinking about now?" Cathy asked, having caught the furrowed brow.

"I was just thinking about the Muldoons and the way they believe," Maddie said honestly, not sure what Cathy would say.

"Thinking about it in what way? Worrying about it?"

"Some worry, I guess, but mostly wondering how our beliefs could be so different."

"We're not so different," her aunt surprised her by saying. "We don't believe in murder or stealing. I know there are some issues where we don't see eye-to-eye, but I try to keep my focus on where we do agree.

"After all, Maddie," Cathy said matter-of-factly, "we're none of us heathens. We're all going to the same place. Why should we argue about such small things, most of which we can't do anything about?"

Maddie had never heard her aunt talk like this. She was not a person who criticized others with every breath she took, but she wasn't always very opened-minded either.

The conversation soon shifted, and Maddie didn't mind. She knew if she kept it up, she would be losing her appetite and pestering Jace all over again when she got home. And he was tired these days. Much as he loved the mill work, it was taxing.

Maddie looked forward to seeing him at noon each day, but he couldn't linger as he did at other times of the year. Woody had been with him a year ago, and Maddie knew that Jace felt the pressure this year of doing all the mill work and farm work on his own.

The topic she had raised with Cathy, however, stayed on her mind all day. She wasn't upset, and because she wasn't feeling desperate or ready to cry, she felt safe in bringing it up to Jace during tea.

"How was Mrs. Muldoon?" he asked as soon as they'd sat down.

"Doing very well. The baby is so cute. I got to hold him."

"What did they name him?"

"Jeffrey."

"That's nice. I knew a Jeffrey when I was growing up."

"Hey, Jace," Maddie asked, her voice telling him she was not upset. "What will we teach our children about God?"

Jace smiled at her. "Are you trying to tell me something?"

Maddie blinked at him, not sure what she'd missed. Jace's brows rose and he waited.

"No," Maddie told him when she caught on, her eyes growing a bit. "I won't keep that a secret from you. I promise."

She shook her head at his rascally grin and went back to her food. But Jace had not forgotten her question.

"I don't know what we'll teach our children. It might be fair to let them figure out what they believe on their own. I'm not sure anyone can know anything to be certain."

"But what if they don't believe in God at all? I wouldn't want that."

"I don't think that will happen. I think they'll believe much as we do. After all, I believe the way my parents did, and you have followed Doyle and Cathy."

"But now your sister is so different, Jace."

"I've thought about that," Jace said, and Maddie realized she didn't think Jace ever had. "And I guess I'll just make up my mind when the time comes."

"How does that work?"

"Well, I haven't heard anything that makes me think I have to know all this right now. When the time comes, I'll decide."

"That's why you're able to stay so calm about it," Maddie guessed.

"It must be. I hadn't really considered that."

Maddie had at least a dozen more questions she wanted to ask, and the temptation to pepper him with more was hard to resist, but he was weary—she could see it in his face.

Maddie finished tea, letting Jace lead the conversation. She wasn't worried, however. Her husband was right. They were going to be fine, and she was going to enjoy her life with Jace Randall, come what may.

Twenty-One

Jace didn't know when nine days had ever dragged on so long. Maddie and Cathy had gone to Boston, and Jace missed Maddie as though he'd never been without her. Both he and Doyle were at the train station when the train pulled in, feeling as though life had returned to their hearts.

Both women were full of stories about Boston in the spring and how the Nunley family was doing. The men listened long after the train pulled away and then realized that the wind was not as warm as it first seemed. With a wave goodbye, Jace took his wife home, ready to tell her she could never leave again. He was also ready to hear about every moment of her trip, but Maddie had questions about his time alone.

"Did you have time to go into town at all?"

"Yes, one day. I stopped at the livery and then picked up a newspaper at the printer. Did you know that the printer's wife has left him?"

"Is that what he told you?"

"Yeah. I don't know how it came up, but he's pretty upset."

"Where did she go?"

"I don't know. I don't know if he knows."

"Do they have children?"

"I'm not sure. He didn't say."

"What a shame. Did you go and see Doyle too?"

"Yes, and he already knew about it. I also saw Mr. Muldoon with two of his sons before I got to the store."

"Which ones?"

"I'm not sure of the names. One looked to be about five."

"That's Martin, I think."

"They're good kids," Jace commented thoughtfully.

"What makes you say that?"

"They do exactly as he tells them to do, and they don't get upset about it. While we were talking, the older boy wanted to go with some friends who had stopped to speak to him, and Mr. Muldoon said no. I watched his face. He was fine with it—no pouting, nothing."

Maddie watched Jace's face. She knew he'd not been overly impressed with Mr. Muldoon in the past and wondered whether he might be changing his mind.

"And how did Doyle do while we were gone?" Maddie asked next.

Jace laughed. "I think he got himself invited someplace nearly every evening, and when he was alone, he took himself to the tavern."

"And you would never have done that." Maddie barely covered her sarcasm.

Jace smiled. "Of course not. I had Clara coming to take care of me."

Maddie smiled knowingly and Jace caught it. He reached for her hand and pulled her over to sit in his lap.

"Was I actually the one who suggested that you go to Boston with your aunt?"

"That's how I remember it."

Jace slowly shook his head. "Never listen to that kind of stupid suggestion again."

Maddie could have had a good laugh over this, but suddenly she was too busy. Jace had pulled her down for a kiss.

∞

"How are you doing with praying for all men as we're commanded to do? Are you being faithful?" Douglas asked the congregation on Sunday. "Are you remembering? When you're standing in your kitchen and someone walks past the window, do you pray for him or her? When you hear the train coming into town, do you ask God's forgiveness on those dear folks on the train?

"Remember what we're trying to accomplish here, my friends: faithfulness. Some of us sow and some of us reap, and some do both. But of the two, I would have to say that reaping gets more attention. It gets more notice. For that reason it's harder to be a sower, one who's willing to keep praying for all men.

"We must pray as Jesus did: Father, forgive them. If anyone could have called them each by name, it was God's Son, but He didn't do that. He said, Forgive them. That's what I pray too. I don't know everyone in Tucker Mills. If I know a person, I pray for him by name, but if I don't, I don't need to worry about that. God knows that I'm asking Him to save that person and work a miracle in his life with His saving grace."

Douglas asked his small group of worshipers to sit quietly for a moment and think of someone they knew, someone who needed Christ. He encouraged them to pray for that person and to ask God to forgive and save him.

Douglas did the same thing. As he was standing there in the kitchen corner with his Bible in hand, Maddie Randall came to mind, Jace right after her. Douglas asked God to save this newly married couple who seemed to be searching but not yet ready to find.

Early summer had come and the days were warming up nicely when Jace surprised Maddie by asking her to go for a walk. The walk wasn't much of a surprise, but the time of day was.

"It's nearly dark out," she told him, thinking he hadn't noticed.

"Is it?" he teased her, and Maddie knew he was up to something.

Nevertheless, she went along, going with him out the door and holding his hand as they walked toward the millpond. It was a moonless night, and Maddie thought that was too bad. She had seen moonlight on the millpond many times and always found it beautiful.

Maddie was on the verge of mentioning to Jace how she wished there was a moon when he took her off the road and into the trees.

"Watch your head," he whispered as they neared a branch, and Maddie ducked just in time.

"What are we doing?" she whispered as well.

"You'll see," he told her, still pulling her by the hand and heading toward the pond. "Okay," he said, having come to a small clearing at the water's edge, "take off your clothes."

Jace was met with silence. He knew Maddie was still there— he could feel her hand—but not a sound came from her, not even breathing.

"Maddie?"

"What?"

"Did you hear me?"

"Yes, and you have clearly taken leave of your senses, Jace Randall."

"I'm going to teach you to swim," he said softly, and found his hand gripped tightly with both of hers.

"You what?" Her voice rose in panic.

"Shh," Jace found her mouth and covered it, already starting to laugh. "We don't want to be heard."

"I can't swim, Jace," she told him as she pushed the hand away. "This is not going to work."

"Yes, it is. I won't let anything happen to you. Now get undressed."

Jace let go of her then, and she heard the rustle of his clothing.

"Are you moving?" Jace asked, knowing she only stood there.

"We're not actually going to do this, are we?"

"Yes. Now strip down, Madalyn."

Maddie put her hands out and encountered Jace's bare flesh. She knew at that point that she wasn't going to get out of this. Had it been the least bit light, she would have walked home on her own, but she couldn't see a thing in front of her.

"How am I going to find everything again?" she asked with some heat, beginning to work the pins on her dress.

"Just make a pile. It will all be there when we get back."

Jace heard her loud sigh and smiled to himself. It sounded as though she was getting the job done, but he gave her a few more seconds.

"Are you ready?"

"Yes."

Jace put his hand out and found cloth.

"Maddie, what is this?"

"My shift, and I'm not taking it off."

"How long is it?"

"It stops just above my knees.

"That'll probably work. Are your shoes and stockings off?"

"Yes."

"Here's my hand." Jace found hers and began to lead her into the water. They were almost there when Maddie gasped.

"What is it?"

"You're trying to kill me," she accused. "You've changed your mind about our marriage and you want me dead."

Jace's entire frame shook as he found her shoulder so he could laugh into it.

"Your laughter doesn't fool me," Maddie said, fighting some giggles of her own. "You want out of this marriage, and this is how you figure to do it."

"If anyone is going to be the death of someone, Maddie, it's going to be you," Jace told her, still trying to stop laughing. "Come on now."

The water was unbelievably cold. Maddie gasped a few times, but Jace only told her to hush.

"Okay," he said close to her ear, the water to their waists. "It drops off here just a bit, but we're not going out far enough to have it over your head. Okay?"

"Okay," she shivered against him, waiting for her body to acclimate to the water temperature.

Coaxing her deeper into the water, Jace began the lesson. Through muffled laughter and more accusations from Maddie, Jace taught her to stay afloat. She even managed to stay above water on her own for a ways, his hand never leaving her side. They worked on it until Maddie's teeth chattered so loudly Jace knew it was time to conclude the lesson.

Back at the house, Jace helped his shivering wife into a dry nightgown and bundled her with quilts in front of the parlor fireplace. He put on dry clothes of his own and wrapped himself around her for added warmth. Maddie stared into the flames until she felt Jace's gaze on her.

"You were wonderful," he said when she looked at him, the firelight bouncing off her face.

"It was so cold."

"But next time you'll know a little more."

"Next time?" Maddie said, brows raised, but Jace just grinned at her. "Honestly, Jace, I thought a few times there that I was going to drown. You too."

"We won't let that happen," Jace said quietly, pulling her damp head to his shoulder. "I'm not sure if either one of us is ready to die."

Maddie would have sat up and looked at him, but Jace pushed her head down.

"Just get warm, Maddie," he whispered. "And know that I'm proud of you."

Maddie wanted to ask what he'd meant, but something in his voice stopped her. She knew he would not get angry, but she did suspect that no matter what she asked right now, Jace would not have an answer this time.

Epilogue

Maddie was beginning to think that Jace would never get home for dinner. It had been ready for some time, and she'd been pacing the kitchen floor for what felt like an hour. This had not been one of Clara's days off, but Maddie had put dinner together for her and told her to go home.

Clara had looked at her oddly but gone out the door, not overly fazed. And now Maddie waited alone. She checked the food she was keeping warm. She tasted the tea and even some of the potatoes, but still Jace didn't come. She stood in front of the window as long as she could stand it and then paced to another window to peer out of that one.

After what seemed like ages, she spotted him. He was coming from town, and she knew he would have to stable the horses and put the wagon away. She nearly went outside to meet him but then stopped, wanting him to be indoors for this special announcement.

"Hi," Maddie said with a smile when the door opened.

"Sorry I'm late," Jace said in return, giving her a kiss. "Doyle wanted to talk my ear off."

"How is he?" Maddie asked, catching the breathlessness in her voice.

"Fine. Cathy asked me to dinner, but I told her you were waiting. I think she's planning to visit you later this afternoon. She asked how you were."

They were at the table now, Maddie having brought out the warm dishes. Jace began to fill his plate, but Maddie only stared at him.

"Are you all right?" he asked when he caught her.

"I'm pregnant," Maddie said, unable to wait another moment.

"Oh, Maddie." Jace was instantly on his feet, taking her into his arms. "Are you sure?"

"Yes. I looked at the calendar and thought about my soreness right now, and I'm sure of it. Sometime last month, I think."

Jace kissed her ever so gently and then wrapped his arms tightly around her, trying to absorb her into his very being. He stood and rocked her in his arms for a long time.

He didn't want Maddie to know just then. He still had much thinking to do, but the enormousness of his wife's news was hitting him very hard. A new life. A small person completely dependent on them for everything. And what did they know? Jace couldn't think of a thing at the moment.

He wouldn't mention to Maddie just yet what had been going on in his heart for days. He would wait and take good care of her for this time, but soon, before the baby was even born, he knew he needed to make his own trip to see Mr. Muldoon.

ᘒ Glossary ᘕ

I learned many things about life in the late 1830s. Here are just a few…

- **buttery:** pronounced but'ry, it's a room where dairy goods are worked into various products, cheese and butter for example.

- **dinner:** the noon meal, always a full-blown affair.

- **flume:** a long wooden box that carries water from the millpond to the waterwheels below a mill.

- **green:** also called the center or common, it's the middle of town—a grass area around which homes and shops sit in a square or rectangle. I know of one in Connecticut that's a mile long.

- **hard cider:** fermented apple juice.

- **meetinghouse:** a building for public assembly, including the church on a Sunday.

- **millpond:** the pond of water that feeds the mill and is fed by spring thaw, or in the case of Tucker Mills, by a huge river that doesn't run dry in summer.

- **millrace:** the canal where the water from the pond enters the flume.

- **parlor** or sitting room: where people sat in the evening, entertained visitors, and unless the house was very large, ate their meals. The table in the kitchen was mostly for work and not for eating.

- **pew rental:** the way the pastor was paid in some meetinghouses.

- **pins:** straight pins were often used to hold dresses on. Buttonholes were a lot of work, and women avoided making them.

- **tea:** also called "snack"—this was the evening meal, which used leftovers from dinner.

Dear
Reader,

Some of the roads people go down before coming to faith are longer than others. This has been one of those roads. Reflected in Jace's and Maddie's search for meaning is the search that many of the people you and I touch daily are facing. I invite you to read the next book in the series. I hope you'll enjoy the next phase in Jace's and Maddie's lives.

Books by Lori Wick

A Place Called Home Series
A Place Called Home
A Song for Silas
The Long Road Home
A Gathering of Memories

The Californians
Whatever Tomorrow Brings
As Time Goes By
Sean Donovan
Donovan's Daughter

Kensington Chronicles
The Hawk and the Jewel
Wings of the Morning
Who Brings Forth the Wind
The Knight and the Dove

Rocky Mountain Memories
Where the Wild Rose Blooms
Whispers of Moonlight
To Know Her by Name
Promise Me Tomorrow

The Yellow Rose Trilogy
Every Little Thing About You
A Texas Sky
City Girl

English Garden Series
The Proposal
The Rescue
The Visitor
The Pursuit

The Tucker Mills Trilogy
Moonlight on the Millpond

Other Fiction
Sophie's Heart
Beyond the Picket Fence (Short Stories)
Pretense
The Princess
Bamboo & Lace
Every Storm